D1164110

JANITORS

JANITORS

TYLER WHITESIDES

ILLUSTRATED BY
BRANDON DORMAN

SHADOW
MOUNTAIN

Text © 2011 Tyler Whitesides
Illustrations © 2011 Brandon Dorman

Visit us at ShadowMountain.com

Library of Congress Cataloging-in-Publication Data
Whitesides, Tyler, author.
  Janitors / Tyler Whitesides.
     pages cm
  Summary: A sixth grader stumbles upon a secret that threatens to turn school-children everywhere into mindless automatons.
  ISBN 978-1-60908-056-3 (hardbound : alk. paper)
  [1. Students—Fiction. 2. Monsters—Fiction. 3. School custodians—Fiction.
4. Schools—Fiction.] I. Title.
  PZ7.W58793 Jan 2011
  [Fic]—dc22   2011007692

Printed in the United States of America
Publishers Printing

10 9 8 7 6 5 4 3 2 1

For mothers and custodians everywhere,
who seem to sweep and vacuum endlessly.

And for Connie, who swept me away.

CONTENTS

CONTENTS

CHAPTER 1

"YOU'RE GOING TO GET AN F."

S pencer shifted the papers on his school desk and looked for a hundredth time at the graffiti in the corner. Last year's occupant of the desk must have spent hours etching the message into the wooden surface.

Mrs. N Smells like cabbige

Dummy, Spencer thought. *Couldn't even spell cabbage.*

Truth be told, Mrs. Natcher did smell a little like cabbage sometimes, but she was still tolerable. Today, however, a strong Bath and Body Works fragrance filled the sixth-grade classroom and Mrs. Natcher was nowhere to be seen.

In her place was a thin, younger woman who had short, stylish hair streaked with pink highlights. She

1

wore high-heeled red shoes and a skirt so short that Mrs. Natcher would have croaked. Turned out that Mrs. Natcher *had* croaked—well, almost—which was why Miss Leslie Sharmelle had been called to Welcher Elementary that morning.

Spencer glanced at the clock on the wall. Only a half hour until lunch! The morning had flown by. After a lesson on geography, Miss Sharmelle had started the students creating maps of imaginary lands. Spencer traced a crooked line from his pencil-sketch mountains to the coast.

"Keep working on your maps, boys and girls," Miss Sharmelle instructed. "I've got to buzz over to the copy machine for a sec." With half a dozen papers in her hand and her heels click-clacking on the floor, she disappeared into the hallway.

Instinctively, Spencer swiveled his head to glance at Dez Rylie. Sure enough, there was already a soggy wad of paper coming out of the boy's big mouth. Only a desk away, Spencer's map was an easy target. But with the substitute out of the room, Dez wouldn't settle for a small target like Spencer. Dez was going to spread the fun (and the spit) to everybody.

With a whoop, he tossed the mass of chewed paper into the air. It made a lazy arc across the room, showering everyone below with drops of Dez-juice. The spit bomb made a fast descent and landed with a *splat* on Jen McNeal's new back-to-school shoes.

Jen screamed, jumping up and shaking her foot wildly. She danced in the aisle as though an army of ants had decided to bunk in her sock. The vigorous foot shaking sent out a spray of spit, and the wad dislodged, flinging sideways and skidding across Juan Rivera's map. Desperate to save his island, Juan snatched up his map and flipped the spit wad forward.

The wad (no longer soggy, but still unpleasantly moist) rolled off Juan's desk and quickly came to a halt between the backrest of the chair in front of him and the girl sitting in it. Instantly, she began to cry.

As the back half of the classroom erupted into chaos, Dez Rylie threw his head back and laughed at the ceiling. Spencer, who was still shielding his map, noticed that almost everyone else who wasn't dancing, screaming, or crying was doing the same. Those who had escaped the first onslaught were watching Dez like rabbits in headlights.

Everyone except Gullible Gates.

Daisy Gates was seated in the front left corner of the classroom, far out of spit's way. She might have been humming softly, as she often did, but there was too much noise in the room to be sure. One thick, sandy-colored braid reached halfway down her back. She sat hunched over the desk, her nose an inch away from the forest she was drawing. She scribbled more pine needles onto a tree, somehow oblivious to the upset in the room.

Dez scowled when he saw her. Spencer opened his mouth to shout a warning, but cringed, unwilling to make himself the target. Dez pushed himself out of his desk and tromped down the aisle, intentionally treading on somebody's notebook that had fallen to the floor. The back of the room had quieted. Juan was holding his wrinkled map in front of the fan. Jen was alternately blotting off her shoe and drying the tears of her sobbing friend.

It wasn't until Dez Rylie's shadow fell on Daisy's desk that she looked up. Seeing the bulky kid standing before her, she quickly looked down again, vigorously scrawling pine needles. Dez bent down to examine her work and the entire class held its breath. If Daisy had been humming before, she was definitely not doing it anymore. The clock ticked loudly. Twenty minutes to lunch.

"Nice map," Dez said.

Daisy stopped drawing and looked up. A reluctant smile spread across her face. "Uh, thanks, Dez."

"It looks pretty good . . . except for one thing."

"What?" Daisy asked, looking at her map as though it had betrayed her.

"You weren't listening when Miss Sharmelle told us about forests." Dez's fat finger pressed down on Daisy's pine trees. "Forests can't grow next to mountains. You're going to get an F."

Daisy sat stricken for a moment, then fumbled for her large pink eraser. With hasty movements that tore little marks in her paper, she scrubbed at her forest until it was nothing but a gray smudge next to the mountains.

Across the room, Spencer's body tensed. That was wrong. Daisy's forests could grow wherever they darn well pleased. Taking a deep breath, Spencer began to say "Daisy." But all he could manage was "Dai" before Dez silenced him

4

with a threatening glare. Spencer felt the "sy" catch in his throat and he swallowed it down.

"Where *can* I put my forest?" Daisy asked.

"Forests only grow on tiny little islands a hundred and two miles from the coast. In geography, we call them Gullible Islands." Laughing, Dez snatched Daisy's pencil and drew a big *F* at the top of her map.

"You're so dead, Dez." Jordan Height broke the silence. Jordan wasn't as tall as Dez; no one in the class was. But Jordan was usually the first to stand up to the bully.

"Shut up, pretty boy," Dez replied, folding his beefy arms.

"I mean it," Jordan said. "Miss Sharmelle's going to drag you to the principal's office so fast."

"I don't care," Dez shrugged. "In fact, I kinda hope so. Maybe Miss Sharmelle will hold my hand. She's a hottie."

The students gasped collectively and Spencer averted his eyes, ashamed to even be sharing air with Dez Rylie.

"You *will* be going to the office, Dezmond." Miss Sharmelle's voice cut through the gasps. She was in the doorway, a large stack of papers in her hand. Her face looked a little flushed, but not as red as Dez's.

The bully turned to face her, regaining his composure. "Let's go," he said.

Miss Sharmelle crossed the room, set the papers on her desk, and returned to the open doorway where Dez was waiting for her with a stupid grin on his broad face.

"And *no*," she punctuated, "I will *not* be holding your hand."

CHAPTER 2

"THAT SOUNDS NEAT."

The yellow school bus rumbled to a stop and released a hiss of air before the door opened. Four children with matching brown hair and a smattering of freckles moved to the front of the bus. James took two steps per stair because he was in first grade. Holly held the handrail and descended by hopping on one foot because she was in third grade. Erica jumped down all the steps because she was in fourth grade. The last one thanked the driver and moved down the stairs like a civilized human. Because, after all, Spencer was in sixth grade.

Once outside, the bus driver checked her mirrors and motioned the kids across the street. Spencer herded his siblings, wondering why the driver had even bothered to check the mirrors. There was never a car on this road anyway.

When the children were safely across, the flashing red stop sign tucked away and the bus ambled down the road.

Without a sidewalk to follow, the four kids moved along the weed-infested edge of the road. September was brown in southern Idaho, but the farmers still fought it with huge sprinklers that launched water in glittering, sunlit arcs across the fields.

They passed a rundown farmhouse and Spencer turned his siblings up a steep side road. Suddenly, the neighborhood changed. This newly developed area on the hill seemed too fancy for the rest of town. Like pearl earrings on a pig.

Two blocks into the wealthy subdivision, the kids arrived at their gaudy, three-story home. A few months ago, the lot had blended nicely with the neighborhood. Green lawn and tidy landscaping. But, for better or worse, Spencer's family had a way of making things their own.

In the weeks since they'd arrived, the lawn had withered to a dry and crispy brown. A clunker station wagon was parked mostly in the driveway, with one wheel on the dying grass. The car meant Mom was home. The bad parking job meant she was in a hurry.

The house, too, had once been a monument to wealth. Now it looked recently blown in from Kansas. On the porch, cobwebs hung scalloped from pillar to pillar like someone had hired Spider-Man to do the decorating. The "welcome" mat didn't look too welcoming, all caked in dry mud so that only the *w* and *e* were legible.

Spencer opened the door and stepped inside, his little

brother and sisters following. There was a clank of pans from the kitchen and Spencer heard his mother's voice. Probably on the phone.

A three-year-old rounded the corner with a bottle of soapy bubble solution in his hand. The other hand waved a bubble wand, flicking soap onto the hardwood floor.

"What the . . . ?" Spencer grabbed the wand from the child's hand. "Who are you?" A second later, two more three-year-olds came careening into view, one with a butter knife, the other with a pair of scissors.

"Whoa!" Spencer said, seizing his littlest brother by the arm and prying the scissors from his grasp. "If you're going to play inside with friends," Spencer lectured, "then you have to be respectful of Aunt Avril's house."

Max merely hissed at his older brother, exposing a chipped front tooth. He made an attempt to grab the scissors back and then ran off.

Spencer was alone in the entryway. His other siblings had dumped their backpacks on the floor and quietly crept downstairs. Afternoon cartoons on the big flat-screen TV attracted them like moths to a porch light. Not the porch light at Spencer's house, though. It had been left on 24-7 and burned out weeks ago.

Spencer sighed. For a house with so many windows, it surely seemed dark. He crossed the room and twisted the wooden blinds to let some light in. Something darted out from behind the leather sofa, nearly stopping Spencer's heart. It was a cat. Since when did they have a cat?

Spencer picked up a toy dump truck and kicked some

stuffed animals out of his way. The mess in this house was maddening. He would clean things up after dinner, but right now, Spencer needed some time in his sanctuary.

"Spencer!" his mother called as he headed toward the stairs.

"Here, Mom!" he answered as if she were calling roll.

"Spencer, come in here and tell me about your day."

Resignedly, Spencer left his backpack on the first step and walked into the kitchen. His mother was a whirlwind. Alice Zumbro was stooped down, digging for the colander while balancing a steaming pot of noodles in one hand and trapping a spatula between her knees as she pinned the phone to her shoulder with her cheek. Her apron nearly tripped her when she stood up, colander in hand, and crossed to the sink.

Spencer stood obediently near, wishing he could help, but knowing that his mother preferred to do everything on her own. Especially since Dad had left.

Finally she turned to him, her face moist from the steam of the noodles and her hair sticking in strands to her forehead.

"How was school today?" she whispered around the phone.

"Fine."

"What did you do?" she asked.

"Mom," Spencer protested. "You're on the phone. I'll tell you later."

Alice shook her head. "Tell me now. It's just your Aunt Avril." She carried the dripping noodles across the room and set them on the table, steaming water still oozing out of the colander. "Well?" she mouthed as she passed him on her way to the stove.

"Well?" echoed Spencer. "The bus ride was boring this morning," he began. "Boring and long."

"Uh-huh," his mom responded, though Spencer wasn't sure if it was intended for him or Aunt Avril.

"I sat by myself because James and Holly and Erica have all made friends."

"Uh-huh."

"Mrs. Natcher was gone and we had a substitute named Miss Leslie Sharmelle. She was nice, but some of the kids were mad because we didn't get morning recess."

"Oh, Avril, don't worry about that," Alice scolded into the phone. Then she looked right at Spencer and gave him a very clear "uh-huh," answering his question about who the grunts were intended for.

"Then this big kid, Dez, went berserk and chucked spit wads all over, so Miss Sharmelle took him to the office."

"Uh-huh."

"In P.E., I was picked last for kickball. I ate lunch by myself and accidentally spilled ketchup on my shirt, see?" Spencer stretched his shirt to show his mom the red spot. She tried to glance, but got distracted by the can opener.

"Then, at lunch recess I met some aliens. They were pretty cool and showed me their ray guns and stuff. So I zapped everybody except Daisy Gates, 'cause everybody picks on her. Then the aliens gave me a lift back to our *real* home in Washington."

"That sounds neat, Spence," Alice answered. She gave him a dismissive smile, said, "Oh, I know," to Aunt Avril on the phone, then said "Shoot!" because she realized that she hadn't put the noodles in a bowl and the colander was leaking hot water everywhere.

Spencer ducked out of the cluttered kitchen—*Aunt Avril's* kitchen—and made his way back to the stairs. His backpack was still there, but someone had flicked soapy bubble solution on one of the shoulder straps. Spencer picked it up carefully and jogged up the stairs, dodging piles of dirty clothes and an open can of soda as he went. He moved quickly, hopeful that there would be no more distractions.

With a sigh of relief, Spencer opened the door and stepped into his bedroom. Everything was clean. Everything had its place. And everything was *always* in its proper place . . . except for a heap of pillows in the middle of the floor!

"Max," Spencer muttered disapprovingly as he put the pillows back—two on the bed and two in the padded window seat. Spencer hung his backpack on a hook and sat down on a chair to remove his shoes.

It was Monday. Two lonely weeks at Welcher Elementary were over and another had just begun. Fifty more weeks until Aunt Avril and Uncle Wyatt would return from business in Thailand and claim their house back—or whatever was left of it.

Spencer wanted a snack. He had some treats in his top drawer, but he hadn't washed his hands from school yet. He couldn't bring himself to snack without washing and he couldn't wash without leaving his tidy sanctuary. For a moment he sat perfectly still. He closed his eyes, letting the school day settle behind him.

Something wet flicked across his face. For a terrible moment Spencer thought that Dez Rylie had somehow thrown a spit wad so far that it had penetrated his sanctuary. Spencer's eyes opened and he saw one of Max's friends emerge from hiding, bubble wand in hand. The kid was making a break for the door, giggling wildly.

Spencer would have zapped him if he'd had a ray gun.

CHAPTER 3

"DISGUSTING."

M iss Leslie Sharmelle gave them morning recess the next day. It was only a ten-minute break, but at least it was ten minutes that Spencer could get away from Dez's grubby hands. The big bully had been poking Spencer all morning. His trip to the principal's office obviously hadn't been enough to inspire good behavior.

Spencer cursed the seating chart after recess as Dez plopped down beside him again. Miss Sharmelle had thrown out Mrs. Natcher's lesson plans and decided to teach algebra. Daisy Gates, who had only briefly heard about algebra, thought it was some kind of deep-sea creature. Dez encouraged the myth, giving life-sucking tentacles to the dangerous algebras. Daisy, who had wholeheartedly forgiven Dez of his cruelty the day before, was ready to believe him.

But then the lecture started and Miss Sharmelle (wearing a shirt that said X + Y = XOXOXO) shot down the myth.

Miss Sharmelle, who had previously been so exciting, suddenly delivered the most dreadfully boring lecture possible. Spencer's head began to bob like a basketball dribbling in slow motion. The first time it drooped, he jerked up, embarrassed. He'd had this problem in his old school—falling asleep even when he really wanted to learn what the teacher was explaining. Glancing around, Spencer noticed that several others were fading too.

Not Dez. He slouched forward with a melty handful of M&Ms. Carefully, he placed a candy up his nose. Plugging the other nostril, he exhaled hard, blowing out the M&M and catching it on his waiting tongue.

"Disgusting," Spencer muttered. Repulsed beyond description, he turned away from the brute. He tried to focus on Miss Sharmelle's voice. His head bobbed again . . . and again. Spencer almost wished that Dez would start poking him again—if the bully washed his hands first.

Finally unable to resist, Spencer put his head onto his desk, X + Y equaling Zzzzzzz.

CHAPTER 4

"WEIRD."

Spencer felt someone shaking him. His eyes were sticky and he had to squint against the light. Suddenly remembering where he was, he shot upright in his seat. The glue seal on his eyes snapped and he glanced around the classroom.

He was alone.

Well, not alone, because Miss Sharmelle had a hand on his shoulder, bringing him around. But all the other students were gone!

"I'm sorry, Miss Sharmelle," Spencer said. "I don't know . . . sometimes I . . . I'm sorry."

Miss Sharmelle smiled attractively. "It happens, Spencer. Algebra affects everyone differently."

"What time is it?"

"The bell just rang. I bet your classmates aren't even in the lunch line yet."

Spencer shook his head in shame and began scooping his belongings into his backpack. "I won't fall asleep again, Miss Sharmelle. I really am sorry."

"Don't worry about it. I won't tell Mrs. Natcher or anything." But then, as Spencer stood and faced her, Miss Sharmelle gasped. Her green eyes, under a pair of fashionable fake glasses, studied his cheek and forehead.

"What?" Spencer asked, his stomach sinking. "What's wrong with my face?"

Without answering, she motioned him over to her desk. From her pink leather purse, Miss Sharmelle withdrew a round makeup compact, flipped open the lid, and held the mirror out for him. Although the mirror was marked with several smudges and dusted with powder, Spencer caught the reflection of his left cheek. $X + Y = Z$ was sloppily tattooed in black marker across his face. On his forehead was another algebraic equation, and by his chin, a third one had been started but left without an answer, probably because the bell had rung.

"Dez," mumbled Spencer angrily. He told Miss Sharmelle that he would wash it off in the bathroom and gave her the mirror back.

"Terrible thing, permanent marker," she said, examining her own reflection before replacing the makeup mirror in her purse.

"It'll come off," Spencer said.

"Good luck."

The nearest bathroom was just across the hallway. Spencer kept his face down and walked—fast. He pushed open the door with his elbow and stepped inside just as someone flushed the toilet and turned to face him.

Dez.

"Hey, Doofus," the bully said. Spencer paused, trying to decide whether he should flee immediately or attempt to get past Dez and wash his face.

"Nice equators," Dez smirked.

"What?" Spencer asked, his fist clenched like a grenade.

"Maybe you should look in the mirror, smarty-pants," Dez answered. "You've got math equators written all over your face."

"*Equations*," Spencer said. "Math *equations*."

"Yeah, whatever. You still look like a dork." Dez snorted and Spencer was afraid for a moment that the bully would launch a gob at him. Nothing came out, so Dez shifted gears. "You thought about standing up for Gullible Gates yesterday, didn't you?"

"That's why you drew on my face?" Spencer asked.

"No," said Dez. "Actually, I drew on your face because Nancy Pepperton thought it would be funny." Dez dug in his jeans pocket (a difficult task when the jeans are a size too small) and withdrew a crumpled strip of paper. "She passed me this during algebra."

Half expecting the paper to grow teeth and bite him, Spencer took it from Dez's hand.

Spencer is so out. Draw something on his face.
—Nancy

Spencer crumpled the paper and stuffed it into his own pocket. He barely even knew Nancy! What did she have against him?

"Anyway," Dez said. "Stay out of my fun with Gullible Gates and life will be easier for you. I like to play with her mind. It's soft like Play-Doh but doesn't dry out as fast. Next time you think about being a hero, I'll spell a different equator for you. It's called Fist + Nose = Blood. Deal?" Dez extended his beefy hand to seal the bargain, but Spencer just stared, trapped.

"Deal?" Dez repeated, unaccustomed to having his victims think before they agreed.

"Deal," answered Spencer finally. "It's a deal."

"Why won't you shake on it?" Dez demanded, his hand still extended.

"Well," Spencer hesitated, wondering if honesty would win him a face-plant in the toilet. "You just went to the bathroom and you haven't washed your hands yet."

Dez exhaled a breathy puff of disbelief that turned into a mocking laugh. Spencer stood rigid, ready for anything. After a good chuckle, Dez reached out and gently patted Spencer's cheek. "Washing's for sissies." He pushed Spencer aside, flung open the bathroom door, and announced his arrival in the hallway with a loud belch.

As soon as the door clanged shut, Spencer took three quick steps to the sink and turned on the water. Dez's bathroom hands were a second incentive to a thorough face washing. In the mirror, Spencer saw the ink equations more clearly. He must have been sound asleep not to feel Dez's marker.

Grateful that no one else had seen the math-work, Spencer splashed his face with water. Reaching over, he gave two solid pumps to the soap dispenser on the wall.

Nothing.

Spencer began pumping violently on the dispenser, but it was hopeless. There was no soap. Spencer scanned the room desperately. The next bathroom was all the way down the hall and around the corner. He would never make it without someone spotting Dez's artwork.

Spencer's eyes suddenly fell on a small bottle resting on the edge of the next sink. His face still dripping, Spencer reached over and snatched it up, hopeful that it might contain something that could remove his facial graffiti. Turning it over in his hand, Spencer saw that it was actually a hotel shampoo bottle from a Best Western. Quickly deciding that shampoo might do the trick, he unscrewed the cap.

There was the tiniest bit of gelatin-like substance in the bottom of the bottle. Spencer squirted the glob onto his palm, surprised to see that it was bright pink and looked more like soap than shampoo after all. The soap smelled fresh, if a little chemical.

Spencer worked the pink gel to a foamy lather between his hands. He rubbed his cheek, watching X and Y melt away with surprising ease. Then he closed his eyes and lathered his whole face.

Burning hot!

Icy cold!

"Yaaaaaggghh!"

Spencer frantically began rinsing his face. The soap was in his eyes now, stinging like crazy. He plunged his entire face directly under the faucet, letting the lukewarm water flush out his eyes. Spencer reached out blindly and pumped a roll of paper towels. Blotting his face with the paper helped make the tingling sensation fade.

Spencer opened his eyes and stared back at his reflection. The front of his shirt was soaked from his rapid and reckless rinsing. His brown hair was damp and clinging to his forehead. And his face . . . it was as red as a tomato and still burning. But at least there was no sign of Dez's algebra.

Spencer picked up the bottle, blinking rapidly in hopes that his eyes would stop stinging. He smelled the soap again. It was strong—definitely not Best Western shampoo. It might have been paint remover, for all he knew. Whatever it was, Spencer decided he was allergic. He was lucky to have found it first. What if some little baby first grader had washed his hands with the napalm soap?

Feeling like he was doing the world a favor, Spencer tossed the bottle into the garbage can, where it sank out of sight beneath crumpled paper towels.

Suddenly, a flash of movement caught his eye in the mirror. Spencer blinked, still trying to focus. The stall door was open, but he thought he'd seen something duck out of sight.

Spencer took a cautious step toward the bathroom stall

and peered in. Seeing nothing, he gently pushed the door. It swung on its hinges to reveal an empty stall, nothing but scraps of toilet tissue littering the hard floor.

"Weird," Spencer muttered, still blinking against the eye-tingling sensation. Dispensing another small piece of paper towel, he used it to open the bathroom door. Then he headed for the lunchroom.

CHAPTER 5

"BETTER HURRY UP."

Miss Sharmelle's afternoon lessons were back up to par. The students sat on the floor for the last twenty minutes of class listening to her read aloud from some novel about the Civil War. Spencer had read the book on his own the year before, but he didn't mind hearing it again. Anything was better than algebra.

As Miss Sharmelle turned another page, her voice escalating with the narrative, Spencer glimpsed movement by the bookshelf. There was something crawling across the top of the books!

Before Spencer could say anything, something sprang forward, unfolding leathery, batlike wings. It had the bald head and hooked beak of a vulture. The rest of its black body, no bigger than a softball, was covered in short, bristly hair.

From the bookshelf, it flew in a jagged arc over the students, turning only inches away from Miss Sharmelle's pink-streaked hairdo.

"Ahhh!" Spencer cried, flattening himself to the ground. "Look out!"

As soon as the words left his mouth, the winged creature arched back and dove as fast as a falcon behind the teacher's desk.

"Spencer?" Miss Sharmelle said, looking up from the novel. "Is something wrong?" The other kids were staring at him, some trying to suppress giggles.

What? Impossible! Of course something was wrong! Some hideous bat thing had just come out of the bookshelf. Spencer glanced toward the teacher's desk. The creature was hiding now. Probably waiting for the perfect moment to swoop down and scoop out everyone's eyeballs.

"I thought I saw something," Spencer said. "Did anyone else . . . I mean . . . did anyone see anything?" His classmates slowly shook their heads with looks on their faces that might have condemned him to a lifetime in the loony bin.

Finally, someone broke the silence. "Yeah. I saw something." Spencer turned. It was Dez. "I saw some doofus put his face on the floor and shout, 'Look out!'" This won laughter from several kids, but Miss Sharmelle killed it.

"Spencer, what exactly do you think you saw?"

"Well," Spencer said, unsure how to explain it. "It was kind of hairy, with black wings and a sharp beak."

"Like a bat?" one of his classmates asked.

"Yes!" Spencer said. "Kind of like a bat."

"Uh, bats don't have beaks, Doofus." This was from Dez, who clearly thought everyone was taking Spencer too seriously.

"It came out of the bookshelf over there," Spencer explained, rising to his feet. "It flew right down here, close to Miss Sharmelle. But when I saw it, the thing just shot down behind the teacher's desk."

Instant stampede. About half the kids in the class rushed over to Mrs. Natcher's desk, surrounding it from every angle.

"There's nothing here!" shouted Daisy. "It's gone."

"Of course there's nothing," answered Dez. "Spencer just imagined it. See, Daisy. He's got that flu I was telling you about. The only way to stop it is by doing this." Dez stuck his thumbs up his nose and put his pinkies in his ears. Then the bell rang and he jumped up, grabbed his backpack, and ran out of the classroom screaming.

As the students poured out of the room, Miss Sharmelle called Spencer over. "I'm a little worried about you," she said. "I don't know what Mrs. Natcher usually tolerates, but you've been kind of disruptive today. Now, I won't tell her about this, or about how you slept through math. But I surely hope you weren't *trying* to make a scene."

"No, ma'am," Spencer promised. "I'm pretty sure I saw something."

"Well, maybe you did. I'll keep my eyes peeled." Miss Sharmelle gave him a heartwarming smile. "See you tomorrow."

Unable to resist, Spencer took a few steps forward and peeked behind the desk.

Nothing.

It took Spencer a few moments to gather his things; by the time he entered the hallway, most of the kids were outside loading into the busses. It would be a long walk if he missed the bus. And Spencer really didn't want to bother his mother for a ride—assuming that the station wagon started in the first place.

Spencer rounded a corner, heading for the main doors, and stopped in his tracks. There it was, nestled in the trash can, its bat wings sticking up over the top edge. Frozen, Spencer watched it rummage through the garbage, poking its bald head in a Kit Kat wrapper.

"Get down!" someone shouted, and Spencer instinctively dropped to the carpet. Dez appeared behind him, waving his hands at invisible objects above his head. "Save us, Batman! They're everywhere!"

Dez's sixth-grade buddies showed up laughing. "Good one, dude." Dez stopped swinging his arms and joined in the laughter.

One of the bullies pointed as Spencer scampered to his feet. "That's the weirdo from your class? What a loser."

Spencer looked instinctively at the garbage can. The vulture-headed creature was still there. Lifting a chocolaty beak from the Kit Kat wrapper, it ruffled its wings and flew off down the hallway.

"Come on." The bullies burst through the school doors. Spencer's face still might have been a little pink from the soap that morning, but now it was bright red. Dez was telling everyone! It was bad enough that he didn't have any friends at Welcher Elementary. But it would be far worse if everyone in the school thought he was crazy.

Then, as if to seal his insanity, something else moved down the hallway, scuttling low to the floor. It was the size of a prairie dog but as round and bushy as a bath loofah. It had long, gray fur that was so dingy it looked like a giant mothball rolling down the hallway. The dust gopher stopped in a dirty corner where the carpet met the wall and began chowing down on . . . dust?

Suddenly, a broom sailed out of nowhere and slammed into the corner by the dust-ball critter. Spencer jumped as the gopher ran for it. It dashed to a doorway across the hall, but the way was instantly blocked by a huge, oafish man with a vacuum.

Hearing the vacuum rev to life, the dust-ball scurried back just as the vacuum hose came down. The suction came so close that Spencer saw the creature's fur change direction, bits of dirt tumbling out and rattling up the vacuum hose. In an instant, the dust-ball escaped, racing back toward the lunchroom.

Casually, as though nothing strange had happened, the bearlike janitor dragged his vacuum hose along the edge of the carpet, picking up tiny bits of paper that had fallen near the garbage can. With his other hand, he grabbed his leather belt, laden with a large ring of heavy keys and a walkie-talkie radio. His dirty white shirt came untucked as he hiked up his sagging pants.

"Better hurry up," the man said without looking. "Don't want to miss the bus."

Spencer backed away slowly, unsure if he should feel better because he wasn't hallucinating or worse because there really were demon creatures roaming the halls of Welcher Elementary School.

One thing was sure: No one could see them but him and the janitor. And Spencer had a feeling that he wasn't supposed to be on that list.

CHAPTER 6

"YOU BELIEVE ME?"

The morning was crisp and cool when Spencer coasted into the parking lot of Welcher Elementary School. He'd found a bicycle in Aunt Avril's garage. The tires were low, but he'd found a pump, too. It was still very early— school wouldn't start for another twenty minutes. But Spencer needed that time to investigate.

At home, in his tidy bedroom, Spencer had replayed the previous day over and over again, sorting out all the information and trying to determine what made him different . . . or special . . . or psycho.

It wasn't hard to figure out, just hard to accept. Everything had been normal until he had washed his face. Right after he'd dried his eyes, with his face still tingling unnaturally, he'd seen movement in the bathroom stall. Then he saw the bat thing during reading, then more little monsters after school.

The janitor guy saw them too, which made perfect sense because the janitors were in charge of all cleaning supplies in the school. They must have accidentally left that burn-your-face-off soap in the bathroom.

Spencer chained his bike to the empty rack. He needed to tell someone what he'd seen. His mother was too busy to help. On Monday, Spencer had told her that he'd been abducted by aliens on the playground and she had said, "That sounds neat, Spence." No, he needed to tell someone who would take time to listen. Spencer hoped it would be Miss Sharmelle.

Spencer wiped a bead of sweat from his forehead. The morning was cool, but it had been a long ride from his house to the school. He tugged on the door.

Locked.

"They'll open it in five minutes," said a voice from behind a tree. Daisy Gates appeared, book in hand. "I always like to be the first one in the school, so I get here early and read until they open the doors. I don't live far away. Just like three blocks."

"Yeah," Spencer said. "I wanted to get here early too." He studied Daisy. Her long, thick hair was in its usual braid down her back. She was taller than some of the boys, and when she smiled big, her mouth was full of teeth. Despite her extra height, she still seemed small. She looked truly impressionable, which made sense since Spencer knew that she believed anything anyone said.

Gullible Gates. Suddenly, Spencer realized that she was exactly who he needed.

"Hey," he said, walking over to the grass. "There's something I've been meaning to talk to you about."

"About Dez?" she said, tucking a bookmark into her novel. She looked down and began backing away. "I know. People tell me all the time that I shouldn't believe him. But sometimes he says some really interesting things."

"Actually," Spencer said, "it's about yesterday. Remember when I said I saw something during the read-aloud?"

"Yeah."

"Well, I'm *sure* I saw something."

"The little bat?"

"It was more than a bat. It was . . ." Spencer took a deep breath, putting all of his hope in Daisy's gullibility, "a little flying monster."

All right. Now that he'd said it aloud, it sounded absolutely stupid. Daisy stared at him for a long time. Her eyes got wide.

"What did it do?" she asked intently.

"You believe me?" Spencer cried in disbelief.

"Wait a minute, are you tricking me?"

"No! No. I'm serious."

"How come no one else saw it?"

"The janitor did. He tried to vacuum one up after school, but it got away."

"Marv," she said.

"What?"

"The janitor. Was it the big guy with a shaggy black

beard and a bald spot on his head?" Spencer nodded. "His name is Marv Bills," she said. "He's really nice. Marv does most of the work, but John Campbell is really the head janitor."

"You're friends with the janitors?"

"No," Daisy said. "I just study the yearbook and memorize people's names."

Spencer wanted to tell her that was kind of weird. But then, he'd just told her that he saw flying monsters, so he had no room to talk.

"Yeah." Daisy nodded. "The yearbook's great. You probably don't have one yet 'cause you're new around here. Anyway, did you have monsters at your old school?"

Spencer couldn't believe that she was taking him seriously. But that was Daisy's greatest weakness. "It all started when I found some magic soap . . ."

That was it. Spencer had pushed it too far. He saw Daisy's eyebrows furrow in skepticism. If he'd only said "special soap" or "unusual soap"—but no. He'd said the "m" word.

"You're tricking me."

"I swear I'm not," Spencer pleaded. Daisy turned and put her book into her backpack. "Come on," he begged, "I'm not like Dez. I don't stick M&Ms up my nose."

"Why don't you prove it? I'd love to see little critters crawling on the walls."

"It's not really fun, Daisy. It's actually kind of freaky."

"How do you expect me to believe you if I can't see them?" she asked.

"Well, I don't know," said Spencer. "You seem to believe Dez just fine."

Daisy stalked away, pushing open the now unlocked door to the school.

Great! Spencer thought. *Even Gullible Gates doesn't buy my story.* But what if he *could* show her? He could show Miss Sharmelle, too. And the principal. They could call an exterminator!

Spencer caught up to Daisy halfway down the hall. Other kids were entering and Daisy had failed at her daily goal to be the first one inside.

"I've decided to show you, Daisy."

She raised her eyebrows as they walked side by side. Spencer could tell she was having some kind of internal battle: the Daisy who got tricked a lot versus the Daisy who wanted to learn something important. Silently, Spencer rooted for the latter.

"Come with me," he said. "Let me get the soap out of the garbage and you can try it for yourself."

They walked in silence. When they reached the bathroom, Spencer pushed open the door and ran inside with the urgency of someone who'd been "holding it" for hours. He reached the garbage can . . . and his hopes shattered.

A fresh sack lined the can. All of yesterday's garbage was gone—disposed of by the janitors. Spencer's plan was falling apart.

"It's not there," Spencer said, emerging slowly from the bathroom.

"That's okay," Daisy said. "I'm sure the janitors have more."

Spencer paused thoughtfully for a moment. "That's a good idea, Daisy," he said. "Come on. We've still got ten minutes."

In a moment, the two kids stood at the top of a few stairs. The short flight descended into the janitorial area. It was a large space for storing extra garbage cans, trash bags, chemical cleaners, wax for the tile floors, and, Spencer hoped, magic soap.

"Wait!" Spencer caught Daisy's arm at the top of the stairs. "Why do we need the soap?"

Daisy looked at him as though he were an idiot. "So I can see the little critters and you can prove that you're not lying to me."

"Well, yes," Spencer said, rolling his eyes. "But we're not going to tell the janitors *that*."

"What're we going to tell them, then?"

"Well, *I* needed it because I had marker on my face. The soap took it off, no problem." Spencer quickly unzipped his backpack and pulled out a ballpoint pen.

"What are you doing?" Daisy yelped as he reached for her face.

"I'm giving us a reason to ask for soap."

Daisy whimpered at first, but gradually became more co-operative. It was over in a flash. Daisy had blue ink flames leaping up her cheek.

"I'll do the talking," Spencer said. "Come on."

The two kids quietly descended the stairs until they

stood at the doorway to the large storage closet. From this angle, Spencer could see a small desk with a computer nestled among the janitorial boxes, bottles, and canisters. It seemed that the closet doubled for an office.

"Hello?" Spencer called into the dimly lit room.

Almost immediately, a head of shaggy black hair popped over a stack of boxes. Marv Bills stepped out, studying the two kids skeptically. He dusted off his hands, clapping them together like two thick slabs of meat.

Marv wore the same dirty white shirt as the day before. If anything, his faded jeans were sagging further down his behind. He looked a few years older than thirty, but it was hard to tell with his bushy beard. Really the only difference between Marv and a grizzly bear was that Marv could speak.

The burly janitor took a few steps forward, the massive ring of keys at his side tinkling like the bells on Santa's sleigh. Marv grunted when he saw Daisy's face. "Tattoos? In elementary school?" He shook his head and muttered, "What's this world coming to?"

"It's not a tattoo. We need soap," Spencer blurted. Instantly, he wished he'd made some small talk or said something to make it sound less desperate. "Hi, how are you?" he tried again, but it was like telling the joke after the punch line.

"Soap?" Marv asked. "There should be plenty in the girls' bathroom. I filled the dispensers yesterday."

"But she's got ink on her face," Spencer said. "We need soap that'll take it off fast. You know, the strong stuff."

Marv folded his arms. "You kids shouldn't be down here."

"Sorry," Daisy said. "We'll go."

Spencer grabbed her arm. "Not till we get some soap." Spencer stared at the janitor. With a swift motion, Marv reached over and grabbed something off a shelf.

"Think fast," he said, tossing a small rectangular box across the room. Daisy caught it, then fumbled, but caught it again before it hit the ground. Spencer reached for it anxiously, but she evaded his grasp and turned to read the label on the box.

Irish Spring.

"What?" Spencer muttered, finally pulling the box from Daisy's hands. He tore open the little flaps on the end and dumped a green bar of soap into his left hand.

"Not this." Spencer shook his head at Marv. "I want the *special* stuff. The pink gel soap that takes off marker and makes your face tingle."

"Why don't you just be glad for what you got and scram?" Marv flicked his wrist at them. "One kind of soap works just like another. There's no special stuff down here."

With those words, Daisy suddenly went rigid. Warily, Spencer glanced over at her. The blue ink flames outlined on her cheek were turning red. She slowly twisted her glare to meet his eyes.

"Bully," she whispered. Her eyes looked like they might be sprouting tears sometime in the next ten seconds.

"No, Daisy, I promise, I—"

"Dez tells me that forests only grow on islands and tricks

me into putting my thumbs up my nose. But you—you pretend to be my friend so you can draw doodles on my face and scare me into thinking that little monsters roam the school." The first tear departed, running down her cheek and sizzling on the flames. "Gullible Gates! Yeah, right! I'm not believing anyone anymore." Daisy turned and ran up the stairs, covering her graffitied cheek with one hand. Spencer started to follow, but a firm hand gripped his backpack.

"What do you know about monsters?" Marv hissed in his ear.

"Let me go!" Spencer slipped out of his arm straps and began a tug of war with his pack. Daisy had blown his secret!

"Where'd you get this special soap?"

"*You* know!" Spencer said. "You left it lying around!"

Marv suddenly released his backpack and Spencer staggered sideways a few steps. "You've got yourself into real trouble, boy," Marv whispered. "Stuff like that's not meant for you."

The bell rang to announce the beginning of class. Spencer moved toward the stairs.

"I haven't seen the last of you," Marv said. "But tomorrow, we've got an even bigger problem, so you'll have to wait. What's your name?"

"I'm not telling!" Spencer raced up the stairs.

"Then I'll find out!"

CHAPTER 7

"LOOK OUT BEHIND YOU!"

When Spencer reached the classroom, the Bath and Body Works fragrance of Miss Leslie Sharmelle had been replaced by a slight odor of cabbage.

Mrs. Natcher was back.

"Good morning, class," Mrs. Natcher said.

"Good morning, Mrs. Natcher," the class recited in unison.

Along with smelling like a steamed veggie, Mrs. Natcher was very conservative and formal. In her late fifties, she didn't bother to dye her graying hair or paint her nails. After Miss Sharmelle's flash and flare, Mrs. Natcher seemed drab and boring.

Daisy ignored Spencer all morning. The liquid soap in the girls' bathroom had taken the blue flames off her face—mostly. Her cheek was scrubbed raw and her determination was clearly set. Even Dez knew something was wrong with Daisy when she refused to believe that his tennis shoes had once belonged to the president of the United States. Gullible Gates had finally decided that *no one* could be trusted.

With the events in the storage closet as a prelude to his day, Spencer stayed far away from the janitor's stairwell. Before lunch, he entered the boys' bathroom to wash up, ducking past Marv in the hallway.

In the bathroom, he encountered a third type of creature. This one was slimy, pale yellow, and looked like a salamander. It was perched on the rim of the sink, its long black tongue working at some grimy film that had built up next to the tap. Spencer froze to watch, but the creature quickly sensed him and slid into the bowl of the sink. Its body flattened as though bones were optional and quickly slithered down the drain.

A few minutes later, Spencer was looking at a tray of mediocre cafeteria food, trying not to think that gross little creatures might live in the kitchen.

"'Sup, Batman?" Dez turned away from his food, shouting at Spencer over his shoulder. Dez was surrounded by his usual knucklehead buddies. "See any bats with beaks today?"

Spencer froze, his lunch tray gripped firmly. *Don't even look over there*, he told himself. *Just keep walking.* But it was a good thing he looked, because there *was* a bat monster perched right on Dez's milk carton. Its bald head bobbed as it wedged a sharp beak into the carton for a slurp of milk.

"Look out behind you!" Spencer shouted at Dez,

winning the attention of everyone in the cafeteria. Whether it was the sincerity in Spencer's voice or the suddenness with which he shouted, Dez whirled around in genuine surprise. His clumsy turn tipped the milk carton, sending the invisible creature into the air and cold milk into Dez's crotch.

The noisy room erupted with laughter at Dez's blunder. Across the cafeteria, Spencer glimpsed Daisy looking up from her sack lunch. Spencer watched the creature's jagged flight pattern until it ducked out the doorway. When he looked back down, Dez was coming right for him.

Sudden loss of appetite, coupled with the urge to run, made Spencer dump his lunch directly into the nearest garbage and head for the door. Bursting outside, he raced across the playground, not daring to check over his shoulder until he reached the far side of the soccer field. There was no sign of pursuit, so he slumped against the goalpost.

Tears were trying to surface. Spencer shut his eyes. His sixth-grade year was turning out to be worse than he could have imagined and he wanted to shut it out, to pretend he was at his old school. But shutting his eyes wasn't such a bright idea, since he was surrounded when he opened them.

Spencer scrambled to his feet, ringed in by Dez's friends. The bully stood right before him, an embarrassing wet mark down the front of his shorts. In his hand was a new milk carton that he tossed from left to right like a hot potato.

"So," Dez said. "You tried to get me with the oldest, stupidest trick in the book?" He held up his hands in mock fear. "'Oh! Look out behind you!'" he shouted in a high-pitched voice. "That's what *you'd* better be doing, Doofus. Because I'm going to be right behind you from now on."

"But it wasn't a trick," Spencer said. "I really did see something on your lunch tray. It flew off when you turned around."

"Whatever," Dez said. "You made me look bad in the lunchroom and you're going to pay for that." Dez took a step forward. "Do you know what this is?" He held the carton close to Spencer's face.

"Milk?" Spencer hoped.

"Yeah, it's milk. But take a look at the inspiration date."

"Very inspiring," Spencer said. "But it's actually the *expiration* date."

"Whatever," Dez said. "The point is—it's old. Steve's been keeping this in his desk since the first day of school. Should be nice and rotten by now. We've been saving it for a special occasion. This might be special enough. Unless . . ."

"Unless what?" Spencer asked. He stared at the deadly milk carton. Swimming inside were countless bacteria and germs galore. "What do you want from me?"

"Just a simple apology," Dez answered. "And explain to my homies that you lied about the invisible bats."

"But I didn't lie . . ."

"Hold him, guys."

The nearest bullies grabbed Spencer's arms. He tried to jerk free, but their grip was tight. Dez peeled back the cardboard flaps on the milk carton and gagged at the rotted smell. Then he slowly tipped the carton forward.

"Wait! Wait!" cried Spencer. "I'm sorry, okay? You're

41

right! I didn't see anything on your lunch tray. I never saw anything in the classroom. I lied about all of that. I was just making it up to get attention!"

Dez grinned and stepped back. "That's what I thought." Spencer tried to relax as the bullies released his arms. "See, Batman," Dez continued. "Isn't it easier when you do what I say? We both get what we want. I get to hear you confess about your dumb lies. And you? Well, this should get you plenty of attention."

With that, Dez hurled the milk carton. It struck Spencer in the chest with an explosion of putrid milk. The bullies ran off, laughing and whooping.

Spencer stepped away from the spot where the carton fell, glugging out yellowish milk. His shirt was ruined. It absolutely reeked. He wiped his face and noticed someone standing near.

It was Daisy. She looked sad and upset. Spencer was grateful that at least one person cared. But then she opened her mouth.

"You really did lie to me," she said, and Spencer knew she wasn't sad about him. "I heard you say it. You just made it all up for attention. *And* so you could draw on my face."

"Look, Daisy," Spencer said, rising to his feet, "I never lied to you. I really did see a creature on his lunch tray. I just had to tell those guys that I made it up so they'd leave me alone."

"Why?" she said. "If it's true, why did you tell them it wasn't? No one will ever believe you if you don't stand up for what you know is true."

"But you saw. They were going to dump bad milk on me."

"So you denied it."

"Yeah. I denied it to them."

"And they dumped bad milk on you anyway." Daisy shrugged. "Either way, you got bad milk. Seems like it would have been better to stand up for the truth." Daisy waved awkwardly, as if she were bidding him farewell forever.

Spencer stood alone on the soccer field. "Man," he said. "This stinks."

And it did.

CHAPTER 8

"WHAT KIND OF MAINTENANCE?"

Spencer started the next day at school with the secretary's voice crackling through the old intercom. "Good morning, boys and girls. We have a few announcements to make. Tomorrow there is a morning assembly. D.A.R.E. Officer Jacobs will be teaching us how to stay drug free.

"After-school clubs will not convene today. The Bureau of Educational Maintenance will be meeting with the janitors immediately after the bell. We ask that everyone leave the building as quickly as possible so the folks from the Bureau can do their routine checks. Have a great day."

Click.

Spencer, who had been twirling his pencil around his thumb, stopped suddenly, and the pencil rolled off the edge of his desk. Bureau of Educational Maintenance? Like, *building* maintenance? A bureau of janitors, perhaps? If that was true, maybe he could get some info about them at lunch.

Spencer felt tired through all of Mrs. Natcher's morning lessons. Not algebra-tired, like before, but still tired enough to ruin his focus. He hadn't slept much the night before. Every time he closed his eyes, the scene with Dez and the milk carton replayed.

When he watched the instant replay in his mind, Spencer bravely stood up for what he knew was right and took the rotten milk like a man. Then Daisy believed him and together they tried to convince responsible adults to acknowledge that Welcher Elementary had a major pest problem. Together they investigated the janitors and found out more about the creatures.

But that version of the story wasn't real. Spencer had denied the truth, shattered any hope of Daisy believing him, and still been hit with the sour-milk bomb. He was too ashamed to even tell his mom. The stinky shirt had gone straight into the garbage.

Spencer felt like a real loner. Dez hated him. Daisy wouldn't believe him. If he wanted to learn more about the janitors, he would be doing it alone.

When the lunch bell rang, Spencer made his routine stop at the restroom to wash up. Then he kept an eye out for big Marv as he quietly made his way to the front office.

Spencer had entered the office only once before, with his siblings, a few days before school began. They'd been living in Aunt Avril's house all summer, but of course his mom had waited until the last possible moment to register them and fill out the paperwork so the four Zumbro kids could be admitted to their new school.

"Can I help you?" asked the same voice that gave the announcements. Without the crackle and pop of the intercom, the secretary sounded much younger. Spencer had always imagined that the voice belonged to someone with an extraterrestrial in her family tree, but Mrs. Hamp was actually far too normal looking.

"Hi," Spencer said. "I had a question about the announcements this morning." He stayed a few apprehensive feet from her desk.

"After-school clubs will *not* be convening today. To 'convene' means to meet. Put it together. No after-school clubs today, sorry," she answered mechanically, as though a dozen other kids had already been in to bother her about it.

"I know. I'm not in a club. I just had a question about the bureau that's coming."

"The Bureau of Educational Maintenance?"

"Yeah," Spencer said. "What do they do?"

Seeing that his question was a cut above those of the pesky kids complaining about the cancellation of their clubs, Mrs. Hamp pasted on a friendly face. "The BEM is a very old agency. It oversees the maintenance of schools across the U.S."

"What kind of maintenance?"

"Structural integrity, environmental conditions, HR," she began with an I-know-big-words-and-you-don't look on her face. She chuckled at her overabundant wisdom and glanced at Spencer with a look of feigned apology. "In other words, they make sure the building is safe and sound and everything is running correctly. The BEM is in charge of hiring and firing janitors across the nation."

Then she tilted her head sideways and absently picked up a stapler. "But mostly they just do mundane things like deep cleaning and checking to make sure all equipment is functioning adequately."

"And someone from the Bureau will be here after school today?" Spencer pressed. "To meet with Marv?"

"Marv?" Mrs. Hamp asked. "I think not. I would imagine they'll meet with John Campbell."

"Because he's Marv's boss?"

Mrs. Hamp set down the stapler. "My, you have a lot of questions," she said, regaining her initial level of annoyance.

"I'm just interested in that kind of stuff," Spencer lied. "Maybe someday I'd like to work for the BEM."

"Ho, no," Mrs. Hamp said, shaking her head. "You want to scrape up chewed gum and shampoo carpets for the rest of your life?" She tipped back in her chair. "Close the door when you leave. I have to eat lunch too, you know."

Spencer could see that he'd exhausted Mrs. Hamp's knowledge of the BEM, but it was enough. He shut the office door and headed to the lunchroom. He replayed his confrontation with Marv the day before. *Tomorrow, we've got an even bigger problem, so you'll have to wait.*

One thing seemed clear: Marv was nervous about the BEM's visit. And since he had said *"we've got a problem,"*

Spencer guessed that John Campbell was also involved. But what could the janitors at Welcher Elementary possibly have to hide?

To Spencer, the answer was right before his eyes, scuttling across the carpet, leaving a wake of gray dust.

CHAPTER 9

"THERE!"

Spencer's focus was even worse after lunch. Knowing that he might get answers from the BEM gave him anxious stomach butterflies. He also knew he would be breaking a rule to talk to the BEM, since the school was supposed to be empty for the routine checks. But Spencer was already planning a way around that.

Mrs. Natcher was droning on about what makes America great when Spencer felt drowsiness pull at his eyelids.

Not again! He sat up tall in an attempt to ward off the sleepiness. Then he caught a dreaded flash of movement that made his gut turn over. There, under the chalkboard, where white dust fell thickly to the carpet, Spencer saw a creature. It was one of the dust gophers, really enjoying a meal of carpet dirt and chalk dust.

Spencer stared for a moment, then glanced hopefully at his classmates. The creature must have truly been invisible, because to Spencer it sat in plain sight, only a yard from Mrs. Natcher's boring shoes.

Ignore it, Spencer thought. *Just ignore it and it will go away.* But even as he thought this, Spencer pointed a silent finger toward the creature.

"There," he whispered. The word was inaudible, but once he felt it form on his lips, it was easier the second time.

"There." The word got some attention this time and a few kids, including Dez, started looking where Spencer pointed.

"There!" This one was almost a shout and stopped Mrs. Natcher midsentence.

"If you have something to say," she instructed, "please raise your hand and I'll consider calling on you."

"THERE IT GOES!" Spencer jumped to his feet as the dust gopher took off across the room. He traced its run with his finger.

"What is it?" one student shouted.

"A spider?"

"A mouse?"

In seconds, the classroom was out of control. Kids were screaming and climbing onto their chairs. To add to the chaos, Dez knocked over Jen's desk, spilling pencils and notebooks.

Spencer watched the creature disappear into the hallway. He looked to see Daisy's reaction, but all he saw was

Mrs. Natcher coming right for him. She took him by the arm and dragged him to the front of the room.

"Class! Class! You will be silent in three, two, one." Mrs. Natcher clapped her hands and, like magic, the room fell quiet. "I'm sure Spencer would like a chance to explain himself."

Not really, Spencer thought. But it was too late now. Mrs. Natcher wasn't giving him an option. "Well, I thought I saw something."

"Not again," Juan moaned.

"*Again?*" Mrs. Natcher inquired. "Has this happened before?"

Cutting Spencer off, Dez took over. "While you were gone, Spencer thought he saw a bat. But just like this time, he was making it up." Dez turned to the class. "Come on, did anyone actually see anything?"

"Nope."

"Nothing."

"That's right," Dez said. "Nothing to see. Spencer made it up for attention. Told me so himself."

Mrs. Natcher clucked her tongue at Spencer. "That behavior is inappropriate and unacceptable in my classroom. Apologize to your classmates."

Spencer shifted uncomfortably. Couldn't they tell he was speaking the truth? Why would anyone make this up? Sure, he was getting attention, but it wasn't the good kind.

"Sorry," Spencer said. "I didn't mean to be disruptive. I thought I saw something, but maybe . . ." Then Spencer made the mistake of looking at Daisy Gates. Her eyes were trained on him, bolts of energy piercing him. *No one will ever believe you if you don't stand up for what you know is true.*

"I . . . I mean . . . I . . ." Each stammer was like the crank of an engine, slowly building up the power to take off. He looked at Dez. The bully was massaging his fist, like he was itching to pound somebody.

"I see creatures in the school. Some are slimy, some are furry, some have wings. I don't know why the rest of you can't see them. I'm trying to figure that out. I don't want to freak you guys out, but I had to tell you what I've seen."

Dead silence.

Then, like an avalanche: laughter. *Laughter!* Even Mrs. Natcher was chuckling in her own stuffy way. Spencer looked from face to face, sheer embarrassment and disappointment in his eyes. Then he saw Daisy, the one who wasn't laughing. Instead, her brown eyes gave a silent applause.

CHAPTER 10

"WALK WITH ME."

Spencer leaned his head against the pop machine and felt its steady vibration. Was that the machine's way of laughing at him too? Spencer could barely see the clock from where he was hiding. A half hour after school ended and Spencer could still hear his whole class laughing at him. Mrs. Natcher's tone lingered in his mind: "Sit down and remain silent."

All that had hurt deeply. But hurt wasn't the only feeling in his heart. A thread of courage had formed when he told the truth. Courage to stand up for what he knew was right. Courage to move forward with his plan to meet the BEM after school.

He was wedged between two vending machines in the teachers' lounge. Spencer had never even been in a teachers' lounge, let alone hidden out in one. But he'd also never seen demon dust gophers and slimy lizard things lurk-ing around the school. Desperate times called for desper-ate hideouts. The bus was long gone, carrying his younger brother and sisters back to Aunt Avril's house.

With no idea how long the BEM's routine checks would last, Spencer could afford to wait no longer.

Spencer slithered out of his hiding spot. His backpack had gone home with his sister Erica so he would be able to maneuver swiftly if he needed to. He walked past a table and two couches before gripping the doorknob.

Spencer's plan was simple. He would secretly locate one of the BEM representatives and share his concerns about Marv and the creatures. It might be tricky to isolate one of the reps, but Spencer was willing to wait for the opportunity to arise.

Silently, Spencer pushed open the door, hopeful that the coast was clear. Instead, he found himself face-to-face with shaggy Marv. Beside the janitor was a man with a sin-ewy neck, thick as a tree trunk. His blond hair was buzzed in a military crew cut.

Spencer's first thought was to scurry like a dust gopher back into the teachers' lounge. But that was a dead end. He could try to dart past them and sprint for the front doors. Hopeless. So Spencer decided to change his tactic altogether.

"You from the BEM?" Spencer asked the man with the thick neck. The stranger wasn't very tall, but he seemed as tough and bulletproof as Kevlar. Next to Marv, the man looked sharp and clean, no trace of whiskers on his square chin.

"Garth Hadley, regional representative for the Bureau of Educational Maintenance," the man affirmed with a curt nod.

"No kids allowed in the school right now," Marv ordered. Spencer could tell that Garth Hadley made the grubby janitor nervous and twitchy. Marv began chewing on his fingernails, which were, Spencer thought, probably not very clean. Neither man seemed to mind that a sixth grader had just walked out of the teachers' lounge.

"I'm working on a project," Spencer lied, racking his brain. "It's about . . . mops."

"Mops?" Garth Hadley repeated.

"Yeah." Spencer smiled. "Mops through the ages. It's for a history unit. I heard you were going to be here and I wondered if I could interview you, Mr. Hadley, sir."

Marv, shaking his dark head, took an intimidating step toward Spencer, his hairy belly peeking through a hole in his white T-shirt. "Get moving!" Marv said in a tone he might have used to scare a stray dog.

Spencer felt a chill run through him. There was no telling what the big janitor might do to keep Spencer away from the BEM rep. Spencer backed away from Marv's intimidating bulk. The boy was silently pleading that Mr. Hadley would intervene before the janitor used Spencer's face as a prototype for a new mop.

"Mr. Bills," Garth Hadley said to Marv. A slow smile spread across the man's square face, and one muscular hand gestured for Marv to back off. "I'll see that the boy gets outside," he said, directing Spencer by the shoulder. "And we'll talk mops on the way."

Instead of taking Spencer to the nearby front doors, Hadley led him down a long hallway to the exit that opened on the parking lot.

"How old are you? Eleven?" the man said.

"Twelve, actually. I just had a birthday at the end of August. I'm old for my grade."

The small talk was nice, but Spencer had more important things to discuss. Glancing over his shoulder, Spencer made sure that Marv's hulking form was out of earshot.

"It's not mops, really," Spencer said quietly. In his peripheral vision, Spencer caught sight of a winged vulture-bat cutting a jagged path toward the lunchroom. "It's the janitors, Mr. Hadley."

"What about them?" asked the thick man.

Now that Spencer had Mr. Hadley alone, he didn't know exactly how to say it. He couldn't risk becoming the brunt of another joke. The last thing he wanted was for this new stranger to have a laugh at his story. Spencer decided to start small and go from there.

"The janitors are . . . weird."

Mr. Hadley snorted. "Every profession has its drawbacks."

"No." Spencer decided to approach from a new angle. "It just seems like they can see things that other people can't."

"Like an extra layer of grime around the sink in the restroom?"

"Yeah," Spencer said, preparing to dive in. "Like an extra layer of grime that can tuck back its tail and slither down the drain."

Garth Hadley froze, one hand on the metal bar of the door. He was apparently in some kind of deep meditation. Spencer studied his clean, strong face but was unable to read the emotions there.

"Get outside," Hadley said firmly. At first, Spencer thought the man was angry. But to the boy's surprise, Mr. Hadley also stepped out, closing the school door behind him.

The September afternoon was hot and dry. Spencer could feel the sun's rays soaking into the asphalt parking lot, making the few remaining vehicles shimmer.

"What else have you seen?" Garth Hadley whispered, intensity in his eyes.

Spencer felt a rush of exhilaration. Mr. Hadley was believing him! Of course, Daisy had believed at first, but Spencer had gone too far and she was thrown off. Spencer chewed on his lip, carefully deciding how to pace his story.

"Sometimes I see bats in the garbage can . . . and rodents scurrying down the halls."

Mr. Hadley shook his head. "But they're not quite bats, are they? And they're not really rodents." He stooped to look directly into Spencer's eyes. "It's important that you tell me *everything*."

With this encouragement, Spencer spilled all. He

started at the beginning, with the soap he'd found in the bathroom. Then he explained each creature in detail and told how Marv could see them too. He told about his conversation with Daisy Gates and his confrontation with Dez and the sour milk. He ended with his confession to the class and the resulting bitter laughter.

Telling the whole story made it sound even more unbelievable, but the grave look on Garth Hadley's face assured Spencer that he was right about everything.

"Your story confirms our suspicions," Mr. Hadley said. "Walk with me."

They crossed the sweltering parking lot to a white van. On the driver's door was a circular seal with the United States eagle, *e pluribus unum* written on a banner in its beak. In one talon it held a broom; the other clutched a dustpan. "Bureau of Educational Maintenance" was scribed in fancy letters above the eagle's head. Other than the seal, the van was blocky and plain, with no other windows and no additional doors except at the rear.

Garth Hadley pulled Spencer around to the back of the van, the vehicle's shadow cooling their legs. Hadley dug in the back pocket of his black pants and withdrew a wallet. Spencer saw his driver's license and legal BEM certification card. After rifling through the contents for a moment, Hadley produced a photograph.

"Have you seen this man in or around Welcher Elementary School?" Hadley asked, passing Spencer the photo.

The person in the picture was old—at least mid-sixties.

The man's hair was wavy and white. His face was lean and wrinkled, with a full mustache and goatee. It looked like a professional photo with a blue cloth background. The paper it was printed on was dull, the borders showing jagged scissor marks. Clipped out of a school yearbook, perhaps.

"Never seen him," Spencer said, handing the photo back. "Who is he?"

"His name is Walter Jamison, but we have reason to believe that he's going under the alias of John Campbell."

"John Campbell?" Spencer asked. "The secretary says he's the head janitor here. But I've never seen him, just Marv. What does he have to do with the creatures in the school?"

"The little monsters you've been seeing are very dangerous, especially to children. They inhale brain waves of young people and exhale certain toxins that affect children's ability to learn. Walter Jamison has been gathering them with the intent to extract, shall we say, *magical* properties from the creatures."

Spencer stared, dumbfounded. An adult had just dropped the "m" word in all seriousness. This was awesome. Spencer was finally getting some answers.

"So Marv is helping him?" Spencer clarified.

Hadley nodded. "You told me that Marv was trying to capture that dust gopher in the hallway after school. They are wild little beasts. Very difficult to contain. The few you've seen around the school must have slipped through Walter's fingers."

"So why don't you just fire Marv and Walter?" Spencer

asked. "Isn't the BEM in charge of hiring and firing janitors all over the U.S.?"

"I'm sure he'll be fired soon. But it would be unwise to fire Walter now that he is finally within our grasp." Mr. Hadley tapped his square chin in thought. "Walter Jamison has grown very powerful. Should we fire him now, he would vanish for a time, then pop up again somewhere else. Like a bad weed. But we have a chance to cripple him here and now—to put an end to his experiments before it's too late."

"What are you going to do?"

"I'm going to finish my routine inspection of the school and leave. While representatives of the BEM are around, the janitors will be overly cautious. It will be impossible to do what it takes to break Jamison."

"If you guys aren't going to do it, then who is?" Spencer asked.

"I was hoping *you* might help us." Garth Hadley opened the back doors of the van. Spencer was too stunned for words. Maybe he would end up with a career in the BEM after all. And sooner than he thought. Spencer's thread of courage was growing, bolstered by these newfound answers.

"What do you say?" Hadley asked, crawling into the back of the van. Instead of seats, the van was full of custodial equipment. There were two different kinds of vacuums, several brooms, some dustpans, and a couple of boxes full of miscellaneous items.

"Sure," Spencer managed at last. "What can I do?"

CHAPTER II

"SWEET."

It's pretty complex," Garth Hadley explained. "Walter Jamison can only perform his warlock experiments within the walls of this school. He has fortified Welcher Elementary, using an ancient hammer to drive a bronze nail somewhere into the structure. The hammer gives him power, and the nail sets up a link with the building."

"What do I have to do?" Spencer asked.

"I need you to pull out the nail," Hadley explained, "with the same hammer that put it in."

"Whoa," muttered Spencer. "I don't know. I'm not really great with tools."

"You can do it," Hadley said. "It will be difficult. We have every reason to believe that Jamison keeps the bronze hammer on him at all times."

"That's why you want me to get it? Because he won't suspect me until it's too late?"

"Right," said Hadley. The man was on his knees, digging into a box in the back of the van. Spencer stood awkwardly by the bumper.

"Once I get the hammer, where will I find the nail?"

"We don't know. That is part of the reason we've scheduled these inspections." Hadley seemed to have found what he was looking for and began a backward crawl out of the van. "Once we get more details, I'll contact you and instruct you how to proceed."

Garth Hadley stood up and held out the two objects he had gathered from the box. His curiosity piqued, Spencer accepted the offerings. One was a small plastic flashlight with a red switch, the other, a used latex glove.

"Thought you might need these," Hadley said, shutting the back door of the van.

"Thanks," Spencer said, raising an eyebrow.

"There's more here than meets the eye," Hadley explained. "The flashlight bulb is charged with the same power that fuels Walter Jamison's projects. When you turn it on in the dark, you might not think it's doing much. However, other magical items will draw out a strong beam of light. That should help you find the nail and hammer.

"The glove is a dangerous item that we recovered from a raid of Walter Jamison's last experiment station. Jamison, it seems, somehow knew we were coming and was gone by the time we got there. Much like today, in fact."

"Where is he?"

"Marv said he was out of state at his brother's funeral. An unlikely story. But the glove," Hadley explained, "will be vital to your success."

"What does it do?" Spencer asked, dangling the limp, yellowish glove between two fingers.

"Put it on," Hadley encouraged.

Spencer looked at the used glove with apprehension. Who knew where this had been? What kind of germy hands had slipped into this glove before him?

"Nothing to fear," Hadley said, sensing his hesitation. "The glove won't harm you."

Spencer peered into the opening where his hand was supposed to go. Maybe it didn't look so bad inside. He pulled a face. Anyway, Garth Hadley was waiting for him. Taking a deep breath, Spencer plunged his hand into the glove, finding plenty of extra space at the end of each finger.

Hadley suddenly reached out with a sharp motion and grabbed Spencer's arm above the elbow.

"Ow!" Spencer winced at the iron grip and jerked away. To Spencer's surprise, his arm stretched and slipped easily through Hadley's grasp—as though the man were gripping a blob of Jell-O.

"Sweet," whispered Spencer.

Garth Hadley smiled. "As long as you're wearing that glove, no one will be able to hold you down." Spencer pulled it off, feeling the latex stretch and watching the glove turn inside out, a bit of sweat moistening the rubber.

"One exception," Hadley said, "although it's very

unlikely it will occur. If your opponent wears a similar glove, both become able to catch the other. Understand?"

Spencer nodded, still trying to believe that this was actually happening.

"Even with this gear, you'll need to be extremely clever and fast," Mr. Hadley continued. "You'll need some pretty potent distractions to occupy the janitors while you go snooping around. Be thinking—I'll be thinking too."

"What about Daisy?"

"Who?"

"Remember," Spencer said, "the girl whose face I drew on? I'd really like to show her the creatures. I think she could help me too."

"I thought she didn't believe you," Hadley said.

"She didn't," said Spencer. "But with your help, and some soap, she will."

"You want me to give her soap?"

Spencer nodded.

Hadley exhaled slowly. "Intentionally expose a child?" he whispered to himself, obviously caught in some moral dilemma.

"Out of everyone I've told, she's the most likely to believe," Spencer coaxed. "She wants to believe, but she gets tricked a lot." In his mind, Spencer saw the future playing out more hopefully. He would prove to Daisy that he wasn't a prankster, and at the same time he'd gain a friend to help him with Mr. Hadley's assignment.

Garth Hadley began to nod almost imperceptibly, his lips pursed. He led Spencer around to the driver's door and reached between the seats. He handed a clear plastic bottle to Spencer, half full of the strong pink soap. "Swear one thing," he said.

"What?" said Spencer, noting the intensity in Hadley's eyes.

"That soap is shared with Daisy alone. Once her eyes are opened, you'll give the bottle back to me with the bronze hammer and nail."

"Yes, sir."

"One more thing. As you've probably gathered by now, all this stuff is top secret. That means you'd probably better let things drop with your classmates. For your own good as well as theirs."

Spencer nodded. "They're going to tease me about what I've already said."

"Ignore it. This is dangerous business. We don't want to get anyone else involved. If they tease you, be silent and strong. Focus all your energy on your secret mission and bring Jamison down."

Hadley snatched a paper from the dashboard. He clicked a pen from his pocket. "You have a cell phone, Spencer?"

"Nope."

"How about e-mail?"

"SpenceZ@wahoo.com," replied Spencer. Hadley scribbled it down.

"If you run into trouble, just contact me," Hadley explained. He replaced his pen in his pocket and withdrew a business card with his name, phone number, and e-mail address printed on it. "The BEM doesn't want anyone getting hurt. If you think this is too much, don't hesitate to call. We can find some other way. But personally, I think you'll hit Walter Jamison so hard that he won't know what happened." Mr. Hadley patted Spencer's shoulder. "Good luck."

"Wait," cried Spencer as the man walked back toward the school.

"Go home, kid," Hadley shouted back.

Spencer leaned against the white van, wondering if the president of the United States knew that one of the government agencies had just enlisted a twelve-year-old.

CHAPTER 12

"THEM'S THE WORST KIND OF FOLKS."

The Gates home was small and rundown, the polar opposite of Aunt Avril's mansion on the hill. The single-story structure had been painted blue several times over the five decades that it spanned. The cement walkway sported cracks so large that the path looked tiered. A maple tree had been planted too close to the driveway. Now taller than the house, the tree roots reached far and limbs overhung the front porch.

Spencer found the house easily. After leaving Hadley's white van in the school parking lot, he had biked four blocks to a Chevron gas station. There, shuffling through the pages of an outdated directory at a dilapidated pay phone, he'd found the Gates's address. A two-block ride through the afternoon sun had brought him to the edge of Daisy's property.

The grass was mostly dry and crispy brown—at least Aunt Avril's house shared that feature after three months of Zumbro housekeeping. There was a large garage apart from the house. The garage door was open and a Buick was jacked up inside. There were two other cars parked on the broken driveway and a truck on the street.

Spencer stepped off his bike and put down the kickstand on the sidewalk. He reached into his pocket and felt the little bottle of soap. Would Daisy believe him now that he had told the truth in class? She wouldn't want to get tricked again, but Spencer had a plan to help her believe. The first step was knocking on the front door.

Spencer stepped onto the first tier of the walkway. As though he had tripped some unseen sensor, a black dog came tearing around the corner, barking, teeth bared. Spencer jumped backward off the walkway, but the dog seemed to have dinner on its mind. The boy stumbled into the street, tipping over his bicycle.

There was a sharp jangle of chains and the barking snapped short. Spencer glanced over his shoulder to see the dog, chain pulled tight around its neck, halfway across the yard.

Movement in the garage caught Spencer's eye. A pair of legs was sliding out from under the Buick! The legs gave way to torso, arms, and finally a head as a man stood up, staring into the street and wiping his grease-smeared hands on his blue coveralls.

Spencer stared. The man stared back. In his left pocket,

Spencer was fingering the latex glove and wondering if he could slip through dog teeth if the chain snapped.

"What's up?" the man called, walking down the driveway. His face was round and he was balding. Spencer guessed he was in his late thirties.

"Looking for Daisy Gates," Spencer said. "Does she live here?"

"Most certainly does," answered the man. His voice had a casual drawl. "But she ain't home right now. She's on a business trip to California."

"Dad!" Daisy exclaimed, appearing beside the Buick in the garage. Mr. Gates began to laugh as his daughter strolled down the driveway toward them.

"Aw, shoot," the man said, slapping his leg. "You heard me?"

"Hi, Daisy." Spencer waved awkwardly. It had been two days since he'd drawn blue flames on her cheek. He knew she'd been intrigued, frustrated, embarrassed, and disappointed in the past few days—all because of him. Suddenly, standing in front of her house seemed really uncomfortable.

Daisy gave him an unreadable stare before saying, "Hello, Spencer."

"This a friend of yours, Daisy?" Mr. Gates asked, gesturing at Spencer with a shiny, oiled finger.

"He's in my class," Daisy answered. Spencer painfully noted how he hadn't gained *friend* status yet. "What are you doing here?" she asked Spencer.

"I missed the bus," Spencer admitted.

"So you came to my house?"

"I looked you up in the phone book at the gas station."

Mr. Gates whistled through his teeth. "Darn resourceful, this kid."

"I was really hoping that you might give me a lift home. I live kind of far." Spencer gave Daisy a pleading look.

"You've got your bike." She pointed to the sidewalk where the back wheel of the toppled bicycle spun slowly.

"It's uphill." There was a moment of silence. "Please?"

"Don't look at me," Daisy finally answered. "*I* can't drive." Spencer shifted his plea to Mr. Gates.

"You bet," he said. "It might do me some good to get away from that Buick for a bit." He slapped the empty pockets of his coveralls, then said, "Daisy, run grab the truck keys, will you?"

Spencer quickly spoke up. "I was wondering if I could come inside for a minute. To use the bathroom," he explained, somewhat self-consciously.

"Take him in, Daisy," the mechanic said. "Just look out for the dog. She only bites a few times before she decides if she likes you or not."

Spencer followed Daisy through the garage, across a patch of hard, dry dirt, up some side steps and through a screen door, narrowly missing the dog. They entered through the kitchen. Gratefully, Spencer saw plenty of clutter on the countertop and dining table. Daisy didn't notice as he swiped a small paper and pen from the mess and tucked it into his pocket.

"The bathroom is yours," she said after leading him

down a narrow hallway with old, creaking floorboards. "I'll meet you outside."

"Thanks," he said, stepping into the small bathroom and shutting the door. Immediately, Spencer removed the paper and spread it on the counter next to the sink. There was a grocery list hastily scribbled on one side, so Spencer flipped it over and started to write.

> Daisy,
>
> This is the soap—the real stuff. Wash your face with this tonight. If I'm lying, you have nothing to lose. I'll never know that you used the soap and you never have to talk to me again. If I'm telling the truth, then tomorrow you'll see what I see.
>
> I need your help. Please try it.
>
> Spencer

He read over the note once more, adding a comma that he'd missed the first time. Spencer pulled out the top drawer, revealing a tube of toothpaste, some fingernail clippers, and a single toothbrush. Removing the little bottle from his pocket, Spencer placed the note and the soap in the drawer next to the toothbrush.

A moment later, he was outrunning the dog and climbing into the Ford truck idling by the curb. Mr. Gates had already loaded Spencer's bike in the back. The boy pulled the truck door shut and strapped on his seat belt. Daisy occupied the middle seat, but the cab was still spacious.

Daisy's father put the truck in gear and rolled away from

the Gates home, leaving his garage door up and the house unlocked. The driver's side window was down and the wind blew what hair was left on his head.

"Where we going?" Mr. Gates asked.

"Hillside Estates," Spencer said.

Mr. Gates whistled through his teeth again. "We've got a big shot here, Daisy," he said.

Spencer felt his face turn as red as the truck's paint. He wanted to explain that the house wasn't really his—that they were just living in it because Uncle Wyatt was away on business and Aunt Avril felt bad that Spencer's dad had left them in the lurch. Instead, Spencer just fumed silently for a moment, wishing that *he* had a dad who drove a Ford truck and trusted the world enough to leave the house unlocked.

The silence became awkward and Mr. Gates turned on the radio. When the stations only came in fuzzy, he snapped it off and turned to his silent passengers. "You go to school together, right? Don't you two have anything to talk about?"

"I haven't decided about Spencer yet," Daisy said to her dad as though they were alone in the truck.

"Decided? What do you mean?" her dad asked. With each comment, Spencer grew more uncomfortable. He watched out the window in desperate anticipation for Hillside Estates.

"Well, he's very confusing. He told me the truth and lied to another boy. But that made me wonder if maybe he lied to me and told the truth to the other boy. Now I'll never know for sure. He says some really interesting things, but I'm afraid he might be a chameleon."

"A chameleon?" Mr. Gates slapped a hand to his forehead. "Them's the worst kind of folks."

Spencer cleared his throat to remind them that he was actually still in the vehicle.

"And he drew on my face," Daisy said. "But it washed off."

Another bout of silence hit the truck like a black hole.

"Could someone please explain why I'm a chameleon?" Spencer finally muttered.

"A chameleon," Mr. Gates said as he turned into Hillside Estates, "is a type of lizard that changes color. Might be green one moment and black the next. It changes to fit the environment around it, sometimes to blend in, sometimes to stand out."

"But what does that have to do with me?" Spencer pointed out Aunt Avril's house and the big Ford rolled into the driveway.

"You don't get it?" Daisy asked, a faint smirk on her face. "In our family, a chameleon is someone whose story changes. They might tell it one way, then totally twist it around and tell a different version. People do it when they're insecure. Sometimes to blend in, sometimes to stand out."

Spencer wasn't pleased about being called a color-changing lizard. He had a comeback worked up, but he let it die on his lips. Just wait. The soap was in Daisy's drawer. Soon she'd see that he wasn't a chameleon.

"Thanks for the ride, Mr. Gates," Spencer said, slipping off the edge of the seat. He checked his pocket for the flashlight and the latex glove. With both items secure, he walked to the back of the truck, but Mr. Gates had beaten him there. With a smile, Daisy's dad lifted out the boy's bike. Spencer jumped on and pedaled up the driveway. Ditching the bike on the steps, he opened the front door.

The house was its usual mess. Spencer hadn't seen the station wagon out front, which meant that his mother wasn't home. She would most likely bring back dinner. His mom flaked out on a lot of things, but the kids could always depend on her for some kind of dinner. The house was quiet. Max was probably with Mom. The other kids could be anywhere.

Spencer waded through a three-month-old box of clothes yet to be unpacked and found his way down the hall to the computer room. Photographs of Aunt Avril and Uncle Wyatt flashed across the screen until Spencer wiggled the mouse. Compared to the school computers, the internet seemed faster at Hillside Estates, and he had his e-mail open in no time.

Spencer felt his heart race as he saw that there was one unread message from ghadley@bem.gov. *"Instructions"* was the subject heading.

With a nervous hand, Spencer opened the e-mail.

CHAPTER 13

"I GOT MORE INFO."

Spencer and Daisy crouched behind the corkscrew slide on the playground. Daisy was breathing hard, as if she had just run a half marathon. In reality, she had barely run from the back door of the school to the playground before Spencer had intercepted her on his bike. Now the bike was ditched in the bark next to the tire swing and the two kids were using the slide for cover.

"How can you go in there with those . . . those *things* crawling around the hallways?" Daisy asked again, shaking her head in disbelief. The second bell rang, making them both officially tardy for Mrs. Natcher's class.

Spencer was relieved and delighted that Daisy had tried the soap. Now that she had seen the creatures for herself, Daisy was the best listener. Spencer had told her all he'd learned from Garth Hadley about the BEM and how he'd been enlisted to stop the janitors at Welcher Elementary.

"So they want you to do dirty work for the Bureau of Educational Maintenance?" Daisy asked. "I don't know." She sighed. "I met John Campbell when he came to Welcher at the end of last year. He doesn't really seem like the magical-experiment type of guy."

"You don't believe me again?" Spencer cried. "You think I'm still being a chameleon?"

"I know *you* are telling the truth," she said. "But what if the BEM is wrong about the janitors?"

"Don't be crazy," Spencer said. "The Bureau's a government agency." He opened his backpack. "I got more info," he said, handing Daisy a printed e-mail.

She read intently, mumbling every fifth word or so. But Spencer didn't need her to read it out loud. He'd read the message so many times he almost had it memorized.

To: SpenceZ@wahoo.com
From: ghadley@bem.gov
Subject: Instructions

Spencer:

I believe we were able to determine the location of Walter Jamison's bronze nail. At the end of the hallway by the gym is a boy's bathroom. The restroom has been labeled "out of order."

The door is normally locked, but I managed to jam the lock during our routine inspection. Somewhere in the bathroom is the nail. Before you go for the hammer, you must know exactly where the nail is. Here's the plan:

At precisely 11:06 tomorrow morning, the power will go out at Welcher Elementary School. The power will remain off for eight minutes. You should be able to get inside the bathroom without anyone seeing. Also, with the lights off, your flashlight will come in handy. Use the flashlight to locate the nail, then get back to your classroom and wait for more instructions via e-mail. Be careful, and watch out for the janitors!

Garth Hadley
BEM regional representative

"I always wondered about that bathroom by the gym," Daisy said. "It was out of order for months last year. Wonder why the janitors haven't fixed it yet."

"Because it's not broken," Spencer said. "They just *say* it's out of order so they can hide the nail in there and nobody will go in." Spencer checked his watch. "Hmm—11:06. That's only two hours from now. Are you coming with me?"

"You only have one glove," Daisy said.

"We shouldn't need it," Spencer answered. "Remember, this time we're just scouting for the nail."

"Yeah." Daisy swallowed hard. "I'll come."

CHAPTER 14

"TAKE THE HALL PASS."

By the time the clock showed 11:00, Spencer's hands were sweating. He kept glancing at Daisy. Her eyes shifted nervously from the clock to her worksheet and back to the clock. What was she doing? Daisy was supposed to be out of the classroom with the hall pass by now.

Spencer checked his wristwatch. The digital screen showed 00:00. Since Mr. Hadley's 11:06 might not be the same as Mrs. Natcher's 11:06, Spencer was ready to hit "start" on his watch the minute the power went out. From there, he would have eight minutes to rendezvous with Daisy in the hallway, check the "out of order" bathroom, and get back to the classroom. If Daisy would ever leave!

Finally, at 11:01 and a half, Daisy's hand shot up, the gesture screaming urgency.

"Yes, Daisy?" Mrs. Natcher said, peering over her glasses in the usual manner.

"May I please go to the restroom, Mrs. Natcher?"

Mrs. Natcher breathed deeply through her nose as she looked at the clock. With three pairs of eyes on the clock, Spencer wondered if the minute hand would freeze under pressure. Evidently deeming it a good time to grant Daisy's wish, Mrs. Natcher simply said, "Take the hall pass," and looked back at the computer screen on her desk.

Mrs. Natcher, for some odd reason, used a bald baby doll wearing nothing but a diaper for a hall pass. Whatever the teacher's reasons, the doll (nicknamed Baybee) usually embarrassed students enough to prevent unnecessary trips out of the classroom. But at 11:02, Daisy leapt up, snatched Baybee without reserve, and disappeared out the door.

The next four minutes passed like hours for Spencer. His worksheet was untouched on his desk. He quietly clicked his tongue with each movement of the red second hand. Dissatisfied by the sluggish tempo of the clock, he began clicking twice for each second.

"Shut up," Dez grunted at his side, but Spencer didn't hear him.

Five . . . four . . . three . . . two . . . one . . .

11:06.

Nothing.

Spencer glanced up at the fluorescent tube lights on the ceiling. Not so much as a flicker. Spencer's stomach began to twist nervously.

Then, without a sound, the lights turned off. The fan

in the back of the room gradually slowed and Mrs. Natcher looked up from the black screen of her computer with an annoyed look, as though the power outage was planned. Well—it *was*, but Mrs. Natcher had no way of knowing that.

Spencer hit the button on his watch and the seconds started rolling.

Dez immediately jumped to his feet and did some awkward dance move while chanting, "Power's out! Power's out! Wahoo!"

The classroom had one large window in the wall, but Mrs. Natcher kept it covered with outdated paisley curtains. Under the curtains was a shade that she'd pulled down the first time the overhead projector was used and she'd never put it up again.

"Everyone sit down," Mrs. Natcher said. "The power will return at any moment." She crossed the room to pull up the window shade and let in the now-needed sunlight.

Spencer waited until Mrs. Natcher's back was turned. The class was still in mild chaos, and he attracted no extra attention as he slipped out the door.

It took Spencer longer than he wanted to find Daisy in the dim hallway. At the sight of Marv, Daisy had retreated to hide in a remote corner, clutching Baybee as if it were her own child. Spencer wandered several halls before they found each other.

Three precious minutes had passed by the time they stood before the boys' bathroom with a wrinkled "out of order" sign thumbtacked to the wooden door. Spencer was holding the little gray flashlight in his hand, but he was afraid to turn it on. Baybee dangled in Daisy's grip by one plastic arm, the doll's diaper crooked from Daisy's run down the hall.

Here, by the gym, it was rather dark. Spencer knew that without a window in the restroom, it would be pitch-black inside. Not willing to waste any more time, Spencer clicked the flashlight's switch with his thumb. A dull, yellow glow appeared at the end of the small bulb. As Mr. Hadley had explained, it wasn't even bright enough to illuminate the door two feet away.

Spencer was reaching out for the door when suddenly a bright white beam of light shot from the flashlight, angling sideways across the hallway. Spencer and Daisy jerked around to see the beam land on a winged vulture-bat. It was hanging upside down from the ceiling, but when the light touched it, the creature took flight. Spencer's light tracked the jagged flight pattern masterfully, even though the flashlight was motionless in his hand.

The flying beast dove and touched the ground. Wriggling forward, it disappeared through the gap under the gym door. The flashlight returned to its dull glow in Spencer's hand.

"What happened?" hissed Daisy in his ear.

"Mr. Hadley said that other magical objects would draw out the light. I guess that means creatures too." Spencer finally pushed open the bathroom door. A small card fell to the hard floor. Hadley must have used it to stop the door from latching.

Spencer picked up the card. "Come on," he urged, using the Indiglo feature on his watch to see that five minutes had passed. Daisy didn't move. "What's wrong?"

She hesitated. "I've never been in a boys' bathroom before."

"Oh, please," Spencer muttered. "They're just like girls' bathrooms, except *we* have couches and entertainment systems with surround sound."

"Really?" Daisy asked, her gullibility setting in again.

Daisy stepped into the bathroom and Spencer inserted the card over the latch and carefully shut the door over it, plunging the restroom into nearly complete darkness. In the dim light from the flashlight's weak bulb, Spencer saw two urinals on the wall next to a single stall. There was one sink with an old soap dispenser and a roll of paper towels.

Suddenly, the flashlight flared to life. The white beam split the darkness, pinpointing its target near the sink. Then the beam flashed a different direction, toward the wall of the bathroom stall. Erratically, the light jumped between two objects.

The target near the sink crawled forward. When the next flash of light highlighted it, Spencer and Daisy saw that it was one of the salamander creatures. The flashlight shifted targets and Daisy backed up, fearful that the little monster would crawl up her leg in the darkness. The next time they saw the creature, it was stretching its pale body through the grate on the floor drain. Then it was gone.

With only one magical target now, the flashlight shone a steady white beam at the silver wall of the bathroom stall.

All of the light honed in on one small area no larger than the head of a nail.

"There!" Daisy whispered. They had just taken a step toward the stall when the wooden door of the bathroom banged shut behind them. Spencer whirled around, but the flashlight changed to a weak glow as he faced away from the nail. Spencer felt Daisy draw closer to him. The boy's bathroom was almost completely dark again.

But *three* people were breathing in the darkness!

"Ha ha!" laughed the intruder. "Gotcha!"

That voice was much too familiar—and the last one that Spencer or Daisy expected to hear.

"Open the door, Dez," Spencer spoke into the darkness. They'd seen the nail and, according to Spencer's timer, had two minutes before the lights came back. Spencer had hoped to take a closer look at the bronze nail, but there wasn't time now.

"That's a wimpy flashlight," Dez said. His voice had drawn a step nearer.

Spencer reached into his pocket and felt the latex glove. Then he quickly withdrew his hand, realizing that Daisy would be stuck in the boys' room alone with Dez if he used the glove to escape. Facing away from the nail, the little flashlight wasn't doing much. Spencer didn't want to arouse Dez's curiosity further, so he switched off the light.

At seeing the dim bulb turn off, Dez laughed. "You can run, but you can't hide!"

Spencer grabbed Daisy's hand and jerked her against the wall as they heard Dez lunge through the blackness.

"Oh, ho." Dez chuckled. "Not bad, lovebirds." The big kid was swiping his arms through the darkness, dirty fingers eager to find them. Spencer held close to the wall, dragging Daisy around the urinals toward the door.

Thirty seconds left on Spencer's watch.

They were almost to the exit, Dez still blundering behind them, when Spencer and Daisy froze. On the other side of the door, they heard a heavy sigh followed by the sound of jingling keys. Someone else was trying to get in! Someone with a big ring of keys. In Spencer's mind, that narrowed it down to two people: Marv, or maybe Walter Jamison himself!

"Back, back!" Spencer hissed in Daisy's ear.

"I *hear* you," Dez whispered back, trying to make his voice low and menacing.

"Listen, Dez!" Spencer warned. "Someone's trying to get in and we've got to hide fast." Spencer was across the room, braving the germs on the bathroom wall and pushing Daisy into the stall.

"What?" Dez asked. Obviously this was the last thing he expected Spencer to say. On the other side of the door, they heard a mumbled curse. It was definitely Marv. And he seemed to be having trouble finding the right key in the darkness.

"Just get in here and shut up," Spencer ordered.

"In where?" asked Dez, taking a step toward Spencer's voice.

"The stall," answered Spencer impatiently. Then, suddenly, the lights went on. Spencer blinked against the brightness and Daisy shielded her eyes. Dez stumbled across the bathroom toward them. Outside, Marv managed to get the key into the lock.

The door opened and Marv stepped in.

CHAPTER 15

"WHAT'S SO FUNNY?"

The bear of a janitor glanced around the bathroom and then snorted. Marv didn't see the three kids and the baby doll balancing silently on the cold rim of the toilet, holding on to each other and bracing themselves against the wall. The stall door was shut and latched, but Marv didn't seem to notice details.

Spencer could barely glimpse the burly figure through the space between the hinges. Marv approached slowly until he stood only inches from the bathroom stall. On the other side of the thin wall, Spencer, Daisy, and Dez held their breath. Marv checked for the bronze nail, grunted unintelligibly, and then turned away.

The kids heard the bathroom door open, then bang closed. They heard the muffled sound of keys in the lock.

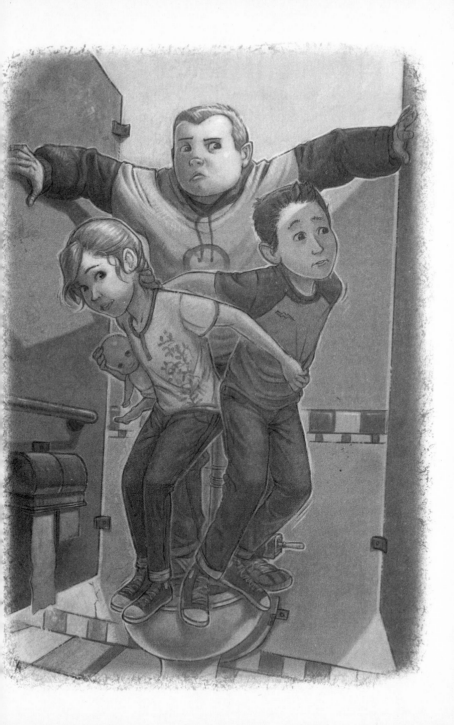

Marv snorted once more, apparently trying to dislodge something from his sinuses. Then there was silence.

Of course, Dez was the first one to move. He jumped down from the toilet seat, chuckling to himself. "Good thing I told you guys to hide. We'd have been busted. That dude looked like he wanted to eat someone."

"Quiet," Daisy whispered. "He might still be out there."

"Relax," Dez said. "He didn't see us."

Daisy and Spencer stepped off the toilet seat as Dez unlatched the stall door. "We've got to get back to class," Spencer said. "Mrs. Natcher's going to freak when she sees that three of us are gone."

"You're not going anywhere," Dez said, stepping in front of them. "I've still got to clean out some toilets with your heads."

"Get out of the way," Spencer said, brushing his hand at Dez like he was a pesky fly. A few days ago, Dez had been the most intimidating foe. But ever since the milk incident, ever since Spencer had discovered the courage to stand up for the truth, Dez seemed smaller. Indeed, compared to the wicked janitors and demented creatures that Daisy and Spencer were up against now, Dez looked about as frightening as Baybee.

"Hold it," Dez said, unaccustomed to people ignoring his threats. Spencer and Daisy stepped past him and Spencer pulled on the bathroom door.

Locked.

Marv had locked the deadbolt, making sure to keep everyone out while unintentionally trapping Spencer, Daisy, and Dez in. Unwilling to believe, Spencer pulled again . . . and again. But the door was secure. They weren't going anywhere.

Dez began to laugh.

"What's so funny?" Daisy said.

"It's perfect," answered Dez. "It's the perfect excuse not to go back to class . . . and to give you lovebirds endless swirlies."

Ignoring Dez, Spencer and Daisy began brainstorming. Hitting the door and shouting for help was out of the question. Picking the lock was impossible. Daisy got on her hands and knees, putting her cheek dangerously close to the bathroom floor, and tried to peek under the door.

"Hey." She carefully reached forward. A tiny bit of paper was visible under the door. Daisy trapped it with her fingernail and dragged it into the bathroom. It was the card that Garth Hadley had used to stop the lock. Daisy flipped it over. It was Hadley's business card, the same kind that the BEM rep had given Spencer.

"Yes!" Spencer said, taking the card from her hand. "That's got Hadley's phone number on it. He told me to call if we get in trouble."

Daisy smiled, showing her teeth in all their glory. "Hurry up," she said, "call him. I want to get out of here."

Spencer's shoulders slumped. "You don't have a cell phone?"

The girl shook her head, long braid swinging.

"Me neither."

Behind them, Dez emitted an obnoxious, look-at-me

sigh. Daisy and Spencer turned to find the boy operating a cell phone with both hands.

"All right, Dez!" Spencer said. For the first time, he was actually pleased with the bully. "If you let me borrow that for a minute, I can get us out of here."

"Hang on," Dez said. "I'm busy texting the sewer police. Got to tell them to expect two newcomers from toilet number one." He grinned maliciously and snapped the phone shut. "You think I want to go back to Mrs. Natcher's class?" Dez faked a yawn. "Yeah, right."

Spencer and Daisy exchanged a glance. They had to get the phone from Dez before the janitors found out that they were missing from Mrs. Natcher's class. If Marv's threats carried any weight, he would already have figured out Spencer's name and classroom.

"Why are you here, anyway?" Daisy asked, hands on her hips.

Dez tucked the cell phone into the pocket of his shorts and began to chant, "Spencer and Daisy, sitting in a tree, K-I-S-I-N-N . . . K-I-S-I-N-G . . ." he trailed away. "You guys came into class together this morning—late. Then, when the power went out, I figured Spencer went to find you. I usually don't like to watch kissing, but I wanted to know where you were going."

"So you followed us in here," Spencer said.

Dez nodded. "Not a very romantic place for your first date, Doofus. But I thought it might be fun to crash the party. Besides, I've been looking for a way to get back at you."

"For what?" Spencer asked.

"Yesterday's little speech to the class. You can lie to *them* about seeing monsters, but I know you're a fake."

Spencer swallowed and ignored the taunt. Just like Garth Hadley had advised, he focused on their secret mission. "Give me the phone, Dez."

"No way!" Dez pulled out the phone to tempt them again. "Minutes aren't free, you know."

"I'll pay you back," Daisy promised.

"You'll pay me now," Dez stated, pointing at the toilet aggressively. "Two swirlies for every minute on the phone. Deal?"

"You're disgusting," Spencer said, wondering if Dez actually had the guts to stick someone's head in the toilet and flush it. He wondered for only a moment.

Dez leaped clumsily at Daisy. She spun aside, and the bully turned quickly. He tripped on an untied shoelace and went down, grabbing Daisy's leg as he fell. Both kids tumbled to the hard floor, Dez struggling to get a controlling grip on Daisy.

Without thinking, Spencer plunged in. He'd never punched anyone before and it ended up hurting his hand a lot worse than he thought. Spencer's fist pounded into Dez's shoulder. The bully released his grip on Daisy and the girl crawled toward the stall. Dez's cell phone spun across the yellow-brown tile and stopped under the sink. Spencer went for it, but Dez's big foot kicked out, catching Spencer in the knee and sending him to the floor.

Dez grabbed the phone and jumped to his feet. His face

was twisted in anger like Spencer had never seen before. One punch from those meaty hands would probably put Spencer out cold on the floor—the dingy, *germy* bathroom floor.

Losing his courage, Spencer retreated to the stall, where Daisy quickly shut the door and latched it tightly. The walls of the stall didn't reach all the way to the ground, so there was still room for Dez to crawl under. But Spencer was prepared to stomp on any part of Dez that appeared.

"You're dead, Doofus. Sooner or later you'll have to come out—and I'll be waiting."

"Sooner or later, you'll give us that phone so we can all get out of here," Spencer said.

"Whatever! I'll wait a week if I have to."

"Without food? Yeah, right."

Dez fell silent. Apparently he hadn't thought about long-term food storage for his siege on the bathroom stall. Spencer and Daisy watched him pace for a while, then slump down against the wall. He pulled out his phone and, judging by the sound effects, started playing Pac-Man.

Spencer pulled Daisy aside and whispered in her ear. "I'm going to get the phone. Stay here."

"What?" Daisy shrieked.

"I hear you," Dez said, ending his game. But before he could slip the phone into his pocket, before Daisy could protest any further, Spencer threw open the door and lunged at Dez.

Spencer's right hand closed around the cell phone, jerking it free of Dez's grip. Instantly the bully had a heavy hand on Spencer's arm, twisting it painfully. Then Spencer stretched and slipped free, passing through Dez's grasp like his arm was made of Jell-O.

Spencer's left hand was sweaty inside the oversized latex glove. He had the phone and was only a few steps from the safety of the stall.

Dez sprang, grabbing both of Spencer's legs. But it was useless. Spencer's feet kept moving, his legs tearing free of Dez's hands without effort. Dez was left facedown on the dirty tile as Spencer flung himself into the stall, Daisy pushing the door shut.

"Here!" she shouted, thrusting the BEM business card at Spencer. He tore off the glove, flipped open the phone, and rapidly started punching in the numbers. Just as he hit the green *send* button, Dez's head appeared under the stall door. Daisy screamed and swung Baybee like a sledgehammer. The plastic doll smashed into Dez's face.

"Mr. Hadley?" Spencer asked. "We need help—quick!" he paused. "Yes, we found it. But we're locked in the bathroom with the nail!"

Daisy was going wild with Baybee. Dez's hands protected his face and he struggled to retreat. With one swing, Dez managed to grab onto the doll, and the two kids played tug-of-war with the hall pass. Dez came out with Baybee's torn diaper and Daisy fell onto the toilet with the unclothed doll.

"Thanks," Spencer said into the phone. "Okay, we will. 'Bye!" As soon as the conversation was over, Spencer closed the cell phone, bent down, and slid it along the floor. Dez turned like a dog going for a ball.

"You all right?" Spencer asked, helping Daisy to her feet. The girl nodded, hefting the nude hall pass like a club. "Good job," Spencer praised her combat skills.

"What'd Hadley say?"

"He's sending someone to get us out."

"When?"

Dez suddenly punched the stall door, causing both kids inside to jump. "Not before I'm done with you!"

CHAPTER 16

"THE ISSUE HAS BEEN RESOLVED."

To: ghadley@bem.gov
From: SpenceZ@wahoo.com
Subject: Thanks

Dear Mr. Hadley,

Just wanted to thank you for bailing me and Daisy out of the bathroom yesterday. We found the bronze nail and we're ready to go for the hammer. Do you have any ideas on how we can get to Walter Jamison? I think we should act fast. The janitors are already suspicious of me. Let me know what you want us to do.

Thanks,
Spencer

Spencer moved the cursor and clicked *send.* In a moment, the sent mail was confirmed and Spencer went to log off. He sat staring at the monitor for several moments, thinking. It was Saturday, and his siblings were all outside enjoying the warm weather and open spaces that their Aunt Avril's home in Welcher provided. His mother had gone to the store an hour ago. Spencer had spent the morning cleaning up the disheveled house, wiping down the mirror and sink in his bathroom, and vacuuming up a colony of ants that was working away at a long-abandoned cookie.

Yesterday was still vivid in his mind. After his phone call to Garth Hadley, Spencer and Daisy had spent a good half hour keeping Dez out of the bathroom stall. At last, help had arrived in the form of a nineteen-year-old, pimply guy with a shaved head and skinny legs. The guy was wearing the orange vest of a Welcher Elementary recess aide, but Spencer and Daisy had never seen him on the playground before.

The recess aide had opened the bathroom door and ordered Dez out. Once the bully was gone, Spencer and Daisy left the stronghold of the bathroom stall. The guy said he was undercover for the BEM. He'd swiped an aide vest and gone to the janitors, claiming to need their keys to unlock a door and get basketballs for the kids outside. With the keys, he had opened the "out of order" bathroom and rescued the kids.

The imposter recess aide had even given Spencer a slip of paper that he presented to Mrs. Natcher after lunch.

"What's this?" Mrs. Natcher took the note, plucking it out of Spencer's hand with two fingers. She unfolded it and read aloud: "Please excuse Spencer Zumbro, Daisy Gates, and Dez Rylie for their unexpected disappearance from class this morning. I had quite a discussion with them in my office. The issue has been resolved—Principal Poach."

Mrs. Natcher raised her eyebrows. "I hope you three learned your lesson. The principal is known to be harsh when occasion arises."

Spencer studied the carpet. The note had nearly convinced Daisy that she'd actually been to the principal's office. Dez had remained silent, brooding, probably waiting for the perfect opportunity to strike Spencer.

Which was another reason why Spencer was grateful for Saturday.

The weekend came just in time. It would provide two full days with no angry Dez. Two days without janitors and creepy crawlers. Two days without Welcher Elementary.

Spencer dug into a drawer and rifled through some computer games. He didn't feel like fighting evil Jedis, and the strategy games would make him think too hard. Spencer abandoned the idea and went to the internet again. Only a moment had passed, but why not obsess over his inbox?

There it was. Sent only two minutes ago.

To: SpenceZ@wahoo.com
From: ghadley@bem.gov
Subject: RE Thanks

Spencer,

Glad to be of help. Thanks for being willing to get the hammer. I think we have a working plan.

On Monday evening, there is an ice cream social at

the school from six to eight. The social will be held in the cafeteria, with games on the lawn outside. Other than the cafeteria and entry hallway, the school is supposed to be closed off. Marv Bills and Walter Jamison are both scheduled to work the event.

Spencer, you need to make a mess in the cafeteria—a large mess. It needs to be something that cannot be ignored. Something that will require both janitors to clean it up.

Meanwhile, Daisy needs to clear a path to the bathroom. That means opening doors, so she'll need to pick up a master key. Every teacher should have one.

Once Daisy gets the doors open, shine the flashlight on Walter Jamison. The beam should show you where he is carrying the bronze hammer. Wearing the glove, you need to grab the hammer and run to the bathroom. Once you've pulled the nail, I'll meet you at the southwest corner of the school in a blue Toyota to help you get away.

Good luck!

Garth Hadley
BEM regional representative

CHAPTER 17

"YOU *ALWAYS* MAKE A MESS."

Monday came. Spencer didn't think it would, but it certainly did. After letting his anger stew for a whole weekend, Dez was sure to make Spencer eat wood chips on the playground. Spencer had been lucky to evade the janitors on Friday, but there was no telling what secret councils had been held to get Spencer on Monday morning. That was why Spencer had decided to be sick.

He'd already made plans with Daisy on Sunday afternoon. Spencer had biked to her house, eaten pie with Mr. and Mrs. Gates, and secretly given Daisy the printed e-mail. They had solidified their plans for the ice cream social and then Mr. Gates had given Spencer a ride home, tossing his bicycle in the back of the red Ford truck again.

Spencer felt comfortable in the Gates home. Aside from its being ten times quieter than his house, Spencer felt relaxed and accepted there. Daisy, being an only child, received more attention from her parents in one day than Spencer did in a month.

Mr. and Mrs. Gates talked to Spencer like he was an honored guest, a fact that Spencer later found out was true. Daisy, in all her six years of schooling, had never had a friend come to visit. He was a valued commodity in the Gates home.

Every moment, Spencer was more grateful for Daisy's help. She'd given him courage in the beginning and now she was proving rather courageous herself. It would just be impossible without her.

Spencer's siblings had been home from school for over an hour on Monday before their mother returned. She entered the house, her face beaming. She'd been to a job interview with Quick 'n' Speedy truck stop and Mr. Aldez had hired her. It was her fifth interview in a month, and her success warranted a celebration. Alice had passed the school on her way home and seen folks putting together a giant, blow-up bouncy castle for the ice cream social. Her unexpected announcement made Spencer's stomach do a pirouette.

"We're *all* going to the ice cream party tonight!"

Max toddled up and began cheering for ice cream. Holly's head appeared around the corner, eyebrows raised.

"Yes! We're *all* going," Alice announced as though she'd just won a million dollars. "Now, let's eat some supper and head out."

With her victory at Quick 'n' Speedy and her offer to take the kids to a school activity, Alice had overlooked dinner. She hastily prepared some pasta from a box and microwaved some frozen peas. Hard rolls rounded out the dinner as five hungry kids sat shoulder to shoulder at the table with their elated mother.

Spencer had little appetite. His task of making a giant mess at the social had been daunting before. Now that his whole family would be there, Spencer wondered how he could do it without shaming his mom.

Before he had the answers he needed, the six Zumbros were piling out of the old station wagon in the school parking lot. There were already a lot of kids at the party. On the lawn outside was the bouncy castle with a pile of shoes beside it. A line of kids snaked toward the entrance, each anxious for a turn to bounce.

"Let's try to stay together," Alice said, ushering her children up the back cafeteria steps like ducklings. Spencer absorbed every detail along the way, wondering what would be to his advantage in mess making. Before he entered, Spencer got his bearings and scoped out the southwest corner. There was no blue Toyota yet.

As they entered through the cafeteria's back door, an oldies song assaulted them through tall speakers against one wall. The tables and chairs in the cafeteria had been arranged in a U shape. There were big white buckets on the center tables—gallons of ice cream in a variety of flavors. On the adjacent tables were bowls of optional toppings. Through gaps in the people, Spencer saw cookie crumbs, gummy bears, M&Ms, nuts, and an assortment of sticky syrups. At the end of one table were two ice chests brimming with cans of root beer for those who wanted to make a float.

Spencer studied the crowded cafeteria. There were no janitors on guard, and, gratefully, no sign of Dez Rylie. Spencer checked his watch. It was almost six-thirty. Daisy would be waiting for him by the front door. Now he just needed to get away from his family.

"I'm going to grab a drink real quick," he said.

"Good," his mom replied. "Take little Max with you; he's thirsty."

Without a word, Spencer grabbed Max's hand and led him out of the cafeteria toward the drinking fountain. In the hallway, the chatter of the crowd and the beat of the song faded. Spencer peered left down the entry hall. The janitorial storage closet that was also the janitors' office was at the end of the hall just before a set of double doors that closed off the rest of the school. At the other end of the hallway was the school's front entrance.

Spencer led Max to the drinking fountain. He boosted his three-year-old brother and the little kid began slurping up water. Soon he reverted to splashing water onto the floor and Spencer had to set him down.

"I want some ice cream!" Max shrieked, his cute little face smiling mischievously, showing off his chipped front tooth.

"You'll probably get it everywhere," Spencer said. For every ounce of effort that Spencer put into cleaning, Max threw down a pound of destruction. "You *always* make a mess." Spencer suddenly paused, staring at his little brother with newfound appreciation.

Suddenly, the sound of footsteps approached from behind. Spencer whirled around.

"You're late," Daisy said. "Are you ready?"

Spencer exhaled, relieved to see that it was only Daisy. He patted his pockets to show her that he had the flashlight and glove.

"Good. Here's the soap we're supposed to give back to Mr. Hadley today." Daisy handed Spencer the little bottle. "You should keep it."

Spencer shoved the soap bottle into his pocket as Daisy pointed at Max. "Who's he?"

"Oh, this is my little brother, Max."

"You brought your little brother?" she asked.

"I didn't mean to," Spencer said. "But he's great at making messes."

Daisy nodded, understanding the importance of Max's talent. "Well." She took a deep breath. "Let's get started."

CHAPTER 18

"IT'LL BE TOO LATE TO STUDY."

The first person Spencer and Daisy saw when they reentered the cafeteria was Mrs. Natcher. She wore a denim dress, and her gray hair was wound up in a bun. There was a purse dangling on her arm and a small bowl of plain vanilla ice cream in her hand. Yeah, that seemed right. Mrs. Natcher was a plain-vanilla kind of person. To Spencer's mild surprise, the dowdy teacher scooped a conservative helping of crumbled peanuts and let them cascade down her ice cream.

Spencer and Daisy exchanged one final you-be-careful glance before parting ways. Spencer headed toward his family, who stood huddled in the corner.

"Hey, Mom," Spencer said, "I'll help Max get some ice cream, okay?"

"Actually, Spencer," she said, "we're going to have a

bounce on the castle before ice cream. I don't want you kids getting sick on a belly full of sweets."

Spencer swallowed. His mom was supposed to say, "That sounds great, Spence. Thank you very much." But Spencer wasn't ready to give up so easily. He bent down to eye level with his small brother. "Do you want to bounce, Max, or do you want ice cream?"

"I want ice cream!" he shouted. Well, at least the three-year-old was going along with Spencer's plan.

"Spencer, did you really just . . ." Alice put her hands on her hips and took a deep breath. "If you have ice cream now," she told Max, "you can't bounce later."

"I want ice cream!" the stubborn little guy demanded. That seemed to settle the matter. Alice led the other kids out the back door of the cafeteria toward the blow-up castle while Spencer led Max to the ice cream table.

●　　●　　●

As Spencer and Max accepted bowls of caramel cashew and chocolate chunk, Daisy began some negotiating of her own.

"Hello, Daisy," Mrs. Natcher said, examining the girl below the rims of her glasses. The teacher always seemed to look over or under her glasses, never through them.

"Oh, Mrs. Natcher. It's a good thing you're here. I left my spelling review sheet in my desk after school. I need to study it tonight. I was wondering if I could go get it."

Daisy had often spread false information, believing it

was true. But to tell an outright lie would almost be impossible for honest Gullible Gates. Which was why she had *purposely* left her review sheet in her desk after school.

"The school is all locked up. Just get your review sheet tomorrow."

"But the test is tomorrow, Mrs. Natcher. It'll be too late to study."

Mrs. Natcher ate a nibble of ice cream, thinking. Then she sighed. "Pneumonia," the teacher said expectantly.

"P-N-E-U-M-O-N-I-A," Daisy answered.

"Correct," said Mrs. Natcher. "Aqueduct."

Daisy crossed her fingers, hoping that Mrs. Natcher wasn't going to drill her on all twenty words. Daisy began the word correctly before suddenly realizing the need to misspell. "A-Q-U-A-D-U-C-K."

"Incorrect," Mrs. Natcher said with a frown. Then the teacher gave the correct spelling and said, "Colonel."

"K-E-R-N-E-L."

"Incorrect." Mrs. Natcher began to correct her, then frowned deeper. Digging in her purse, she produced a ring of keys. "Goodness, you *need* the review sheet," she said, handing Daisy the keys. Daisy accepted with sweaty hands. "Bring those keys right back or you'll be in an undesirable P-R-E-D-I-C-A-M-E-N-T. You understand?"

Daisy nodded, backing away from Mrs. Natcher while trying not to let the look on her face betray her success. Before she exited the cafeteria, Daisy glimpsed Spencer and Max, who had moved on to the toppings. Then she broke into a speed-walk down the hallway.

• • •

"Okay, Max," Spencer said. "Do you want chocolate syrup on yours?" Max hadn't refused a single topping and his ice cream was unseen beneath a layer of goodies. As expected, Max nodded vigorously.

"Here's what we'll do," Spencer whispered to his brother. "These four syrups are just for us, but I need you to take them to that table over there, okay?" Spencer pointed to the table farthest away across the cafeteria. "Can you do it?"

"I think so." Max nodded with excitement. There were strawberry, caramel, butterscotch, and chocolate—four bottles of syrup just for him!

In a flash, Spencer untwisted the squirt caps on all four syrups. Then he set the caps loosely on top of the plastic bottles, only the sticky residue holding them in place. Spencer quickly loaded the bottles into his little brother's arms. Max toddled away, struggling to keep a good grip on all four bottles while still carrying his Styrofoam bowl of loaded ice cream.

As soon as the disaster was on its way, Spencer changed directions and headed for the ice chests full of root beer cans. He casually grabbed two cans, shook them, and slipped them into his pockets. A second later, he snatched two more cans.

"Whoa!" someone shouted, and Spencer heard Max's syrup bottles hit the floor. A shout went up and all of the adults in the room reached for Max. Their arms shot out like frog tongues going for a fly. Max was whisked away from the multicolored, sticky mess, dropping his ice cream in the process.

Parents converged on the syrup spill, each armed with a roll of paper towels. In the confusion, Spencer snatched as many soda cans as he could and retreated to the opposite side of the cafeteria.

Across the room, Max was attempting to recover his inverted ice cream. The mess was good, but the janitors hadn't been summoned yet. Of course, the parents thought they could handle it.

Spencer had his cans lined up—eight on the floor, with two more in his pockets. The cans were pressurized and ready to burst. Spencer had shaken each one for ten seconds. In the middle of the cafeteria, a stranger had Max by the arm, asking him where his parents were.

Just as the adults thought they had the syrup mastered, two cans of pressurized root beer slid across the cafeteria floor. The top was punctured just slightly to allow a tall geyser of brown soda to spurt out. Two more soda grenades followed, spraying root beer onto kids, parents, and all over the floor.

Spencer cracked two more soda cans and lobbed them into an adjacent corner. Kids were crying, parents shouting. The cafeteria had been plunged into Dez-worthy chaos.

Spencer had the seventh can opened when the first parent saw him crouched behind a table and stack of chairs. It was time to go. Spencer tipped over the tower of chairs to block his retreat, then sprinted out of the cafeteria into the entry hall.

Marv had emerged from the janitors' storage/office and was racing toward the cafeteria like a firefighter on call. There were several other people in the hallway. If Spencer could turn his back to Marv, he might blend into the crowd. He walked casually toward the drinking fountain, but his insides were trembling. Spencer lowered his lips to the stream of water, but he was too anxious to actually drink. With his head cocked at the fountain, Spencer kept his eyes trained on the hallway.

Marv entered the cafeteria to begin cleaning up. But where was Walter Jamison? The head janitor had not emerged according to plan. Any minute, the angry, root-beer-soaked parents would flood the hallway in search of Spencer. He waited only a second longer before deciding it was time to improvise.

Spencer hoped that Daisy had all the doors open as he jogged toward the short stairway that led to the janitors' storage/office. He dug in his pocket for the flashlight and glove, maneuvering around the extra cans of root beer that jostled at his side. By the time he reached the top stair, Spencer was wearing the latex glove.

Spencer crouched on the steps, trying to see into the huge storage area. The dim stairway was the perfect place to use the flashlight. But Spencer needed to get Walter out of the basement first.

Shouts up the hallway confirmed that the parents were looking for him. He knew he didn't have much time. Taking both cans of root beer from his pockets, Spencer began to shake them vigorously. He felt the contents pressurizing, the aluminum cans turning as hard as the shell of an airplane.

Spencer cracked the top of the first can. The soda shot out, dousing his shoulder. Spencer quickly set the can on the top step, positioning it on its side so the fountain of brown liquid shot into the storage area. He set the second can beside the first one: dual guns.

With the bait set, Spencer edged around the corner. He was out of Walter Jamison's sight, but the parents up the hall spotted him instantly. Spencer held his position as the adults converged on him. If Jamison didn't take the bait in the next ten seconds, Spencer knew he would have to break cover and run.

Suddenly, Spencer saw a hand close over the root beer can, setting it upright and averting the stream. Spencer spun around the corner, the flashlight flicking on. An older man was on the stairs. At first it didn't look like the Walter Jamison from the picture. He was wearing khaki cargo pants and a red button-up shirt with a pressed collar. A big ring of keys dangled at his side. This man was totally bald and clean shaven, but the face was the same. Wrinkles around the tired green eyes, lean features well worn.

The flashlight's white beam erupted and found its mark instantly. In the dim stairwell, the light outlined the shape of a small hammer in a cargo pocket by Walter Jamison's left thigh.

Spencer didn't hesitate. He flung the flashlight into Jamison's face and leapt down the stairs at the man.

Spencer's hands grasped Walter's leg as the old man caught the boy by the neck. Spencer grunted in pain but didn't pull away as he managed to plunge a hand into the cargo pocket. He felt the hammer, cool and hard on his fingertips. As soon as Spencer had a firm grip on the hammer, he twisted away, turning to Jell-O in Jamison's hands.

The old janitor gasped as Spencer staggered up the steps. The parents were waiting for him, but no one seemed to be able to get a tight grip on the boy. He flowed through their fingers like a fish through water. He sprinted across the hall to the doors that sealed off the rest of the school. If Daisy had succeeded, the doors would be . . .

Open!

Spencer burst through, running wildly down the dark hallway. He held the bronze hammer before him like an Olympic torch. Behind him, the door opened and several figures dumped into the hallway. Spencer was running too hard to be sure, but he guessed that one of them would be Jamison.

Spencer passed through another set of should-be-locked doors, praising Daisy's name all the way to the boys' bathroom. He kicked open the boys' room door. The light was already on, and Spencer dashed toward the nail. Hitting the stall wall, Spencer reached up with the hammer.

For the first time, he hesitated, unsure how to pull the nail with such an antique tool. Unlike modern hammers, this one lacked the hooked prongs on the back. It was a primitive tool that seemed to have the capability only to pound nails.

Sounds of pursuit were catching up in the hallway. There was no more time for hesitation. In desperation, Spencer placed the hammer against the head of the bronze nail. A burst of golden light suddenly formed between the two objects. A pulse of power surged through Spencer's arm. Then, like a piece of metal picked up by a strong magnet, the little bronze nail popped out of the wall and fell with a tinkle to the tile floor.

CHAPTER 19

"HOLD MY HAND!"

Daisy burst outside into the fresh evening air. Behind her was a wake of unlocked doors in the school. She ran the length of the school, gasping for breath until she reentered through the front door. The scene in the entry hall was utter chaos, which meant, of course, that Spencer had done his job.

Daisy clutched her spelling review sheet in one hand, the corner wrinkled from the sweat of her grip. In the other hand, she jingled Mrs. Natcher's keys. Daisy's hair was matted with sweat from her short run. She was breathing hard and feeling awful about telling Mrs. Natcher a half-truth. The sooner Daisy returned the keys, the better.

The girl pushed open the cafeteria door. The place was a complete disaster. A collage of pink, tan, and brown syrups still decorated the center of the room. Everything else was laced with streaks of sticky root beer. Daisy spotted Marv in the corner, firing up a machine that squirted water and sucked up messes.

Mrs. Natcher stood nearby, gazing into the syrup splash with a mournful expression. Whether she was mourning over the ruined ice cream social or the wasted syrup, Daisy wasn't sure.

"Got my review sheet, Mrs. Natcher," Daisy said, snapping the teacher out of her reverie. "Thanks." Daisy held out the keys.

The teacher took the keys and dropped them into her purse. "You missed a real disaster," Mrs. Natcher said with a grave expression.

"Looks like it." Daisy turned toward the exit. She needed to get to the rendezvous spot to meet Mr. Hadley.

A firm hand suddenly gripped her arm. "Coincidence?" Mrs. Natcher said. "Coincidence that Spencer, your trouble-making friend, would be up to no good while you made off with my keys?"

Daisy suddenly looked paler than vanilla ice cream. A cold fear rushed all the way to the soles of her feet.

"You've got some explaining to do." Mrs. Natcher dragged her across the cafeteria, Daisy struggling uselessly to get away.

Then, out of nowhere, Dez Rylie appeared, a heaping bowl of mostly melted ice cream in his hand.

"Gullible Gates!" Dez's eyes narrowed to a glare of revenge. "I can't find your boyfriend, so I'll have to settle for you!" With one swift motion, the bully shoved the bowl of dripping ice cream into Daisy's face.

Shrapnel from the ice cream bomb splashed onto Mrs. Natcher's cheek, and the force of the impact knocked them both back. Mrs. Natcher took a step backward to steady herself, but the teacher's shoe came down in the syrup swamp. The slick mess tested Mrs. Natcher's ability to skate . . . and she failed. The boring woman went down, her gray hair bun acting like a mop for the strawberry topping. Daisy came loose in the process, but she staggered, blinded by the ice cream.

Daisy wiped her eyes. The rest of her face was still sticky and white, as if some kind of spa facial mask had gone wrong. She had to make it to the rendezvous spot with Garth Hadley before the janitors got her! Leaving Dez in shock and Mrs. Natcher in syrup, Daisy crossed the cafeteria and exited out the back door. There were kids in the bouncy castle, some giggling, some crying, all totally oblivious to the war inside.

Daisy leapt down the steps and ran past the castle. A huge form suddenly appeared around the edge of the bouncy building. Big hands reached for Daisy, but she turned sharply, running back up the steps.

"You're supposed to be cleaning the mess inside!" she screamed as Marv came after her.

"The mess isn't going anywhere," the janitor answered. "But it looks like the mess makers are."

Daisy flew back up the steps, her retreat totally cut off. She entered the cafeteria at the same time Spencer burst through the opposite door. The two kids ran toward one another, each pursued by a dangerous janitor, with Mrs. Natcher standing up in the middle.

"You got it?" Daisy shrieked.

"Got it!" Spencer answered.

Spencer and Daisy met in the center of the cafeteria. "This way!" Spencer retreated to a corner. Daisy followed, drops of melted ice cream still flinging off her face.

"What now?" Daisy asked. The two kids had their backs to a wall. The two janitors slowed, spreading into attack formation Alpha Beta and coming slowly toward the children.

"We're cornered," Daisy moaned.

"No!" Spencer gritted his teeth. In desperation, he pulled off the latex glove.

"Spencer Alan Zumbro!" his mother's voice pierced the cafeteria. "You come here this instant!" But Spencer wasn't listening. He couldn't, or his mom's voice would break his heart. *Focus on the secret mission.*

"Hold my hand," Spencer whispered to Daisy.

"Wha–?"

"Just do it!"

Daisy grabbed Spencer's hand. Walter and Marv pounced. Mrs. Natcher hung back in case the kids managed to break free.

And they *did* break free!

In the last possible instant, Spencer had shoved the latex glove over their clenched hands. The janitors' grasp held them for only a moment before Daisy and Spencer slid easily between their fingers.

It was awkward to run holding hands, trying to keep their palms close so the stretchy glove wouldn't slip off. The mob of parents had filed outside along the back cafeteria steps. It was difficult to navigate the crowd, even though no one could hold them. With the parents forming a barricade, there was only one place to run.

"You have to take off your shoes!" the bouncy castle worker screamed as Daisy and Spencer dove through the mesh flap into the air-filled arena. There were three first graders bouncing reluctantly, but they quickly vacated the castle as Spencer and Daisy leapt inside.

The big inflatable castle was square, with four blowup turrets, one on each corner. Mesh walls connected the corners, but the top was uncovered. Spencer glanced up. If they could get over the back wall, it would be an open field to the rendezvous site.

The inflated floor suddenly shifted. Spencer went down as Daisy went up. The motion caused their hands to release, and the latex glove fell to the floor.

The cause of the disruption was Marv's great bulk, leaping ungracefully through the castle entrance and displacing a lot of air as he landed. The entrance flap, designed for elementary-school-sized children, had proven to be tighter than Marv had apparently expected, and he was tangled up in it.

As the janitor struggled, Spencer handed the nail and hammer to Daisy. Interlocking his fingers, Spencer made a quick stirrup for her. She stepped into his cupped hands and, with a bounce, he sent her over the wall.

Daisy didn't fly too gracefully. On her way up, she screamed, dropping both items. Daisy landed hard on the grass outside, but the hammer and nail landed with a bounce on the castle's inflated floor.

Spencer caught the bronze hammer on the first bounce. But before he could recover the nail, Marv jumped.

It was like fighting on the moon. Spencer bounced out of reach. Marv came down, sending Spencer higher on his next bounce. Walter Jamison climbed through the castle flap, his gaunt face set with determination.

The bronze nail was like a single kernel of corn in a popcorn popper. Every time someone landed, the nail went in a new direction.

Spencer went for the glove, possibly his last chance of escape. Walter beat him to it, dive-bouncing across the castle floor. As Walter landed, Marv went up. The big janitor lost his balance and came down on his belly as the nail rolled under him. The sharp nail pierced the tarplike material of the bouncy castle with a tearing sound. Marv rolled away from the split and a gush of air went up. The castle turrets began to fold and tilt inward.

The irate bouncy-castle worker shouted and switched off the air machine that kept the castle upright. As the castle collapsed, Spencer made a final leap and vaulted over the sagging mesh wall.

Spencer ran so hard he felt sick. His legs pumped across the field till they were numb. He didn't look back to see if the janitors were pursuing him. He didn't want to imagine his family—his mom—so disappointed and upset. She

wouldn't understand what he was doing, why he had ruined the ice cream social and fled the premises.

The blue Toyota was idling at the rendezvous corner. As Spencer got close, Daisy threw open the door and he dove into the car. Garth Hadley was at the wheel. Even before the door was shut, the car was speeding down the street.

"Well?" Mr. Hadley asked. His clean, square face was anxious for the report.

Spencer held up the bronze hammer. It was one solid piece of metal, very plain, with no special designs or jewel-encrusted handle.

"We got the hammer," he said. "And here's the soap we borrowed." Spencer dug the little bottle from his pocket and handed it over.

"What about the nail?" Garth Hadley asked. "Did you get it?"

"Nope," said Spencer. "The bouncy castle did."

CHAPTER 20

"YOU'RE JUST LIKE YOUR FATHER SOMETIMES."

It was a quarter to midnight when the blue Toyota pulled into Hillside Estates and came to a gentle stop in front of Aunt Avril's house.

After their escape from the ice cream social, Garth Hadley had driven the kids out of Welcher to a small neighboring town. There, he bought them a late dinner at a twenty-four-hour dive. The bathroom was as dingy as they come, and Spencer held his breath the whole time as he washed his hands. The food was greasy, but as the adrenaline of the evening wore off, Spencer and Daisy found they were hungry.

Garth Hadley was pleased with their work and assured them that Walter Jamison had been stopped—at least momentarily. He still had the nail, but without the hammer there was no way for Walter to set up a link with the school again.

Hadley explained that the BEM would stay in town until they found a way to get the bronze nail, leaving Walter Jamison totally powerless.

"We could really use your help," Garth invited. "You two were great at the ice cream social."

"No, thanks," Spencer said quietly, poking at his last bite of country-fried steak. Daisy just shook her head.

"That's all right, kids," Hadley said. "The BEM is in your debt. You've been instrumental in crippling a criminal. Just let me know if you change your mind."

The drive back to Welcher was quiet and awkward. Daisy dozed in the backseat. Garth Hadley said nothing, his broad face studying the road ahead. Spencer watched the black night go by, wondering what kind of trouble he would be in with his mother, with the janitors, with the principal, with the angry, root-beer-stained parents . . . the list went on.

Had it been a mistake to help the BEM? It had gotten him in serious trouble, and he'd dragged Daisy down with him. Part of Spencer wished that he'd never spoken to Garth Hadley. But the world of the janitors was also fascinating and enticing: magical creatures roaming the halls, a latex glove that made the wearer slip through enemy fingers. . . . What other awesome tricks might exist that Spencer was completely unaware of?

Hadley dropped Daisy off first, the Gates's savage dog greeting them with a chorus of barking. Daisy, ashen-faced at the prospect of meeting her parents, jumped quickly out of the car. Light illuminated the windows of the little house. Daisy's parents were undoubtedly waiting up.

Aunt Avril's house, however, looked pitch-black from the street. For a hopeful minute, Spencer thought he might be able to slip upstairs to his bedroom and pretend like nothing had happened.

Spencer opened the car door and put his feet out.

"Hey." Garth Hadley reached over. "You've got a career in the Bureau of Educational Maintenance if you want one, kid."

Spencer looked back at Mr. Hadley, BEM regional representative. Spencer wanted to smile, but the things he'd done at the ice cream social pulled at the corners of his mouth. "I'm only twelve."

Hadley laughed, showing straight, white teeth. "I'm just saying . . ." He trailed off. His face resumed a more businesslike look. "As you've discovered, the BEM does a whole lot more than scrape gum. There's another world out there, Spencer. You've only tapped the surface, but you show real talent."

"Thanks," Spencer muttered, and he stood up. Garth Hadley was examining the bronze hammer again. Spencer thought he might say something more, but before Hadley had the chance, Spencer shut the car door.

Spencer stood alone on the dead grass as the blue Toyota drove out of Hillside Estates. The wealthy country neighborhood was alive with the chirrup of crickets. Somewhere in the distance, Spencer heard the *ch-ch-ch* of a large sprinkler. With a sigh, he walked up the steps, opened the front door, and locked it once he was inside.

"We have to talk."

Spencer's heart jumped, pulling his feet off the ground in surprise. His mother was seated on a scratched leather couch, enveloped in darkness.

"Mom! What are you doing in the dark? You totally freaked me out!"

"I freaked *you* out? Spencer, it's nearly midnight! Where have you been?"

Spencer didn't know what to do—ignore her and walk away, or spill everything and see what she believed. He needed time in his tidy bedroom. Time to sort everything out and decide what to do next.

"Can we talk about this tomorrow?" Spencer tried.

"Are you kidding? You're twelve years old, Spencer. I'm your mother and I have every right to know what's going on. You made a huge mess, left your little brother covered in ice cream toppings, popped the blow-up castle, and then ran away from—"

"I didn't pop the castle. It was that fat janitor guy."

"Don't make excuses for your poor actions! You're just like your father sometimes!"

Her words hit Spencer like a splash of icy water in the face. Comparing Spencer to Alan Zumbro evoked high emotion from both mother and son. Alice was trembling. Spencer didn't know whether he should feel insulted or proud.

They stared silently at one another, two dark silhouettes

in an oversized living room. Spencer had never felt so ashamed, so afraid of tomorrow. It was dark enough to cry, wasn't it? His mother was already doing it, so Spencer let a tear fall too.

"I'm afraid," he whispered. "I don't know what to do."

Alice held out her arms. Spencer shuffled toward her, uneasily at first, like a toddler learning to walk. Then he collapsed on the couch and felt his mother's arms wrap around his shoulders.

"It'll be all right," Alice whispered. "Just tell me what's going on."

Spencer swallowed hard. How much could he tell his mother before she decided that his childish imagination was out of control? Besides, Garth Hadley had told him not to talk about the creatures anymore. And Spencer's confession to the class had been met with laughter. Laughter that deeply hurt. If his mother didn't believe him, if she laughed . . .

But he had to tell her *something!* He needed to know what to do next and wanted someone else to decide it for him. Alice gave Spencer a comforting squeeze.

"Last Thursday," Spencer began. He wiped his eyes and took a deep breath. "After school, I met a guy from the Bureau of Educational Maintenance. Garth Hadley. He said the BEM needed my help to get something from the janitors. Something they . . . stole."

Spencer had to fib a little here. In the silent moments before he spoke, Spencer had already decided that telling the story would be much easier if he left out the *magic* altogether. There was no reason to mention the creatures. No reason to tempt his mother to laugh. After all, the janitors were the real problem. That was where he needed help.

"I did what Mr. Hadley said and took a bronze hammer from the janitor. I don't know what it was for. Maybe it was worth a lot of money or something."

Alice took a deep breath through her nose. One hand went to her forehead. "This isn't helping my headache at all," she muttered. "I'm worried, Spencer."

"I know." He bit his lip. "Me too. The janitors will probably be waiting for me tomorrow."

"It's not the janitors I'm worried about," Alice said. "It's Garth Hadley."

CHAPTER 21

"IS THIS TRUE, SPENCER?"

But Mom," whined Erica over breakfast, "I don't see why Spencer gets a ride to school while the rest of us have to take the bus."

"It's about last night," Holly guessed. "What Spencer did at the ice cream social."

Spencer stared at his soggy frosted flakes and tried to pretend that he wasn't in the room. His sister's words were painfully true. Mom was taking him to see the principal.

"We've got to go now or I'll be late for work," Alice said. It was, after all, her first day at Quick 'n' Speedy. "Just dump your cereal in the sink. I'll be waiting in the car."

Spencer climbed into the station wagon and tossed his backpack next to the car seat behind him. Max had already been dropped off at the day care, and all that was left of him were a few fragments of Cheerios on the seat.

They drove in silence. Spencer thought his mother seemed like a force to be reckoned with. She clearly wasn't happy about Spencer's involvement with the BEM. Now she gripped the steering wheel like it was Garth Hadley's neck.

Well before the morning busses arrived, Alice Zumbro pushed into Welcher Elementary's front office, Spencer in tow. Mrs. Hamp looked up from her desk, already planning a greeting that would test this woman's vocabulary.

"Do you require the immediate assistance of someone in an administrative position?" She feigned politeness, poorly.

"Listen," Alice said, clearly in no mood for prose, "we need to see the principal. I've only got five minutes."

"Principal Poach has not yet arrived," the secretary said. "His arrival is undoubtedly postponed by the traffic."

Alice rolled her eyes. "You've got to be kidding me. Traffic in Welcher is a contradiction. When will the principal be here?"

"He always arrives for morning announcements." Mrs. Hamp checked the clock on her computer. "Fifteen minutes, give or take."

"Shoot," Alice said. "I've got to be to work by then." She glanced at Spencer, but he was a statue.

"If you have a pressing concern, I could make a note and pass it to the principal when he arrives."

"My pressing concern," Alice said, leaning across the desk, "is for the safety of my children at Welcher Elementary School."

Mrs. Hamp leaned back defensively. "Has there been some betrayal of your trust in our school, Miss?"

"Don't *Miss* me, missy." Alice was getting worked up. Spencer couldn't decide if he should smile or not. It was kind of cool to hear how much his mom cared about his safety. Cool in an embarrassing sort of way.

"My son was approached by a stranger in this school. Whether the man was actually from the Bureau of Educational Maintenance or not does not excuse the fact that he enlisted my son's help to accomplish illegal acts."

Mrs. Hamp sat forward. Her eyes widened with the practice of someone with years of experience in meddling and gossip. "Illegal acts? Strangers in Welcher Elementary? Elaborate!"

Spencer shifted awkwardly as his mother gave the one-minute version of how Garth Hadley had asked him to steal something from the janitors. When Alice was finished, Mrs. Hamp sat back. Now the secretary's eyes narrowed and a smirk appeared.

"Children," Mrs. Hamp said knowingly, "have a way of leaving out important information."

Spencer slunk back as the secretary's accusatory gaze pierced him.

"Mr. Hadley is indeed a licensed member of the BEM," Mrs. Hamp said. "Last Thursday, he arrived at the school to perform a routine inspection *after* the school had been vacated. If your son did meet Mr. Hadley that day, it would have been due to his lack of obedience in exiting the school when the final bell rang."

Each word she spoke seemed to reduce Spencer. When she finished, he felt smaller than a toothpick.

"Is this true, Spencer?" his mother asked. "Were you in the school after you had been asked to leave?"

Wordlessly, Spencer nodded. Why hadn't he just told his mother the whole truth from the very start?

"But what about the other times he contacted you?" Alice asked. "Where did he meet you?"

Spencer wished it were another yes-or-no question so he could simply nod again. But now his mother had called on him to speak an answer. And oh, how that answer was bound to disappoint.

"I only met him once," said Spencer. "Last Thursday."

"You see!" Mrs. Hamp jumped in. "Welcher takes great pride in knowing every visitor that passes through these doors. Rest assured that Mr. Hadley will not come again, unless on official business for the BEM. And in such an instance, the school will be empty of children. As it *should* have been last Thursday."

Spencer glanced at the clock. His mother's time was spent if she wanted to be on time for her first day of work. But Spencer knew she wasn't done investigating yet. She put a hand on his shoulder.

"Did you contact this Hadley person on your own?"

Spencer nodded.

Then came the dreaded word. "How?"

Spencer looked at his feet as if hoping to find a different answer written there. "E-mail," he finally whispered.

"Spencer Alan Zumbro!" Her hand dropped from his

shoulder. "You know very well the rules of our family! That e-mail account is for contact with your friends in Washington. Anything else—*anything* else!—must be approved by me."

Alice put her hands on her hips. "I'm disappointed in you, Spencer." Mrs. Hamp was smiling at the family tension until Alice pointed a finger across the desk. "And I'm not happy with *you*, either. I don't care who Garth Hadley is. If the janitors stole something from him, it's the police he should contact, not my twelve-year-old son! I suggest a background search on school visitors."

Mrs. Hamp held up her hands in defense. "Don't look at me. Mr. Hadley's a government man. We don't interfere with them."

"Yeah? Well, I'm a *mother*. And you shouldn't interfere with me, either!"

CHAPTER 22

"RUINED BY CHILDISH RIFFRAFF!"

In the noisy moments just before class started, Spencer sat in his desk. A thin smile spread across his face when he recalled his mother chewing out Mrs. Hamp a few minutes ago. But the smile couldn't last, filled as he was with guilt and shame about disappointing his mom.

Daisy didn't look much better, sitting in the corner. She arrived at the classroom much later than usual, her eyes pink from sleeplessness and tears. They glanced at each other only briefly. Just long enough to make sure that they were both still alive.

Neither of them would look at Mrs. Natcher. They didn't want to see if she still had sticky strawberry syrup in her gray hair.

The only troublemaker who seemed unaffected by the events at the ice cream social was Dez. He belched in unison with the bell, trying to make his burp last longer. His expression quickly changed as Mrs. Hamp's crackly voice sounded over the intercom.

"Dezmond Rylie, Spencer Zumbro, and Daisy Gates. The principal has arrived and demands to see you—immediately."

Spencer stood on trembling legs. Daisy tried to get up twice, but seemed frozen in place. As Spencer passed her desk, she found the courage and stood at his side.

Dez moaned obnoxiously but jumped to his feet. Dez seemed to have no trouble walking, having gained his "principal's-office legs" through repeated trips to the front office.

"Take the hall pass," Mrs. Natcher said. She might have added, "You all get F's for the year," and Spencer wouldn't have been surprised.

At the door, Daisy shamefully lifted Baybee from its place on the bookshelf. The doll's diaper was modestly in place once more, but the plastic forehead looked a little scratched from the bathroom tile.

As they stepped into the hallway, Dez snatched the baby doll from Daisy's hand. "I don't trust you with that," he said, tucking the hall pass under his arm.

The three kids walked in silence for a while. But Dez, King of Unnecessary Noise, soon started making squishing sounds with his mouth every time he took a step.

"You know," Dez said, "the principal's not so bad if you know how to handle him." Spencer and Daisy didn't acknowledge, but Dez continued anyway. "He likes it if you call him respectful titles like 'Emperor Fatso,' or 'Honorable Senator Blimp.'"

"Be quiet, Dez," Daisy said.

"Huh?" cried the bully. "What happened to you, Gullible Gates? You used to believe *everything* I said."

"'Cause I used to think you might have something worth saying."

The kids were at the principal's office much sooner than they had hoped. But no amount of lollygagging could postpone the undesirable P-R-E-D-I-C-A-M-E-N-T they had gotten themselves into.

Mrs. Hamp had a pleased glint in her eye as she motioned for the three kids to wait on some benches until the principal was ready for them.

They waited about five minutes, Dez making Baybee dive-bomb off the bench onto her head over and over again while accompanying the scenario with gory sound effects.

Then the principal's door opened and Dez was summoned inside. The bully tossed Baybee onto the bench and went through the door as though he were going out to recess.

Daisy and Spencer waited nervously on the bench. Baybee sat between them, and Daisy held one of the doll's hands while Spencer held the other, feeling the uncontrollable need to hang on to something, even if it was only a lifeless, plastic doll.

Dez appeared a few minutes later, his face a storm cloud brewing with bolts of negative energy. "See you chumps in about a week," he grunted. "Emperor Fatso decided to spend me." Dez probably meant to say *suspend*, but the bully didn't look like he was in any mood to be corrected.

As Dez walked away, Spencer and Daisy's attention turned back to the principal's office. A man filled the doorway, almost as big around as he was tall.

Principal Poach wore a striped collared shirt and pink tie that looked miniature against his portly belly. He had a walrus face, complete with bristly brown mustache.

Principal Poach's eyes were squinty and small as he pointed at Spencer and Daisy with two fingers that looked like microwaved hot dogs. Then the hot-dog fingers wiggled, a gesture that Spencer interpreted to mean "get in my office now."

The two kids arose, Baybee dangling between them, and entered the office. Principal Poach shut the door and waddled to his desk chair. The principal was so round that the only way Spencer could tell he was walking, and not rolling, was by the stripes on his shirt. Once comfortably nestled into his padded chair, the principal stroked his mustache for a moment. Spencer looked for tusks, but didn't see any.

"An entire event—ruined!" Principal Poach said. His voice was high and whiny. It seemed biologically impossible for such a massive body to produce such a piercing voice. "Ruined by childish riffraff!" He slammed a hand onto the desk.

"Twenty-four years I have been principal of Welcher Elementary, and I have never—*never*—heard of such behavior. We do not tolerate it. We cannot abide it."

What Daisy and Spencer didn't know was that Principal

Poach was giving them his memorized speech for first-time offenders. Dez had made it to speech number eight before Principal Poach suspended him.

"During the Edo period of Japan, at the time of the Samurai, criminal punishment included such cruelties as imprisonment, exile, and penal labor. At any rate, the Samurai warriors of Japan saw the need for a corrective course of action to rectify one's misdoings."

The speech, aside from being really hard to understand, made Spencer and Daisy shift uncomfortably in their seats. The parts of Principal Poach's speech that Spencer understood were the bits about imprisonment, exile, and, although Spencer wasn't exactly sure about "penal," labor was never good.

"Thus it is with you, my young friends," Poach continued. "You are in need of guided correctional behavior. Due to the offense, I see fit to . . ."

At this point in the speech, the principal would generally insert a punishment; he had any number of them memorized. But that morning, Principal Poach did something extraordinary. He left the safety of his memorized speech, looked right at Spencer, and began to speak on his own.

"Mrs. Hamp told me of your mother's visit this morning. I find your claims about the BEM highly unlikely. However, safety of the children is our top priority, and we will monitor school visitors more closely in the future."

Great for the future, Spencer thought. *But what about the things that already happened?*

"We can never truly know if Mr. Hadley put you up to

the task of mess making, as you have declared. But *some-one* has to be punished. The ice cream social was a tragedy. I had more than a dozen e-mails from angry parents this morning. The janitors contacted me last night and I . . . I really *wanted* to suspend you." He sighed, his walrus cheeks jiggling.

Spencer and Daisy sat still as the principal rambled. They squeezed Baybee even tighter, feeling like they were barely balancing between suspension and the unknown.

"But I'm not going to," Poach went on. "Suspend you, that is." His hot-dog fingers were nervously interlaced. "I would have, but the janitors encouraged another punishment more appropriate to the offense."

Spencer and Daisy looked at each other, eyes wide. *Please, don't let it be what I'm thinking,* Spencer thought desperately.

The principal regained composure and picked up his speech at the "insert punishment here" line where he had departed. "You shall both spend time in detention with the janitors after school, every day for the rest of the week. I expect your full cooperation in this. Our head janitor, John Campbell, was very kind to dissuade me from suspending you. You might want to thank him."

Thank him? Yeah, right! Spencer felt sick. Daisy's tears finally leaked out. They were being turned over to the janitors. Marv and Walter would be furious about the theft of the hammer.

Spencer knew he would have preferred imprisonment or

exile. Heck, even a samurai execution might be less painful than what the janitors would do.

"In addition," Principal Poach went on, "you shall both write a nice letter of apology to the Parent-Teacher Association, who organized the ice cream social. The parents will be glad to see that you are paying for your wrongdoings. Unfortunately, I must forbid you from attending any PTA activities for the rest of this year."

With some effort, Principal Poach stood up and smiled a walrus smile. "That will be all, children. I expect that no further disciplinary action will be necessary. Do your homework, eat your veggies, and don't go looking for any more trouble."

But Spencer and Daisy didn't have to look far to see trouble. Even as Principal Poach concluded his speech, one of Jamison's creatures, a vulture-bat, crawled out from behind a painting of George Washington and took flight. The little creature swooped down to Poach's desk and landed on the rim of an open can of peanuts. Both Daisy and Spencer had their eyes glued to the creature.

"What?" Poach huffed, following their gaze to his desk. Meanwhile, the vulture-bat folded its wings and dropped into the can, scavenging for nuts.

"Oh," the principal said. "I guess it's not professional to leave my snacks out, is it?" He picked up the can of peanuts. "But I just can't help myself. I *love* a good peanut."

In horror, Spencer and Daisy watched as the hot-dog fingers descended into the peanut can.

"Don't!" Spencer finally shouted. The last thing he

wanted was for the vulture-bat to get a good meal off the principal's fingers. The walrus-shaped man paused for a moment and glanced in the can. Apparently seeing nothing, he plunged in and withdrew a few peanuts. Poach stuffed the nuts into his mouth and crunched noisily.

"What's the matter with you?" the principal asked.

Spencer floundered for an excuse. Poach obviously hadn't seen *or* felt the creature in the can. "It's just that you . . . you forgot to wash your hands."

Principal Walrus chortled, his belly bouncing. "Pish posh," he said, pointing back at his desk. "I use instant hand sanitizer."

Spencer peered around the principal and saw the bottle of sanitizer. It was the kind that doctors claimed killed 99.99% of all germs.

Unfortunately, a slimy yellow salamander creature was wrapped around the bottle, wide mouth drooling all over the top.

CHAPTER 23

"SO FAR I'M GROUNDED FOR A WEEK."

Mrs. Natcher's classroom was relatively peaceful without Dez. At least, an artificial sense of peace could be felt if Spencer and Daisy avoided eye contact with Mrs. Natcher.

The rest of the school day passed normally. Spencer aced the spelling test and Daisy misspelled only *colonel*.

When the bell rang at the end of class, Spencer and Daisy hung back, wondering if it was worth trying to escape before detention. But what did it matter anyway? Sooner or later the janitors would catch them and punish them for stealing the bronze hammer.

The chance to run was shot down when Mrs. Natcher took Spencer and Daisy by the arms.

"The principal informed me of your detention with the

janitors," she said. "Perhaps I could help you find them, so you don't get *lost* along the way."

Mrs. Natcher escorted them down the hall to the waiting hulk of Marv Bills. With a formal head nod, Mrs. Natcher turned them over.

Marv glowered over the kids for a moment. "All right," he said once Mrs. Natcher was gone. "John Campbell isn't here right now, so you kids'll be scraping gum off the desks until he gets back."

"Don't you mean Walter Jamison?" Spencer said. He didn't mean for it to sound so defiant. Spencer just wanted Marv to know that he and Daisy were aware of the janitor's lies.

"Come on," Marv said and led the children to Mrs. Cleveland's sixth-grade classroom. Wordlessly, Marv withdrew two flat razor blades that retracted into a handle by sliding a button back and forth. From his other pocket, he took two pairs of latex gloves.

"You'll need these. I want you to get under each desk, use the blade to scrape off the gum, and then throw it in the trash. If you finish this room, move to the next. I'll come get you when Mr. Campbell arrives." Spencer and Daisy accepted the razor blades and Marv pushed them into the room.

It was a disgusting and intimidating assignment. The classroom had at least twenty-five desks. As Spencer crouched under the first desk and saw four hard, dried blobs, he silently vowed never to chew gum again. For Spencer, there could be no worse punishment than chipping off someone else's ABC gum.

Spencer pulled on his latex gloves. Last time he'd worn one, it had made him uncatchable. These gloves were plain and nonmagical, but at least they would keep the germs off his hands.

Daisy didn't seem to mind the task. She was already on her second desk, holding the fragments of stale gum in one gloved hand while working vigorously with the razor blade in the other. Taking a deep breath, Spencer followed her example and was surprised at how easily the old gum came free.

"I bet your parents weren't too happy last night," Spencer said.

"They were just worried sick. So far I'm grounded for a week. But it will probably be longer once Principal Poach calls to tell them what we did at the social."

"You didn't tell them?" Spencer dodged a piece of gum as it chipped off and fell toward him.

"What could I say? That we were on a secret mission for the BEM?" Daisy shook her head. "My parents have heard all kinds of stories from me. I know what they'd say: 'Daisy, dear, someone was trying to trick you.'"

"That's what my mom told me," Spencer said. "Minus the 'Daisy, dear' part."

"She thinks Garth Hadley was tricking us?" Daisy stopped scraping. "Could that be true?"

"I don't know. We just need to be careful."

They chipped rock-hard gum in silence.

"You sure made a mess in the cafeteria yesterday," Daisy reminisced, as though it were a pleasant memory. "Bet your parents were pretty mad about that. They were there, weren't they?"

"Just my mom," Spencer answered. "But yeah, she was pretty mad."

"What'd she say?"

"Said I was like my dad."

"Isn't that a good thing?" Daisy asked, halting her gum scraping.

"At *your* house it would be," answered Spencer. "But I haven't seen my dad since I was about ten."

"Where is he? On business somewhere?"

"His own business," said Spencer. It sounded too bitter, so Spencer explained. "My dad used to teach biology at a junior high school. His best friend was this scientist guy named Rod Grush. Sometimes they'd travel to do experiments and projects. It really made my mom mad because sometimes he'd be gone for days."

Spencer sat back. It was weird to tell this story. Like sharing a spoon with someone, which Spencer would never do for fear of germs. It seemed to link them together in an extra personal way.

"Got so bad," Spencer continued, "that Mom wouldn't even let us say Rod Grush's name around the house. About two years ago, my dad and Rod went to Texas for a project. He never came back."

"Must be a big project," Daisy said, turning back to her gum chipping.

Spencer felt his face go red. Gullible Gates didn't understand. How could she, with her funny, Ford-driving dad?

143

"No, Daisy," Spencer said. "You don't get it. He's not coming back. Nobody knows where he is. The junior high fired him. Mom says that his projects meant more to him than his family, and that's why he took off."

"What?" Daisy's voice was rich with disbelief. "I don't believe it," she said, a fresh piece of gum sticking to her razor blade.

"What do you mean, you don't believe it?" Spencer asked. He was getting angry, the way he always got when he thought too much about his dad.

"I mean, your dad's *got* to come back. Nobody loves their work more than their family."

Spencer slumped against the leg of a desk, his anger fleeing. His face was still hot and there were tears in his eyes. "I used to think that too. I miss him. He was the coolest guy."

"Did he say he'd come back?"

"Yeah," Spencer said, wiping a stray tear with his shoulder. He kept his head low so Daisy wouldn't see.

"Then you've got to believe him," answered Daisy.

"It's easy for you. You believe everyone."

"Not anymore. I only believe people that I trust."

"Do you trust *me?*"

"Duh," Daisy said. "I think you—"

Daisy stopped short and Spencer's tears dried instantly as the classroom door opened. Marv stepped inside. "John Campbell is ready to see you now. Follow me."

As Spencer tried to regain control of his emotions, the prospect of facing the head janitor made him weak. Daisy came to his side and they followed big Marv until they stood at the top of the janitorial steps. Spencer noticed a few spots of sticky, dried root beer that hadn't been mopped. The stains made polka dots on the stairs.

"Down," Marv pointed. The children obeyed, slowly descending the steps and feeling as if the janitors' storage/office would swallow them like a shark.

The basement room had been tidied since the last time Spencer and Daisy were down there. At the center desk, two chairs sat vacant, side by side. On the other side of the desk was the head janitor. Marv moved into position behind him like an ogre awaiting commands.

Walter Jamison gestured for the kids to be seated. Once they were in their chairs, the head janitor cleared his throat. "Did the principal tell you that I'd recommended detention with the janitors instead of suspension?"

"Yeah," Daisy answered.

"You should thank me," Walter replied. "You have become involved with a very dangerous organization. Being with us is the safest place for you right now."

"Why?" Spencer leaned forward. "So you can poison our brains with your magical experiments?"

Walter Jamison sighed and ran a hand across his bald head. "I need you to inform me of everything that Garth Hadley told you."

Spencer wanted to resist, but Daisy plunged in. Once she started, she seemed unable to stop. After pouring out

145

the whole story, she folded her arms and glanced at Spencer. He smiled briefly at her, grateful to have the truth out in the open.

"Spencer, Daisy," Walter Jamison began, his voice low. "I'm afraid you've been tricked."

CHAPTER 24

"A WARLOCK, ACTUALLY."

Tricked?" Daisy shouted, jumping to her feet. "That's what everyone keeps saying. But how do I know that *you're* not lying? The BEM is a government agency—"

"He's *not* lying," Marv said.

"You won't even tell us your real name!" Spencer said to the head janitor.

"We often use false names to protect ourselves from the enemy," Walter said. "I have been using the alias of John Campbell for several months now, but I assure you, my real name is Walter Jamison, as you've already discovered. Please," he continued, "allow us to explain."

He waited for the kids to calm down, then said, "Garth Hadley has filled you full of half-truths in order to make me into an enemy. He wants the hammer and nail for himself."

Walter held up his hand. "I should start at the beginning." He looked down to gather his thoughts.

"The United States was founded in 1776," Walter began. Spencer instantly hoped that this speech would have nothing to do with Samurai exile. "But even before the nation was formed, many colonists came from Great Britain."

"The pilgrims," Daisy said. "We know."

"All right. Once the American colonies were thriving and schools were established, a certain threat was discovered. Three types of creatures, or Toxites, began to reside in the schools. Pests of the worst kind. You've heard of termites, or dust mites? Well, Toxites are far worse. The winged one is called Rubbish, the furry one Filth, and the slimy one they named Grime.

"Three women spotted the creatures first. Their natural ability to see Toxites marked them as witches. They quickly discerned that, to everyone else, the little pests were invisible. These three witches discovered a correlation between the Toxite population and the learning curve. In other words, if there were more creatures in a school, students did poorly. Determined to fix the problem, the witches set about ridding the schools of Rubbish, Filth, and Grime."

"How'd they do that?" Daisy asked, her gullible side already absorbed by the story.

"Well," Walter said, "they tried sweeping them up, but the Toxites were resilient to ordinary brooms. So the witches developed new brooms that enabled them to crush the critters."

"And let me guess," Spencer said sarcastically. "Then the witches flew off on their brooms."

"Exactly. The magic in the Toxites is indestructible. For example, if a Filth is crushed by a witch's broom, the body turns to dust and the magic goes into the broom that destroyed it. When brooms are powered with Toxite magic, they gain the ability to defy gravity. Do you understand?"

"I understand," answered Spencer. "I just don't buy it yet."

"Let him finish," Daisy said.

"The witches knew they couldn't live forever, but they needed to keep the schools Toxite-free. They developed a way to expose other people to the Toxites' existence. The secret was carried on from generation to generation. When the United States was formed and the country began to expand, the need for Toxite-fighting janitors increased. The Bureau of Educational Maintenance was founded and the secret was kept between those of us in the BEM."

"Those of *us?*" Spencer asked. "You're part of the BEM too?"

"All school janitors are. But only about 50 percent know of the Toxites. You see, the creatures don't live in high schools. Even some junior high schools are bad environments for them."

"Why?"

"Many years after the witches, we discovered that the Toxites inhale active brain waves and exhale waves that interfere with the growing mind. They are most dangerous to younger students. In fact, by the time kids reach high school, the Toxites can't stand to be around them. To the creatures, it would be like breathing in really stinky air compared to the fresh air of the younger schools. It might even make some of them sick."

There was silence in the storage/office while Daisy and Spencer pondered the prospect of Toxites. Finally, Spencer said, "What does this have to do with Garth Hadley and the bronze hammer?"

"Right," Walter said. "You're very on task, Spencer. I like that." He held up three fingers. "There are actually three bronze hammers, each with a nail. Before dying, the witches transferred their knowledge and power into the hammers. I have Ninfa. *Had* Ninfa, I should say. Garth Hadley has her now."

"Why a hammer?" Spencer asked. "It's not like janitors use hammers for cleaning stuff."

"Janitors do more than clean things, kid," Marv said. "If something breaks in the school, who do you think fixes it?" Marv gestured at himself by jabbing a thumb into his chest. "Janitors use hammers all the time."

"Hammers represent the strength and hard work it takes to build something," Walter said. "The three witches were the builders and founders of everything magic. They left their legacy and power in the bronze hammers and nails."

"So, does having the hammer make you a witch?" Daisy asked.

"Well, in my case, a warlock, actually," Walter Jamison answered. "Witches are women. Currently all three hammers are held by men."

Daisy glanced at Spencer, her eyes wide. Gullible Gates had no problem accepting the idea that the school janitor was a magic warlock.

"It's like this." Marv took over. "Each warlock needs a place to do his experiments. He sets it up by pounding the nail into a building. Once the nail is secure, that building becomes the warlock's domain—the only place for him to experiment."

"What are these experiments?" Spencer asked.

"Well, the witches made special brooms to kill Toxites. In our day, the warlocks have developed many new tools to do the job—vacuums and mops, for instance. The three warlocks who hold the hammers receive small shipments of raw magic so they can continue experimenting."

"But you stole one of the hammers from a warlock and set up your own domain here! Didn't you?" Spencer stared into Walter Jamison's hard eyes.

"Yes, I did," the warlock answered. "I had to. Over a year ago, the BEM started withdrawing support from the schools. They instructed all Toxite-fighting janitors to step down and let the creatures take over. I felt strongly that we should continue our war against Toxites, and many other janitors shared my belief. I was able to steal Ninfa and establish myself as a warlock.

"I worked undercover at an elementary school in Arkansas. As a warlock, I received the shipments of raw magic. I began experimenting and creating equipment to kill Toxites. We started an underground operation, distributing Toxite-fighting supplies to janitors who still wanted to protect the kids.

"Unfortunately, our success betrays us. The harder we work, the more our schools excel. Toxite-free students typically do 75 percent better on tests than students that are exposed to the creatures. That's the whole reason the BEM is supposed to exist—to protect education."

"But the BEM's given up." Marv pulled a face, looking as if he wanted to spit. "It's up to us now. Up to the Rebel Janitors to save education."

Walter nodded. "We've been doing our best to keep Welcher Elementary Toxite-free. The best schools in this nation, the schools where kids can still learn, all have janitors from the Rebel Underground. The BEM is tracking us down and firing us one by one. But most of all, they've been looking for me."

Walter rubbed his forehead. "Now, without the hammer to drive the bronze nail, I can't set up my magical domain. I can't experiment. I can't create new Toxite-fighting equipment. I'm a sitting duck. Now all the BEM has to do is wait. It's only a matter of time before our equipment breaks down. Once it does, Toxites will run wild with no one to stop them."

"And if no one controls the Toxites," Daisy said, "all the kids will get stupid?"

"Education will take an irreversible dive." Walter leaned forward and lowered his voice. "Imagine a future without education. No one can do math. Businesses are crumbling. No one understands science and industry. Progression is halted, and then gradually gives way to digression. Things break and no one can mend them. The computer gives way to pen and paper, the automobile to the horse. No one can read. Laws are forgotten but weapons are not. No doctors, no police, no teachers. Terror and chaos reign. Disease, invasion, war. A base and futile fight for survival. That is the future the BEM is creating. That is the future without education."

The image was vivid in Spencer's mind. It didn't seem possible that the Bureau of Educational Maintenance could throw the nation into ruin.

"But," Spencer said, "Mrs. Natcher will teach us. She won't forget how to read."

"Teachers will teach," said Walter, "but the Toxites will be too strong for the kids to learn anything. Once the older generations die, this nation will fall into the hands of today's uneducated youth."

Spencer thought of little Max and shivered. By the time his brother was in school, the BEM's plan would be in full force.

"Why?" Daisy asked. "Why would they destroy the future?"

"We don't know why," Marv said. "Could be revenge. Maybe they're tired of cleaning up kids' messes, year after year, without so much as a thank you." Marv's face contorted in a disgusted expression. "Don't much care about their reasons. It just makes me sick. If the BEM won't give us equipment to kill the Toxites, then it's up to us."

"We have to fight back and maintain the ideals that the

Founding Witches believed in," said Walter. "These are cor-
rupt times."

Spencer tilted his chair back on two legs. The janitors
were either telling the truth or they had just fabricated the
most elaborate lie in the history of lies. Spencer wanted to
believe them, but it didn't seem possible that the Bureau
of Educational Maintenance had gone evil and was letting
kids' brains rot. Walter's picture of the uneducated future
was frightening, but could it be trusted? One glance at Daisy
revealed that she had fallen for the janitor's story, hook,
line, and sinker.

"You're going to have to prove it," Spencer finally said.

Marv stepped forward. "Read the numbers, kid.
Education is falling apart. What more do you want?"

Walter Jamison held up a hand. "Your concern is admirable, Spencer. You've been tricked once and you don't
want to fall into another pit. I've told you everything and
shown you all the proof I can. Just look at the evidence and
trust in your feelings."

Silence filled the storage/office. Silence that became sti-
fling and uncomfortable. After a moment, the warlock continued. "Hadley asked you to do some pretty extreme things:
sneak out of class, create a giant mess, break into locked
parts of the school, steal objects from the janitors. How did
it make you feel to do those things, Spencer?"

Walter had hit a sensitive subject. Nothing about last
week seemed right. Everything Garth Hadley had asked him
to do had ended in disaster. Now he was in detention, nearly
suspended. All on account of the BEM representative.

"All right," Spencer said, ending his guilt-wreaking chain of thoughts. "If I say I believe you, what do I have to do?"

"*Do?*" cried Walter, a grin spreading across his face. "You don't have to *do* anything. That would make me as bad as Hadley, recruiting kids to perform dangerous tasks. No, Spencer. We're here to help you, to keep you safe."

Walter stood, his hands clasped tightly. "The BEM has tried a forbidden tactic—exposing children to the existence of Toxites. There's no telling what else they might do, which is why I think you should prepare yourselves for the worst."

"What do you mean?" Daisy asked. Walter walked across the room. A high stack of boxes leaned against the back wall. Grabbing the boxes, he slid the stack sideways on a hidden metal runner and a door appeared. Painted on the door was the symbol of a large silver ring with at least a dozen keys dangling from it, splaying outward like rays from the sun.

"Boss," Marv whispered, his face nervous. But Walter merely smiled and unlocked the door. Spencer and Daisy stood up and came a few steps closer, trying to peer into the dark room beyond.

"The Toxites are real," Walter said. "And they're not going anywhere. You kids still have a lot of learning ahead of you. If you wish, we can teach you to fight the Toxites and keep yourselves safe from the BEM." Walter motioned for the kids to approach. "There's a whole world of skills to learn. But we'll just start with a closetful."

Walter Jamison flicked on the light.

CHAPTER 25

"TAKE A LOOK, BUT DON'T GET TOO CLOSE."

The room behind the hidden door was as large as the storage/office and had a low ceiling with exposed pipes and naked lightbulbs. The huge concealed closet smelled of sulfur and chili powder.

There were several long tables littered with pieces of janitorial equipment. Mops and brooms hung on one wall. The opposite wall was lined with vacuums: some upright, others little canister vacuums with long hoses. There were racks of spray bottles organized in rows of colors: pink, blue, green, yellow. And there was much more, but Spencer was distracted by a steaming vat in the center of the room.

Spencer took a step toward it, but suddenly, Marv's bearlike body moved to intercept.

"Get back," he grunted.

"Marv's right, Spencer," Walter said. "That container

holds a small amount of raw magic. We call it Glop. Take a look, but don't get too close."

Spencer and Daisy peered over the rim of the vat and saw gray goo, swirling and bubbling as though it were alive. The closet's unique smell definitely came from the Glop.

"That's the stuff?" Spencer said. It looked like someone had mixed pancake batter and concrete and then tried to carbonate it with dry ice.

"With the bronze nail in the wall, this entire school was my domain. Within the walls of Welcher Elementary, I was free to handle and experiment with the raw Glop. Since the nail was pulled, my domain has crumbled."

"What would happen if you touched the Glop now?"

"No one but an established warlock can handle the Glop. If any of us touched the raw magic now, we'd likely mutate into a Toxite."

"There is one exception," Marv said, shutting the closet door. "If Glop is diluted enough—one part Glop to five hundred parts of something else—it can be used to expose newcomers to the world of Toxites."

"So the pink soap was just super-diluted Glop?" Spencer asked. Walter nodded. "It sure made my face tingle."

"You're lucky it was a proper batch. A small error can be fatal when diluting Glop."

"I'm glad you did a good job," Spencer said.

The janitors looked at each other. Finally, Walter spoke. "The pink soap didn't come from us, Spencer. Someone else put it in the boy's bathroom that day. Who? We're not sure yet."

"Dez," Spencer suddenly whispered. "He was in the bathroom before me. Maybe he put it there."

"That's a possibility," Walter answered. "But he wouldn't have done it on his own. There must have been outside influence."

"Garth Hadley gave it to him," Spencer mused.

"If that's true," Marv said, "then we'd better get this Dez down here right now. Is he in your class?"

Spencer shook his head. "He just got suspended for the week."

"We'll check into it when he returns," Walter said. "Thanks for helping us figure that one out. We regret not contacting you two sooner, but things were hectic as we prepared for the BEM inspections. I was out of town for a few days. When I returned, Marv told me of his suspicions about you. By then it was too late. We found this message in the pocket of a recess aide's vest."

Walter took a small paper from a filing cabinet and handed it to Spencer.

Get Spencer out of the boys' bathroom by the gym. Others may be with him. Take a vest and borrow keys from the janitors.

—S.B.

The note was handwritten in black ink. Spencer studied the penmanship. There was something peculiar about it. Something that he couldn't quite put his finger on. He handed the note to Daisy so she could read it. When she was done, Walter placed it back in the filing cabinet.

"Who's S.B.?" Spencer asked.

"We were hoping you could tell us," Walter said. Spencer and Daisy glanced at each other, but the only BEM worker they knew was Garth Hadley.

"When we found that note, we knew you were really involved with the BEM," Marv said. "We wanted to find you on Monday, Spencer, but you didn't come to school. By the time we saw you at the ice cream social, the ball was already rolling."

"You caught us totally unprepared," Walter admitted. "The glove was a brilliant piece of wizardry, no doubt developed by one of the other warlocks."

"Hadley said you made it."

Walter shook his head. "Never seen anything like it. But we have one now," he said, gesturing toward the end table. Spencer saw the used latex glove in a limp pile. Seeing the glove reminded him of the destruction he'd caused the night before.

"I'm really sorry about yesterday," Spencer admitted.

"Me too," added Daisy.

"And *we're* sorry that we didn't get to you sooner. All of this could have been avoided."

Spencer took a deep breath. Knowing the janitor's side of the story made Garth Hadley look unquestionably guilty. Spencer couldn't believe he'd been tricked. He still felt the need to atone for his wrongdoings at the ice cream social.

"We'll help you get that hammer back, Mr. Jamison," Spencer said, his voice ringing with determination.

Walter Jamison smiled. "I can't let you do that, Spencer. Marv and I will do the best we can to recover Ninfa, but you kids need to stay away from the BEM. I'm afraid they might have more plans for you."

"What kind of plans?"

"I'm not sure. And we won't risk finding out." Walter glanced around the closet. He'd been using the room as a makeshift factory for several months now. Thanks to Spencer and Daisy, the entire Rebel Underground would die off and Toxites would destroy education.

"We have you in detention for three more days," the warlock said. "Will you let us teach you what we can?"

Spencer and Daisy nodded in unison. If they had to see Toxites for the rest of their lives, at least they could learn to kill the monsters.

"Good," Walter said, "because there is a war brewing."

CHAPTER 26

"TODAY WE'LL TRY OUT SOME BASICS."

Wednesday afternoon rolled around and Spencer and Daisy met at the top of the janitors' stairs. Unlike the previous day, they were anxious for detention. Marv met them as the school busses rolled away and led them down the stairs.

Grudgingly, Marv broke out two cans of soda and handed them to the kids.

"Walter's out scouting for Hadley's local hideout," Marv said. "He'll be back soon. And anyway, we've got to wait till the school clears out before we can give you an introduction to basic equipment."

Marv dug around in the desk and withdrew a paperback book with tattered edges. "Walter wanted me to show you this." He held it out so they could see the cover. It was drab brown. Embossed in the center was the symbol of a large metal ring with more than a dozen keys hanging from it. It was the same symbol that appeared on the Rebel Closet door.

"*The Janitor Handbook,*" Marv said. "Fifth edition."

Spencer and Daisy almost forgot about their sodas as they thumbed through the contents of the *Handbook*. They skimmed through a chapter about the Founding Witches. There were several pages about the history and organization of the BEM. Much of the book was dedicated to the Toxites, including early and modern sketches of the creatures.

The kids were far from finished with the book by the time Walter arrived. The warlock reported that the school was finally clear, so he and Marv went into the hidden Rebel Closet. A moment later they emerged with a mop, two brooms, and a can of vacuum dust from an upright vacuum.

"So," Daisy told Spencer as they followed the janitors toward the gym. Daisy had *The Janitor Handbook* in one hand. "I'm pretty much grounded for life now."

"Poach called your parents yesterday?"

"I still can't believe what we did at the social."

"Don't remind me," Spencer said.

"What about your mom? Are you grounded too?"

Spencer nodded. "Grounded from the computer. My mom wasn't happy about me e-mailing without permission."

They entered the gym, and Walter locked the doors behind them.

"Today is just an introduction," Marv said. He didn't look overly pleased to be teaching the kids. Marv had been on the front lines, dealing with Spencer from the beginning. Unlike Walter, Marv seemed to be hanging onto a grudge.

"Today we'll try out some basics and let you go home. Tomorrow we'll observe some Toxites. Then, on Friday, hopefully you'll be ready to catch them. All right?" Marv took *The Janitor Handbook* from Daisy.

"Let's start with brooms," Walter said. "These particular sweepers carry a double-T charge. That means two Toxites have been crushed under the bristles."

Walter picked up a broom and held it firmly in both hands. "By hitting the bristles on the floor, some of the magic is activated, pushing the broom off the ground."

To demonstrate, Walter slammed the straw end of the broom against the gym floor. The broom jerked upward, Walter rising weightlessly as it lifted off the ground. He rose, hovered at the peak for a moment, then descended easily.

"For every action," he said, "there is an opposite and equal reaction. The harder I hit the broom on the floor, the higher I'll rise. You don't have to sit on the broom or ride it at all. As long as you're hanging onto the handle, your body will be as weightless as it would be in outer space. Let's practice."

Spencer and Daisy each took a broom. Spencer held onto the wooden handle and gently tapped the other end on the floor. The broom lifted and he drifted about two feet off the waxed wood floor. "That's awesome," he said, touching down again.

Daisy gave her broom a good whack and suddenly jetted into the air. She screamed as she reached her peak about halfway to the ceiling. Daisy drifted down and landed heavily, gasping for breath.

Spencer tried again, a little harder this time. "How do you steer?" he asked as he floated back to the three-point line on the gym floor.

"You don't, really," Marv said. "Whatever direction you take off in, that's where you're going to go."

Spencer and Daisy practiced with the brooms for about ten minutes. It was a rush every time their feet left the floor. Soon they were running, smacking their brooms down, and using their momentum to launch sideways.

"Brooms are helpful when trying to capture Toxites," Walter said. He took *The Janitor Handbook* from Marv and started thumbing through. "Let's see what the glossary says about brooms . . . ah, yes." Walter began reading aloud.

"Broom—swift and mobile, a broom can help you maneuver into tactical positions against which Toxites cannot defend. The strength of the bristles is usually such that a single blow will mete out immediate death to any Toxite. Highly effective in pursuit of winged Rubbish. Alternate uses include flying and sweeping floors." Walter looked up to see if there were any questions.

"Why don't you read 'Mops' while you're at it," Marv said, hefting a dirty white mop head on a long handle.

Walter turned a few pages. "Mop—accurate and constricting, a mop will deal instant death to any Toxite entangled therein. Highly effective in eliminating Filth and Grime. Alternate uses include ensnaring common objects and cleaning hard floors." Walter closed the book.

"Couldn't have said it better," Marv said.

Suddenly, Marv whipped the mop like he was casting a fishing line. To the kids' surprise, the strings of the mop extended, reaching out until they were nearly ten feet long. Spencer tried to step back, but the mop had wrapped around his arm. Quickly, the mop retracted, dragging Spencer forward until he stood only a foot away from Marv. The burly janitor grinned, showing yellow teeth. "Gotcha," he said as the mop unwound from Spencer's arm. "The range and strength will increase with every Toxite you destroy."

Walter set up a few close-range targets—an orange cone, a basketball, and one of Marv's shoes. Daisy went first and found it very difficult to aim the mop. She managed to entangle the basketball, but lost control as the mop reeled in.

Spencer was not much better, but he was determined to snag Marv's shoe. At last he succeeded, tangling the dirty sneaker in the mop strings and pulling it in.

"Last thing for today," Walter said, holding out the can. "Vacuum dust! When you use a vacuum to suck up a Filth or a Rubbish, the creature dies and its magic leaks into the vacuum. This charged dust is particularly helpful in immobilizing an escaping Toxite." He scooped up a small handful. "Run for it, Marv!" he shouted.

Instantly, the big janitor fell into a floor-shaking sprint. Walter made a funnel with his fingers and threw the dust like a Frisbee. The puff of gray shot through the air with the sound of a revving vacuum and struck Marv in the back. The big man stopped, his feet pasted to the ground and his knees almost buckling. His hair and beard were strained downward and the strangest suction sound filled the air.

After a moment, the sound subsided and Marv righted himself, his hair fluffier, like he'd been through a dryer cycle. The janitor scowled at Walter, but the warlock simply laughed.

"The harder you throw it, the more suction it creates on your opponent. Marv is strong, so I couldn't bring him down. But I've seen people with their faces flat on the floor from vac dust suction. Controlling the vacuum dust isn't as easy as it looks. Different hand positions change the distance and spread of your attack." Walter leafed through the pages of *The Janitor Handbook*. "Take a look at this diagram for the different throwing techniques and hand positions."

The Palm Blast (easy)
Wide spread of dust over short distances.

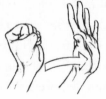

The Funnel Throw (medium)
Accurate and dangerous over long distances.

The Thumb Shot (difficult)
Allows for hitting multiple targets with one throw.

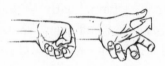

Spencer and Daisy practiced until the can was empty and the last bit of vacuum dust had been tossed across the gym. Marv grabbed a big dust mop and began sweeping up the thrown vacuum dust.

"Can we reuse it?" Daisy asked.

Walter shook his head. "The vac dust is spent. We'd have to get more from the bag before the vacuum maxes out."

"What do you mean by that?" Daisy asked.

"We can't use these things forever," Walter explained. "Glopified supplies have a Toxite kill limit of fifty."

"What happens if you max them out?" Spencer asked.

Marv gave him a look. "What do you think? They stop working. Once a Glopified broom hits fifty Toxites, the only thing you can do is throw that broom into a special dumpster. Someone will be around to collect it and dispose of it safely."

"Who collects the stuff from the magic-filled dumpster?"

"That information is classified," Marv said. "Time to go home."

Spencer didn't want to go home. All he could think about was the unbelievably cool equipment that Walter and Marv had just shown him. He couldn't help imagining Dez with a ten-foot mop wrapped around his face. Then Spencer thought of Mr. Hadley attacking, angry that Spencer and Daisy had betrayed him.

Could a broom lift them out of Hadley's reach?

CHAPTER 27

"FIRST THING YOU'VE GOT TO KNOW ABOUT TOXITES . . ."

Y ou should've put some Glop into a sports car or something," Daisy told Walter Jamison on Thursday afternoon. "That would be awesome. You could fly high, or drive
over water. Who knows?"

Walter smiled, as Spencer found he often did. "It
doesn't work quite like that. Good idea, though."

Spencer and Daisy were in the janitors' storage/office
waiting for the school to vacate so they could train again.

"You see," Walter explained, "the Founding Witches
were afraid that someone in the future would misuse Glop.
They decided to put some limitations on the hammer and
nail. One limitation is that Glop can only be handled by a
warlock in an established domain. Another is that Glop can
only be applied to certain objects that are useful in maintenance."

"So just vacuums and mops and stuff?"

"Those are the obvious ones," Walter said. "There are probably hundreds of possibilities—washers and dryers, keys, machines that wax the floor, buffers that shine it, lawn mowers, weed whackers—anything a janitor might use. I don't know. Exploration is dangerous. Penalties for misusing Glop usually keep warlocks from experimenting too far out of the ordinary. But the latex glove is new. Someone was daring enough to try that and it paid off."

"How'd they make the glove?" Spencer asked.

"Every time a warlock Glopifies something, he has to make a special formula. You start with a bit of raw Glop and carefully add other substances into it. Think of it like a witch's brew. I've seen warlocks add everything from a Rubbish wing to a drop of molten lead to a dash of paprika."

"Sounds like my dad's cooking," Daisy muttered.

"Once a successful Glop formula has been developed, the warlock can send a batch to other janitors. All they have to do is take a new latex glove and dip it into the Glop formula. After that, the glove is Glopified, and makes the wearer uncatchable. It would also make the glove strong enough to destroy Toxites, although I doubt that's its primary purpose. You see," Walter continued, "warlocks are only supposed to Glopify equipment that will aid them in catching Toxites."

"But that's not why they made the glove," Daisy said.

"That's what worries me," answered Walter. "By making the glove, the BEM has developed a Glopified object whose sole purpose seems aimed at attacking other humans. That is dangerous experimentation. I hate the thought, but the time may come when experimentation is all we'll be able to do to keep an upper hand."

"But you can't experiment unless you get the hammer back," Daisy reminded him.

Walter smiled. "Oh, we will get it back."

"We'll help," Spencer offered again. "We already have the BEM's trust; we could trick Hadley and . . ."

"No!" Walter snapped. His face suddenly looked extra weary. "We've already been over this. I don't want you two getting involved any deeper than you already are."

Spencer felt a pang of hurt. Didn't Walter trust them? Wasn't he impressed by their skills at the ice cream social? Spencer frowned. Jamison was just being stubborn, refusing to accept help from a kid.

Marv suddenly lumbered down the steps, slurping from a bottle of cream soda. "Coast is clear," he said. "All's quiet up there. I left several messes that are sure to attract some hungry Toxites."

Spencer and Daisy followed the two janitors up the stairs. They weren't training with equipment today. This was a day for observation.

"First thing you've got to know about Toxites," Marv said, keeping his voice very low and gravelly. "They hate being seen. Toxites thrive on being undetectable."

Spencer suddenly recalled how each time he'd seen a Toxite, the little creature had noticed him staring and scurried away.

"There," Walter hissed, dropping to a crouch in the

middle of the hall. The others followed his example. Spencer and Daisy peered ahead, straining to see what Walter had spotted.

"You see it?" The warlock pointed slowly. Halfway down the hall, a vulture-bat was perched on the edge of a garbage can. "That's a Rubbish. They feed on trash and litter. Those things can palate almost anything—scraps of food, paper, plastic, rubber . . . you name it."

"They don't fly straight, so they're hard to catch," Marv added. "Sometimes you can tangle them in a Glopified mop and that'll crush them. But brooms are best for Rubbishes."

Walter crept forward, staying close to the wall. The Rubbish had hopped into the trash can and was playing in the piled garbage like it was a birdbath. Walter, bent low, approached the can as the Rubbish dove deeper in search of an unseen treat.

Like a pouncing cat, Walter leapt up, grabbed the garbage sack that lined the can, and tied it closed. No sooner was the top sealed off, however, than the Rubbish tore through the plastic sack, wings pounding. A cold, limp French fry drooped from its hooked beak.

Spencer and Daisy reeled back, frightened by the sudden emergence. The Rubbish flapped down the hallway and around the corner.

Marv strode forward, grinning stupidly. "Thought that'd work?" he asked Walter.

"No," he answered. "But I wanted to prove something."

"What?" Marv asked.

"I wanted to show the kids how a skilled Toxite hunter can approach the creatures nearly undetected."

"You're lucky that thing didn't attack," Daisy said. "It barely missed your face when it came out of that bag."

Marv snorted. "Toxites don't attack people. That Rubbish is totally content in this environment. It inhales your brain waves and exhales apathy."

"Apathy?" Daisy asked. She'd heard that people exhaled carbon dioxide and plants exhaled oxygen. But what was apathy?

"Apathy is a lack of interest," Walter said. "When a Rubbish exhales, students nearby suddenly lose the desire to do any work. They become completely disinterested in whatever the teacher is saying. In short, they don't *want* to learn anything."

"Oh," Daisy said, grateful now that she only exhaled carbon dioxide.

"Other than that, Rubbishes don't attack physically," Walter said.

"Unless they're relocated," Marv said. "A few years back, Toxite scientists from the BEM did experiments to see how the creatures would fare in other environments. But the Toxites don't like to be moved out of schools. The scientists relocated some to restaurants, business buildings, and a few other locations. As soon as they were released, the Toxites went haywire and started attacking the scientists.

"An innocent bystander saw it. 'Course, she couldn't see the Toxites, so she thought the scientists were having some kind of spasm or seizure. Looked real creepy. She called an ambulance. Lucky thing, too, since four BEM workers were critically injured. The Toxites escaped, fighting a path all the way back to the school they were taken from. They're very territorial."

When Marv finished, Walter glanced disapprovingly at him. "I don't think that was necessary, Marv Bills," he said. "We're teaching the kids to *defend* against the Toxites, not to *fear* them."

"It's okay," Spencer said, but Daisy indeed looked frightened.

"Just thought they might like to know," Marv said defensively. He trudged down the hall, the other three falling in behind him.

When they reached the corner, Marv stopped, lifting a thick finger to his lips. Spencer and Daisy peered around the corner, eyes scanning the area.

Daisy saw them first—two Grimes relaxing in the drinking fountain. One pale body was curled around the spout where the water came out. The other had flattened its slimy body over the drain and was basking in a pool of stagnant water.

Spencer shuddered, feeling weak in his stomach. He would never, *ever* drink from a school fountain again. He swore to bring a personal water bottle from now on.

"Grimes," Marv whispered. "The only amphibious Toxite. They prefer moist areas like bathrooms and water fountains. But don't be surprised if they show up in a classroom. They can go anywhere."

"What do they eat?" Daisy asked, unable to take her eyes off their nasty little bodies.

"They can live on water alone," Walter said. "But they eat anything wet. The slimy buildup between tiles or around sinks is like candy to them."

"Yuck," Spencer said, trying not to gag. "Kill them already. I can't stand it." Could he ever wash his hands at school again? If the sinks were contaminated, what was the use? Even Principal Poach's instant hand sanitizer wasn't safe from the Grimes.

"They move fast," Marv said. "And they use the pipes like a subway system. Best way to sneak up is by coming directly at them. Their eyes are so far apart that Grimes have a small blind spot directly in front of them. That's why they turn their heads like that."

Spencer peeked around the corner again. Sure enough, both Grimes were lazily moving their heads back and forth, glazed white eyes half open in their relaxation.

"What are we doing here?" Daisy asked loudly. "Where's everybody else? Hey, look at that door, it's so cool!" She started walking down the hall toward a classroom door.

"Marv," Walter scolded. "We've waited too long."

Marv instantly jumped around the corner. The Grimes' bulbous eyes opened and the creatures scattered. Before Marv reached the drinking fountain, both Grimes had folded and stretched themselves to fit down the tiny holes of the drain.

"Whoa!" Daisy said. "Where am I going?" She turned around and rejoined the group.

"Sorry about that," Walter said. "Grimes exhale confusion and distraction. They stop kids from understanding simple instructions and often cause the sudden need to get out of your seat and move around. Teachers hate Grime breath. Don't know about it, but they hate what it makes kids do."

"I don't like it either," Daisy said. "How come Spencer didn't get confused?"

"Certain Toxites work better on certain students," Marv answered. "By the time you reach high school, Toxite toxins probably won't affect you at all. That's why the critters love younger schools."

"Sorry we waited so long to chase off the Grimes," Walter apologized. "We thought we were far enough away that you wouldn't feel the effects. Apparently not."

"What I want to know," Spencer said, "is what would have happened if I wanted a drink?"

"You saw," said Marv. "They run away."

Spencer shook his head. "What if I couldn't see them? What if I was an ordinary student? Would they still scatter?" He was thinking of all the times he'd sipped from a school fountain, wondering if he'd sucked up Grime germs in the process.

"If you can't see them, they aren't there," Walter said.

"No," Spencer said. "That doesn't make sense."

"You'll see," Walter replied. "If a Toxite knows it can't be seen, it'll stay right where it is, breathing in brain waves."

Spencer suddenly remembered Principal Poach's

hot-dog fingers reaching through the Rubbish in the peanut can. "What if someone touches them?"

"If they don't see them, they won't feel them, either. But now that you two can see them, Toxites will probably stay farther away from you."

Marv bent down and took a swig from the drinking fountain. Spencer almost hurled. The big man stood up tall again, water in his black beard. "There's one more kind of Toxite we'd like to show you," he said.

They walked up by Mrs. Natcher's class, then down by the gyms. Marv started to grow impatient as they looped back, the four figures moving stealthily through the hallway. They passed through a set of doors and found themselves in the school library. Using the bookshelves as a shield, the janitors and the kids crawled forward until, at last, they saw what they were searching for.

"Filth," Walter whispered.

Spencer and Daisy took turns looking around the corner of the shelf. A dust gopher was sniffing the floor nearby. It was the size of a guinea pig but, on closer inspection, looked more like a porcupine. Along the creature's back were spiky, dust-covered quills, almost unseen below its long, dusty hair. The rodent face was downturned, and long woodchuck teeth tilled the carpet in search of fresh dust.

The Filth waddled a few steps, found a particularly rich spot, and began scratching at the carpet with its clawed feet. A cloud of dust arose and the Filth snapped and licked at the carpet.

"Can you guess what they eat?" Marv whispered, but Spencer wasn't listening. He was curled on the carpet, his breathing deep and regular.

He was asleep.

CHAPTER 28

"IT DOESN'T SEEM FAIR."

S hoo!" Walter cried, rolling out from his hiding place behind the bookshelf. The Filth's quills bristled, an act that sent up a puff of gray dust. If Walter had brought a Glopified vacuum, the creature would have been a goner. But since he was unarmed, the Filth scuttled away, ducking out of sight beneath the historical fiction shelf.

Spencer revived quickly, distantly aware of Daisy calling his name. He quickly shrugged off the fatigue and sat up, his face reddening with embarrassment.

"What happened?" he asked.

"The Filth got you," Marv said. "That was a big one. Had potent breath."

The four of them stood, Spencer leaning against the bookshelf and yawning.

"Filth breath will plunge you into such a deep sleep, you won't hear a word the teacher says."

A light clicked on in Spencer's mind. All the times he'd been drowsy in class . . . especially during Miss Sharmelle's lecture on algebra. Maybe it hadn't actually been so boring. There must have been a Filth in the room. But why did the Filth breath attack Spencer so hard, while kids like Dez didn't even blink a heavy eye?

"It doesn't seem fair," Spencer said. "Some other kids in my class, like Dez, for example—he doesn't seem affected by *any* of the Toxites. Is he just strong enough to resist their breath?"

Walter gave a half smile, a reminiscent look on his old face. "I was eighteen when I got my first job as a janitor. My mentor was a wise Toxite hunter who answered that same question for me." Walter folded his arms.

"One day, I was observing the Toxites during school lunch. There were two particular boys that I noticed— complete opposites. The first sat in the corner. His table was swarmed with Toxites. The poor fellow was caught between bouts of distraction and fatigue so severe he could hardly eat.

"The second boy sat across the room. He ate his food quickly, and I noticed that not a single Toxite lingered near him."

Spencer could imagine himself in the story, surrounded by Toxites.

"After observing the scene, I commented to my mentor, 'That first boy must be very bad, all surrounded by Toxites as he is. And I'll bet that second child is well-behaved, strong, and smart.'

"My mentor chuckled. 'Walter,' he said, 'how little you understand. The truth is rather the opposite. The first boy is trying very hard. His mind is active and he wants to learn. Those are rich brain waves, and the Toxites swarm around him to feed. That second boy is a ruffian with no desire to be in school. Even in a school that was Toxite-free, that child wouldn't learn a thing.'"

Walter nodded at Spencer and Daisy. "I hope you understand. We're not fighting for the Dezmonds of the school. The Toxites don't waste their breath on kids like him. We're fighting the Toxites for *you*. You are the ones in danger, because you have a great desire to learn and to grow." He sighed. "It may not seem fair. But it's true. Take it as a compliment from the Toxites. Take it as a challenge. There're only two ways to get rid of the creatures. Either you give up and quit learning so they leave you alone . . . or you *fight* for your education." Walter clapped them on the shoulders. "What's it going to be?"

Spencer and Daisy shared a glance. "We fight."

"Good." Walter smiled. "Let's head back to the office. I need to get on with my search for the local BEM hideout."

As they walked down the hallway, Spencer thought back to the time he was employed by Garth Hadley. With the janitors, he felt so positive and confident. Something he'd never felt with the BEM. Walter and Marv never asked Spencer to do things he didn't want to do. They were teaching him, helping him to protect himself. It wasn't something

Spencer could explain with words. It was more of a feeling. A feeling of trust in the janitors.

"I can't believe we saw so many Toxites today," Daisy said, as they rounded a corner.

"That's nothing," said Marv. "The few schools that are staffed by the Rebel janitors are keeping the Toxite population very low. In schools where the BEM has taken over, the hallways are crawling with Toxites. Hundreds of them. Disgusts me. For more than three hundred years, the BEM has kept schools creature-free. Now they're tracking down all Toxite-fighting janitors and firing them. What's this world coming to?"

Hundreds of Toxites? Spencer couldn't imagine what that would be like. What, Spencer wondered, could possibly have motivated the Bureau of Educational Maintenance to withdraw support from the schools? Why did they want the creatures to ruin education? A single Filth had sent him snoring. A single Grime had caused Daisy to take special interest in a door. What would happen to Welcher Elementary if the BEM fired Walter and Marv?

Spencer felt a wave of guilt wash over him. *He* had crippled the Rebel janitors by turning the hammer over to Garth Hadley. Now all the BEM needed was the nail. Hadley was powerful and determined. If he got it, all hope for the Rebel janitors would be shattered.

The seed of an idea rooted in Spencer's mind. It grew as he and Daisy left the school and walked to the Gates home. It probably wasn't a safe idea. It meant doing things he shouldn't do. But it might make all the difference.

"Grab it!" Marv shouted, leaving his vacuum and racing toward the stall.

Spencer stared into the toilet at the immobile Grime. Maybe with a long pair of gloves, Spencer would brave reaching into the toilet . . . but bare-handed?

The vacuum dust wouldn't hold much longer. Spencer reached out his hand and then drew back, unable.

The Grime recovered in a moment and took one stroke toward the back of the toilet. The moment before it vanished down the hole, Marv's bare hand plunged into the depths. He seized the Grime by the tail and flung it to the floor.

The Grime bounced and flopped like a fish on dry land. In a moment it was on its feet again, but a moment was all Marv needed. The vacuum wheels raced forward and the churning, spinning underpinnings of the vacuum closed down on the Grime.

There was a splattering of pale yellow slime. The vacuum sucked harder, seeming to choke on something. Then the machine swallowed and there was nothing.

Marv turned the vacuum off and silence filled the bathroom. Spencer slowly picked up his broom, aware that Marv was glaring at him.

"Why didn't you grab it?" the big janitor asked as they exited the bathroom. "Almost got away."

"I just . . . froze," Spencer answered apologetically. "Maybe the Grime breath confused me." *Or maybe*, thought Spencer, *I just couldn't stick my hand into the toilet.*

They walked silently into the hall. Marv unlocked a set of gym doors. "I set a full garbage bin in the corner of the

The idea was almost fully grown by the time Mr. Gates dropped Spencer at Hillside Estates. He had talked himself out of it two or three times, but it kept coming back. The need to help the janitors, to save education, outweighed all risks.

A quick search of the house assured Spencer that his mother wasn't home yet. She was probably picking up his siblings from day care, so he'd have to be fast. It would be a short message; he already had the words planned out.

Spencer sat down at the computer and swallowed hard. The thought of disobeying his mother caused his heart to sink into his stomach, as if someone had suctioned it with a strong puff of vac dust. Spencer wiped his sweating palms on his pants and tried to overcome the guilty feeling that threatened to undermine his plan.

"For the good of education," he whispered, almost inaudibly. "For the future."

With a cautious glance over his shoulder, Spencer logged into his e-mail and typed as fast as he could.

To: ghadley@bem.gov
From: SpenceZ@wahoo.com
Subject: None

Dear Mr. Hadley,

I changed my mind. Daisy and I can get the nail from Walter Jamison tomorrow after school. People are suspicious of you at the school. Why don't we meet at your local hideout to hand it over?

Let me know where and when.

Spencer

CHAPTER 29

"LET'S HUNT."

Friday dragged on and on. Even though it was the last Dez-free day of class, Spencer couldn't wait for the bell to ring and their final training with the janitors to start. In his backpack, Spencer had the key to their success. It was the printed e-mail, including his original message and Garth Hadley's response.

Spencer had kept it a secret from everyone, even Daisy. At the end of training with the janitors today, Spencer would present the information to Walter Jamison. Garth Hadley's local hideout.

So much anticipation made it hard to sit still.

At last, the bell rang and he and Daisy rushed down to the janitors' storage/office. Walter was seated at the desk, nervously rubbing his bald scalp. Marv was straightening a rack of spray bottles on the wall. The entrance to the Rebel Closet was hidden behind the sliding tower of boxes.

Greetings were short and terse, totally unlike the last few days. Something had happened—Spencer could almost taste it in the air.

"What's up?" Spencer asked, trying to play it cool.

"Things are getting tight without Ninfa," Walter said. "Supplies are running out. The BEM shut down a Rebel school in Colorado last night. Two of our janitors were fired. And Garth Hadley attacked Welcher Elementary at one o'clock this morning."

"What?"

"We were here late, shampooing carpets and brainstorming possible BEM hideouts. Luckily we saw them coming," Marv said. "I stalled them with vac dust while Walter got safely outside with the bronze nail."

"It was too close," Walter said.

"Any idea where they're hiding?" Spencer asked. He couldn't help it, but he was setting himself up to look like a real hero.

"None," Walter said. "My lead last night was a dead end. Welcher's not that big. I've checked everywhere. Garth Hadley must be using an alias."

"We should get started," Marv said. "Time's running out. We need to get these kids prepared."

"Right," Walter agreed as Marv pulled aside the boxes to expose the Rebel Closet. Light glinted on the painted emblem of the janitor key ring as the warlock unlocked the door and strode into the secret closet.

The room looked undisturbed since the last time they entered. Without the hammer to drive the bronze nail, Walter was still unable to touch the swirling vat of Glop in the center of the room.

"Everyone should take a baggie of vacuum dust," Walter said. From the table, Marv retrieved four Ziploc bags, each with a premeasured amount of gray dust.

"And everyone should take a Glopified weapon," said Marv. "I'm taking a vacuum." He wheeled an upright vacuum with a white cord out of the closet. Walter reached for a pushbroom.

Spencer and Daisy walked around the closet like kids in a candy shop. There were so many Glopified, Toxite-killing weapons that the kids had never seen before. Spencer wondered at each one, hoping he could have detention the following week to be trained with more.

"What's this?" Daisy asked, picking up a bulging vacuum bag.

"Careful," Walter warned. "That thing's got more charge than any other object in this room. It really belongs in the dumpster."

"Can't you get some vac dust out of it?" Spencer asked. "It would probably be super powerful."

"That bag's been overcharged. It contains the power of nearly three hundred Toxites. For some unknown reason, it didn't max out at fifty like all the other supplies. We call that bag the Vortex."

"So it has different powers than vac dust?" Daisy asked, examining the thick, papery bag.

"The Vortex is unstable," said Walter. "The dust inside is extremely powerful, but by the time the bag is pierced, it would be too late. Everything in this room would get sucked into the bag. BEM journals account for one other Vortex that was created somehow in the 1980s. When the bag was punctured, the suction was so strong that it pulled the paint off the walls and the carpet rolled up like a burrito. Only the person holding it didn't get sucked inside. Think of it like a black hole inside a vacuum bag."

Daisy set the Vortex gently back on the shelf where she'd gotten it, saying, "I don't think I want to use that today." Instead, Daisy chose a mop with a splintery wooden handle.

Spencer looked at the brooms hanging on the rack before him. Above each broom was a number written in marker.

"Is this the Toxite charge?" Spencer asked.

"Exactly," Walter said, hefting his pushbroom. "This one has a 6T charge. That means I've crushed six Toxites with this pushbroom. Every Toxite I destroy with it will increase the speed and strength of my pushbroom until I max it out at fifty."

"Is a pushbroom different from a normal broom?" Spencer asked.

"Quite opposites, actually," Walter answered. "Instead of lifting me off the ground, my pushbroom will send the Toxites flying, if I hit them right."

Daisy looked back at the spot where her mop had hung.

It had a 1T charge. She quickly put it back on the rack in exchange for a 12T mop.

Spencer picked out a 4T broom with straw bristles. Checking his baggie of vac dust, he followed Daisy and Walter out of the Rebel Closet.

"We'll stick to our usual daily maintenance routes," Walter explained. "I'll take Daisy with me to do the center hallway and the library. Marv, you take Spencer to the north hallway and the gym. Whoever finishes first will come back to work the entry hallway and cafeteria. But be careful—I think Principal Poach is still in the building." Walter checked his watch. "Meet back here in forty-five minutes. Try to catch one of each kind—for instructional purposes." He hefted his pushbroom like a rifle. "Let's hunt."

Spencer waved to Daisy and followed Marv down the hallway. The "out of order" sign was gone from the boys' bathroom. The nail wasn't in the wall anymore, so there was no reason to keep the bathroom closed. Marv plugged his vacuum into an outlet next to the door.

"We'll start here," Marv said. "I'll kick open the door and you run inside. If there's a Grime in there, it'll probably bolt, so you've got to be fast." Spencer nodded to show that he understood.

Marv fired up his vacuum and tilted it so he could race it forward on the back wheels like a chariot. Then he stepped forward and gave the bathroom door a big kick. The door swung inward, testing the strength of its hinges.

In a flash, Spencer was inside. Just as Marv had suspected, there was a Grime perched on the edge of the sink.

Spencer swiped for the slimy creature with his broom. The pokey bristles raked down the Grime's back and the salamander creature fell to the floor. Spencer wielded the broom around like an axe and came down for a fatal chop. His broom hit the floor hard.

But the Grime was gone.

The force of impact sent the broom rocketing to the ceiling, Spencer flying alongside. Below, the Grime slithered toward the floor drain. But escape was blocked, as Marv's upright vacuum dropped over the drain, eagerly sucking.

Without stopping, the Grime redirected. Spencer was pinned to the ceiling, the broom still straining upward. Taking a deep breath, Spencer let go of the broom. Gravity returned instantly and he dropped heavily and crumpled to his knees on the tile.

"The toilet!" Marv shouted, pulling a suction hose from the side of his vacuum.

Spencer recovered and leapt for the open stall door. The Grime was climbing the side of the toilet bowl, bulbous fingertips like suction cups on the slick surface.

Spencer's broom had dislodged from the bathroom ceiling and was floating down. But there was no time to go for it. Hastily, the boy opened his Ziploc bag and gathered a small fistful of charged vac dust.

The Grime was on the toilet seat when Spencer's dust hit from behind. The suction sound filled the resonant bathroom and the force of the vac dust sucked the creature off the rim. The Grime fell with a splash into the water, the force pinning it below the surface.

"Grab it!" Marv shouted, leaving his vacuum and racing toward the stall.

Spencer stared into the toilet at the immobile Grime. Maybe with a long pair of gloves, Spencer would brave reaching into the toilet . . . but bare-handed?

The vacuum dust wouldn't hold much longer. Spencer reached out his hand and then drew back, unable.

The Grime recovered in a moment and took one stroke toward the back of the toilet. The moment before it vanished down the hole, Marv's bare hand plunged into the depths. He seized the Grime by the tail and flung it to the floor.

The Grime bounced and flopped like a fish on dry land. In a moment it was on its feet again, but a moment was all Marv needed. The vacuum wheels raced forward and the churning, spinning underpinnings of the vacuum closed down on the Grime.

There was a splattering of pale yellow slime. The vacuum sucked harder, seeming to choke on something. Then the machine swallowed and there was nothing.

Marv turned the vacuum off and silence filled the bathroom. Spencer slowly picked up his broom, aware that Marv was glaring at him.

"Why didn't you grab it?" the big janitor asked as they exited the bathroom. "Almost got away."

"I just . . . froze," Spencer answered apologetically. "Maybe the Grime breath confused me." *Or maybe*, thought Spencer, *I just couldn't stick my hand into the toilet.*

They walked silently into the hall. Marv unlocked a set of gym doors. "I set a full garbage bin in the corner of the gym after lunch. It should have attracted a Rubbish or two by now."

And sure enough, two Rubbishes were frolicking in the trash. Their beaks snipped at each other playfully and they dove deeper into the bin to see who could surface with the greatest treasure.

Marv slowly worked his way to an outlet on the wall. He plugged in his vacuum but didn't turn it on. Spencer crept up beside him.

"The best way," Marv whispered, "is for you to stay up in the air. If you can make a ruckus above them, chances are they'll come low where I can get them with my vacuum."

"You ready?" Spencer asked. Marv nodded, his finger hovering above the vacuum's *on* switch. Spencer moved away from the wall. He took two running steps in the direction of the garbage and dropped his broom bristles heavily to the floor.

Spencer lifted off at an angle, racing through the air. The Rubbishes spotted him, and the garbage-bin fun stopped immediately. Their vulture-like heads perked up and their leathery bat wings flexed.

Hanging tight to the broom handle, Spencer slammed into the wall above the garbage bin. The proximity made the Rubbishes skittish; one took off, flying low. Marv sprinted in that direction, vacuum wheels turning at maximum speed.

Spencer descended slowly along the wall. In a moment, the Rubbish hiding in the garbage would have a free path upward. Twisting his body around, Spencer tapped the broom bristles against the wall. The opposite reaction sent him gliding sideways across the gym. The Rubbish waited, ruffled its wings, and took flight as Spencer drifted away.

In a moment, Spencer seized an exit sign above the door and pulled himself back to the wall, still clinging to the broom with one hand.

"Got one!" Marv shouted from the center of the gym.

Seeing the last Rubbish escaping higher, Spencer kicked off the exit sign, slamming his broom against the wall at the last minute. The new burst of energy sent him shooting toward the flying Rubbish. One-handed, Spencer scrambled with the little bag of vac dust. Mimicking the widespread palm blast that Walter had taught them, Spencer hurled the dust.

A puff of dark dust billowed out of his hand like a mushroom cloud. The Rubbish was caught in the burst, its wings buckling under the suction. Marv was in position as the creature plummeted to the gym floor.

Spencer, still dangling one-handed from the broom, suddenly realized his mistake. Unable to change his broom's course, Spencer flew straight into the residual dust cloud. The deafening sound of rushing air filled his ears as the vacuum dust fought to bring down the broom. The gravity-defying broom strained upward while Spencer's body was caught in the suction of the vac dust.

Spencer's fingers slipped and he plummeted toward the gym floor. He tried to brace for impact, deaf to all noise except the rushing vac dust. Then, to Spencer's great surprise, he landed on something soft.

Marv.

The bulky janitor wrapped his arms around Spencer, but the downward force was too strong. Marv was flattened on his back with Spencer pinned to his chest. They were stuck for only a moment before the suction from the vac dust suddenly ended.

Spencer rolled aside, moaning. The sound of rushing air was replaced by Marv's idling vacuum.

"You get him?" Spencer gasped, still lying on the floor. Overhead, he watched his broom descend.

"Got you instead." Marv grunted, standing up. "The second Rubbish got away."

"Sorry," Spencer apologized. "I guess I'm not too good at Toxite hunting."

Marv turned off the vacuum and jerked on the cord to unplug his machine. "Look, you're just a beginner." But Marv's tone agreed with Spencer's failure.

"What now?" Spencer stood up and retrieved his broom from the air.

"Quiet!" Marv hissed. A dusty Filth had just waddled under the door and entered the gym.

"All right," Marv said, "here's what we'll do. You go around the side and come at it from the left. I'll get my vacuum plugged in and—" Marv never got to finish.

The gym door flew open and the Filth scurried out of sight. Spencer clutched his broom like a weapon as two figures raced into the gym.

One of them was Garth Hadley.

CHAPTER 30

"GET AWAY FROM HIM!"

As soon as the intruders burst into the room, Marv acted. Tearing open the papery bag on his vacuum, the burly janitor grabbed two fistfuls of charged vac dust, doubling the amount in his Ziploc bag. Marv abandoned the upright vacuum and sprinted to Spencer's side in two floor-shaking steps.

Suddenly, the power went out, plunging the gym into darkness. Two flashlights flicked on. One cast a normal beam that swept across the gym in search of Spencer and Marv. But the flashlight in Garth Hadley's hand cast a white beam that shifted erratically from Spencer's broom to Marv's fistfuls of vac dust and over to the abandoned vacuum.

No doubt about it. Hadley was looking for the bronze nail.

Spencer's eyes adjusted quickly to the darkness. Garth Hadley and his companion, a skinny man with a pointy nose, fanned out to block the gym exits as they moved steadily forward. Each wore a latex glove that Spencer knew was charged. Aside from the flashlight, Garth was toting a mop with a long handle. He held it behind his flashlight so it wouldn't attract the beam.

"Back up," Marv whispered. "Keep heading for the back wall. There is an emergency exit in the northeast corner. Go!"

Marv leapt forward, growling like a grizzly. The two intruders were too far apart for him to attack them both simultaneously, so Marv went for Hadley.

The BEM rep saw him coming, pulled back his mop, and cast the dirty white mop strings flinging in Marv's direction. Just before the mop reached its target, Marv released a puff of vacuum dust. Suction filled the room. The vac dust had just enough strength to knock Hadley's mop off target.

The mop strings dropped and Marv hurdled them like an overweight track star. The second fistful of vac dust, expertly delivered with a funnel throw, struck Hadley in the chest. The strong man shouted and crumpled to his knees. Hadley's clothes were stretched tight against his skin from the downward suction.

Spencer kicked open the emergency exit, flooding the gym with late afternoon sunlight. But the exit was suddenly blocked by a fat man with a broom in his hands. Spencer reeled backward into the gym, noticing the skinny man setting an intercept course. There was nowhere to go but up.

Spencer hit the bristles of his broom against the gym floor, feeling the jerk of the wood in his hands and the unique weightlessness as he lifted. Then the broom shuddered under new weight. The skinny man had seized Spencer's rising ankle, and the broom was struggling to lift them both. The other man charged inside from the emergency exit, pulling a handful of dust from his pocket.

"Ghhhaaaar!" Marv bellowed, pounding into the rising skinny man and sending him sprawling across the gym floor. Spencer shot upward like a helium balloon with its string cut. Glancing down, he saw the fat man from the emergency exit immobilizing Marv with a taste of his own medicine. Across the room, Garth Hadley was recovering. All eyes went upward to the floating boy.

Spencer made contact with the high gym ceiling a little harder than he'd hoped. Below, the three men gathered like vultures to await his inevitable descent. But what if he didn't descend?

Not far away was a basketball hoop hooked into the ceiling with cables. During P.E., the teacher lowered the hoop so the kids could play. The rest of the time, it was folded up against the ceiling. The perfect place.

Still plastered against the ceiling and holding tight to the broom, Spencer used his feet to scrape along, sliding in the direction of the hoop. He was almost there when he felt the broom begin to descend. Kicking off the ceiling, Spencer drifted the last few feet and caught the edge of the backboard. He positioned his legs through the hoop like a very uncomfortable chair, still holding tight to his broom as it became heavy in his hands again.

Below, the BEM workers began mumbling and cursing. The skinny man had his flashlight trained on Spencer. Garth Hadley cast with his mop, the strings lengthening and stretching upward. The cast fell short . . . but not by much. Hadley flicked the mop again. This time, Spencer had to pull his feet up as the hungry mop strings threatened to entangle him and drag him from his perch.

"Get away from him!" Marv cried from behind. In their hopes to reach Spencer, they had left the big janitor unguarded. Marv had recovered from the suction dust and had a trick of his own.

Before anyone could move, Marv used the thumb shot, flicking out tufts of dust like a professional marbles player. The well-aimed dust struck the fat man and the skinny man, bringing them to their faces on the gym floor. The third puff missed Garth Hadley, who countered with an attack from his mop. The strings wrapped around Marv's big belly, tying both arms to his sides and tipping him off balance. The mop retracted, dragging Marv to rest at Hadley's feet.

Spencer knew he had to get away while commotion reigned below. Positioning himself to kick off the hoop, Spencer tapped his broom against the backboard. The boy leapt from his perch, using the gentle tap from the broom to cross the room and descend at the gym door. He touched the floor, his broom still floating beside him. Without looking back for Marv, Spencer ran into the hall.

He dashed toward the middle hallway. The most

important thing was to warn Walter so the warlock could get away with the bronze nail. Spencer stopped at an intersection in the hallway.

To his right were the library's double doors, closed tight. To his left was the middle hallway, with Mrs. Natcher's classroom at the end. Daylight was shining through the exit doors by Mrs. Natcher's room, and Spencer saw the silhouettes of four fighting figures. Grunts and shouts echoed down the middle hallway.

Spencer saw Walter pressing hard to get past three new BEM workers blocking the way. His pushbroom was broken, the handle snapped in half. Spencer scanned the area. Where was Daisy? Wasn't she supposed to be with Walter?

At the sound of running footfalls, Spencer whirled around. Garth Hadley was charging down the hall. Spencer seemed frozen to the carpet. There were too many BEM workers. They'd never get away!

With a shout, Walter leapt for the doorway, but mop strings tangled him just like they had Marv. The warlock slammed against the wall and slumped to the carpet.

Spencer dropped his broom and ran—not left or right, but straight ahead. He needed to find Daisy. He needed to find a hiding spot in the dark school. He needed to run . . . faster!

CHAPTER 31

"I WISH YOU'D JUST CALL ME SARAH."

Spencer rounded the corner and sprinted toward the front doors of the school. But what good was escaping? Marv and Walter had fallen and Spencer needed to help before the BEM hauled them away.

Spencer reeled back as he passed the principal's office. There was a light on—a flashlight or a candle, maybe, since the power was still out.

Spencer had sworn he would never enter Principal Poach's office again. But this was different. Poach could call the cops and they could stop the janitornapping that was happening in the middle hall. Besides, it was a great hiding spot since Garth Hadley wouldn't follow him into the occupied office.

Ducking quickly through the first doorway, Spencer found himself in the waiting area where he and Daisy had once sat on a bench with Baybee. He was reaching for the principal's doorknob when he heard voices floating out of the office.

"Not a problem at all," Poach's nasal voice squeaked. "I'm just sorry about this power outage."

"I don't mind," answered a feminine voice. "I know it wasn't a convenient time for an interview, but thanks for letting me in."

Spencer stopped. *Letting me in?* Through the wavy glass of the office door, he could see only vague outlines and flickering shadows. But whoever was inside the office was about to come out.

It was time to hide.

Spencer crossed the waiting area and threw himself under a computer desk. Pressing his face against the ground, he could see only shoes as the principal's door opened.

A pair of high heels clicked across the floor and paused. A waft of flowery perfume drifted under the desk, reminding Spencer of someone. He just couldn't think who.

Poach's walrus shoes waddled forward. "You are an excellent candidate. Unfortunately, we're not looking to hire right now."

"I understand," the woman said.

"Mrs. Bently—" he started.

"Please," the woman interrupted, "I wish you'd just call me Sarah."

"Sarah," Poach restarted. "You'll be the first to know if anything opens up. I was very . . . impressed."

"Thanks for your time," the sultry voice answered. Then the high heels clicked away.

Spencer didn't dare move. He watched Poach's brown shoes shuffle back into the office. The heavy man sighed, and Spencer heard him gathering papers. Just then, the power returned. Overhead, Spencer felt the computer shudder back to life on the desk. The walrus principal made a contented sound, followed by a little chuckle.

Five minutes later, the principal's shoes reappeared. The office door pulled closed and the man waddled away.

Spencer waited another painstakingly long five minutes before crawling out of his hiding spot. Cautiously, he peeked into the entry hallway. There was no one in sight. The front of the school appeared totally deserted.

Just in case, Spencer opened his Ziploc bag and pinched out the remaining vac dust. His hand was sweaty and the dirty fibers clung to his palm. He wondered how that might affect his toss.

Spencer checked the cafeteria. Empty. He walked down to the middle hall. Empty. The library. Empty. The north hall and gym. Empty. Empty.

Spencer was alone. Garth Hadley had taken the janitors. Why? Why did Hadley attack? Spencer felt his face go red. He had a deal with Garth! They were supposed to meet at the hideout in a half hour, at six o'clock. Spencer thought he had it all mapped out—he would go to the BEM hideout with Walter and Marv, take Hadley by surprise, and steal the hammer back.

Everything was ruined now. Garth Hadley had Walter,

the hammer, and the nail. There was only one thing left for Spencer to do.

Find Daisy.

Spencer wandered back to the janitors' storage/office. It was about the only place he hadn't looked. Spencer jogged down the steps, jumping the last three and landing in the dim office area. No sooner did his feet touch the floor than the sound of a revving vacuum hit him from the side.

Spencer felt a handful of vac dust strike his face. The suction force dragged him to the ground. He writhed on his side, twisting to see his attacker. Why hadn't he been more careful? Of course the janitors' storage/office would be a trap!

Daisy stepped out from behind a stack of boxes, a horrified look on her face. "Oops! Sorry, Spencer!" she cried, running to him. He heard her voice through the rushing sound of the vac dust. "I heard someone coming and panicked." Daisy knelt down by his side. "Gee, I'm glad it's you."

The two kids could do nothing but wait until the suction wore off. At last, Spencer stood up. His brown hair was tousled and he felt like he'd just been chucked out of a typhoon. He sighed wearily. There was no sense in getting mad at Daisy. She'd only been trying to protect herself.

"They took the janitors," Spencer said.

"Walter?" she asked.

"Yeah, they got them both." Spencer dropped his head. "That means they have the bronze nail. Garth Hadley will be long gone by now."

"They didn't get the nail," Daisy said, reaching into her pocket. Triumphantly, she pinched the bronze nail between her thumb and finger, holding it out for Spencer to admire.

"Wh–?" Spencer stammered. "How did you get that?"

"Walter gave it to me. We were in the cafeteria, going for a Grime, when we heard someone coming down the hallway. Walter gave me the nail and his keys and told me to hide. He went out to face them. When the coast was clear, I ran down here."

Spencer felt like hugging Daisy. If Hadley didn't have the nail, he wouldn't leave town. That meant there was a chance to rescue the janitors! And Spencer knew right where Garth Hadley was hiding.

Nearly tearing off his backpack's zipper with excitement, Spencer dug through his pack until he found the paper he was looking for. Pulling it out, he thrust it at Daisy. She took the paper and read quickly, her eyebrows crinkled in concentration.

To: ghadley@bem.gov
From: SpenceZ@wahoo.com
Subject: None

Dear Mr. Hadley,

I changed my mind. Daisy and I can get the nail from Walter Jamison tomorrow after school. People are suspicious of you at the school. Why don't we meet at your local hideout to hand it over?

Let me know where and when.

Spencer

To: SpenceZ@wahoo.com
From: ghadley@bem.gov
Subject: RE None

Spencer,

Good for you. I want you to know you're making the right choice. I knew the BEM could count on you. If you get the nail tomorrow, I'll be waiting for you at six o'clock. Bring the nail to 542 East Maple Street, Apt. 2, right across from Maple Park. If I'm not there, you'll find a spare key under a clay pot on the front porch.

Sincerely grateful,

Garth Hadley
BEM regional representative

Daisy looked up from the printed e-mail, an expression of severe disapproval on her face. She handed the paper back to Spencer and folded her arms.

"You weren't supposed to e-mail him again," she said. "Walter told you not to. So did your mom. Weren't you grounded from e-mail?"

"Who cares right now?" Spencer said. "All that matters is—we know where Hadley's staying."

"What makes you think he'll still be there?" Daisy asked.

"I don't know," answered Spencer. "Maybe he'll already be gone, but I can't think of a better plan right now. Can you?"

Daisy remained silent for a few moments, racking her brain for a better idea. Finally, she shook her head.

"Hadley's not going anywhere without that nail,"

Spencer reasoned. "He might relocate since he knows we're working with the janitors and I found out where his hideout is. But if we hurry, we might be able to catch him unaware."

Spencer pushed aside the secret tower of boxes. "You said you have Walter's keys?" In response, Daisy withdrew the massive ring laden with jingling keys. "Then let's get this open and grab some equipment."

"You really think this is a good idea?" Daisy asked, reluctantly handing Spencer the keys.

"All I know," Spencer said, opening the Rebel Closet, "is that Marv got taken so I could get away. If *we* had been captured, don't you think Walter would come after us?"

"That's different. They're adults."

"We can't trust any other adults. Who do you want to tell? Principal Poach? He's the one who let the BEM in!" Spencer was rambling, anger controlling him. Garth Hadley had tricked him and now the janitors were gone.

Daisy sighed. "You're right, of course. We have to save them. Or try, at least."

"Good," Spencer said. "I couldn't do it without you." He dumped out his backpack on the floor. "Let's gear up and go."

"What should we take?" Daisy asked, studying the room. "There's a lot of stuff in here." She picked up a squirt bottle with blue cleaning solution inside. "What about this?" Daisy set it back on the shelf and lifted a toilet plunger. "Or this?"

"I don't think this is the time to experiment with new equipment. Let's just stick to what we know." Spencer filled his backpack full of vac dust and grabbed a 7T broom and a

14T mop from the rack on the wall. He picked up the discarded latex glove from the table.

"Where's your backpack?" Spencer asked.

Daisy ducked out of the closet and reappeared a few moments later. To Daisy's protests, Spencer dumped everything from her backpack onto the floor. Hastily, he began stuffing it full of vac dust while Daisy picked out a broom and a mop for herself. The backpack was half full when Spencer spotted the overcharged Vortex vacuum bag on the shelf. He quickly placed it in the partially loaded backpack.

"But that's the overcharged bag!" Daisy said. "Walter said that was dangerous."

"I know," answered Spencer. "That's why we're taking it."

CHAPTER 32

"HE'S JUST GOING INSIDE."

D aisy, having lived all of her eleven years in Welcher, knew exactly where Maple Park was located. She often picnicked there with her parents. It was a long walk from the elementary school, and the urgency of their mission made it seem even longer.

They were an odd sight—two kids half jogging down the street with bulging backpacks, each carrying a mop and a broom.

After Spencer had loaded the volatile Vortex vacuum bag into Daisy's backpack, she refused to carry it. Unwilling to give it up, Spencer shouldered her backpack and gave his to Daisy. That was fine for Daisy but unfortunate for Spencer, since Daisy still used the pink princess backpack she had gotten in third grade.

Dez would have had a thing or two to say if he could

have seen them. But then again, had Dez seen them, the bully probably would have ended up pinned to the sidewalk with a mouthful of vac dust.

At last, Spencer and Daisy jogged into Maple Park, careful not to let the bristles of their brooms brush the ground.

"Those are the apartments," Daisy said, pointing across the street. Her forehead was sweaty and she wiped it with her forearm. They moved slowly across the park, passing a young couple who were having a picnic, getting laughs from other kids on the playground equipment. But Spencer and Daisy went forward with determination.

Soon they were close enough to see the numbers on the apartment doors. Number 2 was on the ground level, a small concrete pad making up the front porch.

"Okay," Spencer said, pulling on the latex glove. In addition to the princess backpack, Spencer had pockets full of vac dust. "If it gets bad, you run for it. If I call for help, come fast."

They had solidified their plan during the long walk from the school to the park. Daisy would keep the bronze nail and stay in the park. Spencer would enter through the apartment's front door and rescue the captive janitors . . . if anyone was still there.

"Be careful," Daisy urged, a nervous whine in her voice.

Wordlessly, Spencer jogged across Maple Street and approached apartment 2. He crouched, hoping no one could see him through the apartment windows. Holding his mop and broom like weapons, Spencer felt like an army man running from trench to trench.

Spencer dropped to his knees on the concrete porch

and lifted the clay pot. He felt a rush of relief when he saw the spare key. With his gloved hand, Spencer picked it up. Holding mop and broom in one hand, Spencer stayed on his knees and slowly, silently, inserted the key into the lock.

There were voices inside.

· · ·

Across the street, Daisy bit her lower lip and tensed her muscles nervously. When someone spoke at her side, she nearly whacked the stranger with her broom.

"What's your friend doing there?" the man asked suspiciously. He had nicely combed hair and a yellow polo shirt. Daisy had seen him pushing a child on the swings.

"What?" asked Daisy tensely.

The stranger pointed. "What's he doing?"

"He's just going inside."

"But why's he being so sneaky about it?" The stranger looked annoyed. "And what's with the brooms and stuff?"

· · ·

Spencer turned the doorknob. He took a deep breath, his hand sweating profusely under the latex glove. With one swift motion, he shoved the door open and sprang into the living room.

A suede couch and recliner sat on his left. On the right he saw a dining table and a small kitchen area. A dark hallway angled past the kitchen.

Spencer whirled around, his gloved hand full of vac

dust and his left hand wielding the mop and broom. He surveyed the whole area in a moment and determined that it was empty. The voices he'd heard from the porch turned out to be the Three Stooges yelling at each other in black-and-white on an old TV channel.

There was one place left to look. Spencer strode down the little hallway, past an empty bathroom on one side. Tacked onto a closed door at the end of the hall was a torn sheet of paper. Silently, Spencer read the handwritten note.

Spencer,

This will probably be our last personal communication. I knew you were working with the janitors and I didn't appreciate you lying to me about getting the nail. Since you were waiting until six o'clock, I decided to strike early—when you were least expecting it.

Walter didn't have the nail, so I won't be leaving town yet. Feel free to take what you want from this apartment. This was only our secondary hideout. Did you really think I'd tell you where I've been staying? Anyway, your friends from Welcher Elementary are just beyond this door.

Sincerely,

Garth Hadley

Spencer could barely finish reading. Walter and Marv! Just beyond the door! Anxiously, Spencer grabbed the knob and threw it open.

Spencer suddenly yawned, his mind cloudy with fatigue. He was looking for a comfortable place to lie down when he saw them.

Toxites.

Everywhere.

The nasty little creatures were crawling all over the apartment bedroom. Whatever had prevented them from leaving the room lost effect when Spencer opened the door. The Toxites all turned, baring tooth and claw. Only one thing stood between them and the school to which they desperately wanted to return.

And that one thing was just a boy.

Any hint of fatigue left Spencer immediately as the Toxites rushed forward. He staggered backward, scrambling to get out of the hallway. Behind him, two dozen Toxites were swarming the walls, floor, and ceiling.

When Spencer reached the living room, he spun around, swiping his broom through the air. The bristles struck a flying Rubbish with bone-shattering force. The vulture-bat exploded in a flash of light and Spencer felt a fresh surge of power flow up the broom's handle.

Spencer flicked the mop forward, sending the strings like a net down the hallway. At the same time, he struck the broom on the floor, lifting off the ground as half a dozen Filths scuttled beneath him, dusty quills raised aggressively.

Spencer hit the ceiling as the mop retracted, dragging

a Grime and a Filth to their death. Entangled in the mop strings, the Grime popped with a splat of slime and the Filth vanished in a puff of dust.

Spencer was helplessly pinned next to the ceiling fan, watching three Rubbishes wing a jagged pattern toward him. He felt pain sear through his leg as one sharp beak nipped a bit of flesh from above his knee. The other Rubbish was swarming for his face.

With no other option, Spencer let go of the broom. His weight returned instantly and he plummeted onto the suede couch, hoping that the landing wouldn't puncture the unstable Vortex bag in his backpack.

A Filth jumped onto the couch and snarled. Spencer rolled away, waving his mop clumsily. On the television, the Three Stooges were in the act of bonking each other on the head with a two-by-four when Spencer's mop handle went into the screen. The TV shattered, glass flying across the living room.

Spencer dove forward, emptying a pocketful of vac dust on the way. Two Grimes and a Filth were immobilized. Spencer's broom slowly descended from the ceiling.

A slimy Grime sprang from the back of the recliner and landed on Spencer's right forearm, its suction-cup finger pads latching onto the skin. Spencer screamed and jerked with the pain. He tried to wrench the thing free, but it held with a tarlike grip, slurping and burning. The mop fell to the floor and the Toxites began picking it apart.

Spencer tried to crush the Grime against the wall.

Nothing was strong enough to kill the monster. Only a Glopified object would have the strength to destroy it.

Quickly, Spencer stripped the latex glove from his right hand and stuffed it onto his left. His left hand closed tightly around the Grime. He felt the strength of the Glopified glove . . . and the Grime felt it too. Squeezing for all he was worth, Spencer ripped the monster off his arm and felt the Grime explode in his hand, its energy flowing into the glove.

There was no time for Spencer to be grossed out by the yellowish gunk dripping down his arm. The Grime had left painful purple welts where it had held him.

Spencer went for the mop, tripped, and landed painfully on a bristling Filth. The dusty quills stuck into his side as if he'd fallen on a cactus. Grunting from the pain, Spencer tossed his second pocketful of vac dust, suctioning two more Toxites to the floor. He grabbed the mop and swung it like a club, entangling three more as a Rubbish swooped down and raked a claw along his cheek.

There were too many! He had to get out of the apartment—out of the angry, relocated Toxites' way! Spencer cleared a path across the room with his mop. He needed to reach the broom before the Toxites tore it apart.

Lunging, he caught the handle of the broom in one hand. Two Rubbishes were diving from above, and a Filth bared its sharp, rodent teeth. Kicking off the couch, Spencer slammed the broom against the floor. The door was too far away. But the window . . .

• • •

Across the street, Daisy was doing all she could to keep the stranger from calling the police.

"It's a game we like to play," she lied. "Ya put your right broom in, ya put your right broom out, ya put your right broom in and you shake it all about," Daisy trailed off, wagging her broom in the man's face. "It's kind of weird, I know. But it's actually fun if you give it a chance."

"Seems a little rowdy in there," the stranger said, not willing to put his cell phone away just yet.

"Yeah," Daisy said. "Sometimes it gets a little out of hand. You know, when somebody wants to put the mop in . . ."

Suddenly, there was a shower of glass and Spencer burst through the front window, gripping his broom tightly. He shot across the apartment yard, barely missed a tree, and continued flying across the street.

Daisy and the stranger were both speechless: the stranger, because a boy appeared to be flying across the street, and Daisy, because a dozen Toxites were flooding out of the broken window behind Spencer.

Spencer's feet touched down just yards from Daisy. The boy hit the ground running to keep pace with his descending broom. "Come on!" he shouted at Daisy without missing a beat.

"Now, wait a minute," the man with the polo shirt demanded. He whipped up his phone, apparently deciding to involve the police. But before he could dial the number, a puff of dark dust struck his phone and sent it clattering to the sidewalk, vibrating with the force of suction.

It was a good shot and the stranger stood dumbfounded. Daisy blew on her sweaty fingers, causing a few dusty particles to billow like smoke from a gun.

CHAPTER 33

"YOU'RE A GENIUS."

Spencer drifted over Aunt Avril's dead lawn toward his second-story bedroom window. It was risky to use the broom where anyone might be watching, but it might be far worse trying to explain to his mother why he and his friend had come home with mops, brooms, and backpacks full of vacuum dust.

As the two kids had fled Maple Park, Spencer instinctively turned toward home. Daisy's house was closer, but the savage Toxites were carving a path of destruction to get back to Welcher Elementary and the Gates home was right along the way. It would be safer if they got to Hillside Estates where they could make new plans in peace.

Spencer braced his feet on the windowsill and popped off the screen. He always left his window open an inch so the air in his room wouldn't get stuffy. Spencer waited for his broom's gravity to return before climbing through. He quietly dropped to the floor and waved for Daisy to follow him. She glanced around the neighborhood nervously, then struck her broom on the ground and started to rise.

Spencer propped his mop and broom in the corner and slipped Daisy's pink princess backpack off his tired shoulders. It was good to be back in his sanctuary, where everything had its place. But as Spencer surveyed the room, he noticed several major irregularities. His closet door was open, the hamper overturned, and dirty clothes strewn across the floor. The pillows were off the bed and his checkered bedspread was wrinkled.

Spencer's first reaction was defensive. What if the BEM had somehow sabotaged his room, planting more angry Toxites in case the beasts in the apartment didn't do the job? But upon closer inspection, Spencer realized that the wrinkle pattern on the bedspread was all too familiar— jumping little Max feet.

Suddenly, a head of brown hair popped out from under the bed. Max screamed with delight when he saw Spencer standing by the closet door.

"How you get in?" Max shrieked. "I wanna scare you."

"You *did*, for a minute," Spencer said angrily. "Get out, right now. Did you forget that my room is off-limits to you?"

Max crawled out from his hiding place, lip trembling. "I . . . I just wanna play."

"Out!" Spencer ordered unsympathetically. He stood rigid, his arm pointing to the door. Little Max bowed his head and walked out of the room.

"That was a nice older brother," Daisy said from the windowsill once Max was gone.

"What do you know about it, *only child?*" Spencer retorted, shutting the door and moving to straighten his bedspread.

"I just think you're being kind of rude right now."

"Look," Spencer said, throwing his pillows angrily onto the bed. "*You* didn't get attacked by killer Toxites. *You* didn't get a lying note from the BEM. I have a right to be upset now, okay?"

Daisy nodded patiently. "All right. You did have it rough today. I'll just get out of your way." She leaned out the window, ready to use her broom.

"Wait," Spencer said. "I get it. Don't go."

"Will you be nice to me and apologize to your brother?"

"He should apologize to *me*. Look at the mess he made!"

Daisy folded her arms stubbornly.

Spencer sighed. "Fine. Next time I see him, I'll apologize."

"Good," Daisy said, resuming her usual countenance. She stepped off the window seat, crossed the room, and sat down on Spencer's wrinkle-free bedspread. "How's your cut?"

Spencer lifted a hand to his cheek. He could feel a line of hard, dried blood. "I'm fine," Spencer assured. "What we really need to do is find out where Garth Hadley is holding the janitors."

"I don't know," Daisy said. "Walter searched for a week

and couldn't find him. What makes you think we'll do any better?"

Spencer grunted. "We *have* to find them. It won't be long before the BEM figures out that we have the nail. They'll track us down as easy as pie. What then?" Spencer started gathering the dirty clothes that Max had spread across the room. He hoped that Daisy wouldn't notice his underwear. Angrily, he flung the clothes back into the closet, one piece at a time.

Garth had tricked him—tried to hurt him! Spencer had thought he had everything under control, but the Maple Street apartment was nothing but a setup. Garth Hadley would be laughing. Laughing hard. He'd tricked a twelve-year-old—wow. Would Hadley keep laughing if the twelve-year-old tricked him back?

"Spencer!" Daisy scolded. Without realizing it, Spencer had twisted a shirt in his hands until the fabric began to tear.

"We have to find them!" Spencer shouted, hurling the shirt into the closet.

"Calm down," she said coolly. "Let's sort out what we know."

Spencer stopped straightening his room and rubbed his forehead in thought. "Well, there's like, five or six BEM workers in town. And they could each have a couple of fake names; that seems to be the trend right now."

"But even if they were using real names," Daisy said, "the only one we know is Garth Hadley."

"Oh, good. We're back to where we started." Spencer

reached down, snatched a pair of shorts by the hem, and gave them a good flick into the closet. As he did so, a small piece of crumpled paper fell to the floor. Momentarily intrigued, Spencer straightened it out. When he saw what was written on it, he sighed and crumpled it again.

"What was that?" Daisy asked.

"Nothing," Spencer said, tossing the scrap into the wastebasket by his dresser. "Just some stupid note that Nancy wrote."

"Love note?" Daisy asked, jumping off the bed and reaching into the trash basket. Daisy opened the paper and, to Spencer's annoyance, read aloud:

Spencer is so out. Draw something on his face.
—Nancy

"Yeah," Spencer said, shutting his closet door at last. "Remember the day that Dez drew on my face? I guess Nancy thought it would be funny."

"Nancy Pepperton?" Daisy asked, staring hard at the paper.

"The *only* Nancy in our class."

"Yeah, but . . ." Daisy stammered. "This sure isn't Nancy's handwriting. I know because she's way sloppy and hard to read. Not like this."

Spencer stole the scrap from Daisy's hands, scrutinizing the penmanship with the eye of a detective. It was true. The handwriting was far nicer than anything a sixth grader

221

could conjure. And wait a minute . . . there was something familiar about the way his name was written.

"Yes!" Spencer suddenly shouted, tossing the paper in the air like a single piece of confetti. "This is the same handwriting on the paper that Walter found in the recess aide's vest!"

"Wait. I don't think Nancy Pepperton is working for the BEM," Daisy said.

"Of course not." Spencer rubbed his hands together. All of his anger and energy flowed into this new clue.

Daisy watched him pace for several minutes. Finally she burst out, "Well, who wrote it, then?"

"I don't know," Spencer shouted back. "I'm trying to sort it all out." In that moment, something clicked. It was so obvious! How could he possibly have overlooked it?

"Daisy," he cried, crossing the room till they were only a foot apart. "All this time we were trying to figure out who could have put that little bottle of pink soap in the bathroom."

"Who?"

"It was obviously the same person who wrote the note for Dez to draw on my face."

"*Who?*"

"Leslie Sharmelle! Our substitute when Mrs. Natcher was sick last week."

"Whoa," mumbled Daisy, her eyes bulging as she tried to sort that one out. "But Miss Sharmelle's a girl. She can't go in the boys' bathroom!"

"Oh, please, Daisy!" Spencer slapped a hand to his

forehead. "That's not going to stop her. Even *you* have been in the boys' bathroom."

"What if it was Dez?" said Daisy. "What if Miss Sharmelle gave the soap to Dez and he put it in the bathroom? He had some weird crush on her, remember? Dez would have done anything for her."

But Spencer wasn't really listening. He didn't care exactly *who* had put the soap in the boy's bathroom. He had enough evidence against the substitute teacher anyway.

"Think about it, Daisy," Spencer said. "Leslie Sharmelle was a BEM spy from day one. They needed a kid to work for them inside the school. It was the only way to get close enough to Walter and steal the bronze hammer. The BEM must have poisoned Mrs. Natcher so we would have a substitute. Then Leslie planted a Filth in my desk. That's why I fell asleep after recess that day.

"Once I was out, Miss Sharmelle used Nancy's name and somehow dropped the note on Dez's desk so he would draw on my face. Then she planted the soap—or maybe she gave it to Dez—and the next day she was gone. Miss Sharmelle did her part. The rest was up to Garth Hadley."

"Wait a minute," Daisy said. "The note that the janitors found in the recess vest was signed by S.B. If Leslie Sharmelle wrote it, shouldn't it be L.S.?"

"Fake name," Spencer explained. "While I was hiding out under the desk by Principal Poach's office, a woman came out of an interview. He called her Mrs. Bently, but she said, 'I wish you'd just call me Sarah.' Get it? Sarah Bently! S.B."

"What does that have to do with Leslie?"

"It *was* Leslie! Same clicky high heels and everything. She even wore the same flowery perfume. Leslie staged an interview with the principal so he would open the doors. That's how everybody got inside to capture the janitors."

Daisy thought about it for several minutes. The evening sunlight angled through the bedroom window and a breeze played in the leaves of a nearby tree.

Daisy nodded, finally adding, "Spencer. You're a genius."

"Thanks," Spencer said, grinning. The rage he'd been feeling earlier was totally replaced by hope.

"At least we have three names to work with now," Daisy said. Listing them on her fingers, she stated, "Garth Hadley, Leslie Sharmelle, and Sarah Bently."

"Let's hope that's enough," Spencer said, crossing the room. He shouldered the princess backpack and hefted his mop and broom. "Come on."

"Where are we going now?" Daisy asked.

"To rescue the janitors."

"But where?" She followed him onto the windowsill.

"The Best Western Hotel."

CHAPTER 34

"THERE'S ALWAYS A TURNING POINT."

A shampoo bottle.

Spencer was basing his whole hypothesis on a shampoo bottle. Leslie Sharmelle's little container of pink soap had come from a Best Western Hotel. Daisy reminded him that there were probably hundreds of Best Westerns, any one of which could have provided the bottle. Maybe Spencer was grasping at straws—but it was worth a shot.

They drifted down to the dry grass of Aunt Avril's house.

"Do you have any idea how far away the Best Western is from here?" Daisy asked. She answered without giving him time to speak. "It's, like, a lot of miles. Clear out by the highway, Spencer. I don't think I can walk that far."

"Maybe we can ride bikes," Spencer said. "I think there's an extra in the garage."

Daisy grabbed his sleeve. "You have to remember," she said, "we're only kids. No one trusted Garth Hadley because he relied on kids to do his work when he should have gone to the police. There's always a turning point, Spencer, when we have to hand it over to adults we can trust."

"But the police will never believe us!" he cried.

"I'm not talking about the police," said Daisy. "I'm talking about your mom."

"Mom?"

"She stood up for you in the office. She believed every bit about Garth Hadley."

"That's just 'cause I didn't tell her everything. Only the believable parts."

"So you're a chameleon," Daisy said.

"I'm not a—" Spencer moaned.

"You can't keep changing colors, Spencer. If you tell your mom the whole truth, she'll believe you."

"My mom's not . . . argh!" Spencer grabbed his head. They didn't have time for this. "She really doesn't like *magical* things."

"This isn't about magic. It's about telling the truth so someone will help us save Walter and Marv."

Spencer sighed. She was right, as usual. If his mother was inside, they needed her help. Spencer left Daisy standing on the crispy grass. He entered the house, screaming for his mother.

Alice came around the corner. "What's wrong, Spence? What's the matter?" There was no time to explain everything, such as why he was wearing a princess backpack and holding a mop and broom. She gasped. "My word, you're hurt!" Alice gently touched the scratch on his cheek.

"I'm fine." Spencer pulled away. "But other people are in danger. Garth Hadley broke into the school and kidnapped the janitors. I'm pretty sure he took them to the Best Western Hotel, so we've got to rescue them."

"Hold on," Alice said. "Garth Hadley?"

Daisy suddenly appeared in the doorway, lending credence to Spencer's story. "Saw it with our own eyes, while we were training . . . I mean, in detention."

Alice fumbled for the phone. "This is bad," she muttered. "We need to call the police."

Spencer slumped to the couch, defeated. "Not the police. I knew this would happen."

"Hello," Alice said into the telephone. "I'm calling to report an abduction. Two janitors from Welcher Elementary School."

Pause.

"Yes, janitors."

Pause.

"No, but my son saw it."

Pause.

"Twelve years old. He thinks they're being held at the Best Western Hotel."

"We've got names for a search," Daisy whispered. "Garth Hadley, Leslie Sharmelle, and Sarah Bently."

Alice repeated the names to the dispatcher.

Pause.

"Okay, thank you. 'Bye." The phone went dead in Alice's hand.

"Did they believe you?" Daisy asked.

"They said they'd send someone over. But who's going to believe a twelve-year-old witness?" Alice clapped her hands. "I've got to run to the neighbor's."

"Why?"

"We need a babysitter. Go get in the car."

CHAPTER 35

"THEY'RE HERE, I KNOW IT."

The Best Western stood at the far edge of town, beside the highway that came from Pocatello and went on to Boise. Praised as Welcher's finest hotel, it sported a nice pool and spa along with a continental breakfast for guests. It was a lofty two stories with the lobby entrance under a covered driveway. The parking lot had only a few cars in it. Spencer was disappointed not to see the white BEM van or Garth Hadley's blue Toyota.

It was dusk as the Zumbro station wagon pulled into the hotel parking lot. The front bumper was sagging, crooked from an old accident. One of the headlights had burned out. The car, in its own way, seemed to imitate the expression of its surprised driver.

Alice's mouth was sagging open, crooked in disbelief.

One eye was squinted shut as she tried to process what her son had just explained on the drive from Hillside Estates.

"And you've seen these . . . *creatures* every day?" she verified.

"Yes," Spencer said. "The janitors were teaching us to defend against them when the BEM broke in and kidnapped them."

"And those brooms and mops in the backseat? Those are *magical* weapons?"

Alice pulled into an empty stall near the entrance to the hotel. The car rocked back as she parked it, and she too leaned back against her headrest, running fingers through her hair. "This is absolutely crazy, Spencer. I . . . I don't know what to say."

"We'll show you, Mom," he replied. "But first, we have to rescue the janitors. They're here, I know it."

Daisy leaned forward from the backseat. "And we can't let them get this." She held out her hand, showing Alice the little bronze nail in her palm. "No matter what."

Before Alice had any more time to digest their story, headlights flashed. A police car pulled under the covered awning and two officers casually climbed out.

"Let's go check this out," came the muffled voice of the female officer as they strode into the building.

Spencer glanced at Daisy, who quickly closed her fist around the nail. When he looked at his mom, her expression was determined.

"You two stay here," Alice said. She opened the car door. "I'm just going to be a fly on the wall. Be right back."

Spencer and Daisy watched her vanish through the hotel entrance.

"I knew she would trust you," Daisy said. "It makes a difference when you tell the *whole* truth. No one can trust a chameleon."

Spencer grinned and popped his door open.

"What are you doing?" asked Daisy.

"Preparing for an ambush. I have a feeling that the police won't find anything. When they leave, I want to be ready."

Daisy helped him pull the equipment from the backseat. They stashed the mops and brooms behind a trimmed landscape bush near the entrance. In the fading daylight, the janitorial equipment was hardly visible.

A moment later, Alice emerged from the building. Spencer called quietly from his hiding spot in the bushes.

"They're here," Alice said. Spencer pumped a victorious fist into the air. "They have a room in Sarah Bently's name: 211. Been here for about two weeks." Alice shook her head. "The officers told the receptionist not to worry. The call about kidnapped janitors was most likely a prank."

"No way," Daisy said. "Somebody prank-called about kidnapping janitors? What a coincidence!"

Spencer shared a look with his mom. There was no point in trying to explain it to Daisy. She was obviously in a gullible mood. A mood that Spencer suddenly understood.

Seeing Daisy anxiously chew her lip, leaning against the wall of a hotel full of dangerous enemies, it clicked. Daisy

Gates was most gullible when she was nervous. That's why Dez brought it out in her so often.

Spencer's pity for Daisy melted into understanding. Daisy couldn't help being gullible any more than Spencer could help washing his hands before lunch. It was instinct.

"What do we do now?" Daisy asked.

"We wait for the police to finish their *investigation*," Spencer said.

Spencer glanced at the row of hotel windows. Room 211 would be on the second floor. If this one was like most hotels Spencer had visited, the even rooms would be on one side and odd rooms on the other.

"I've got an idea," Spencer said. "Count by odds for me."

Alice looked puzzled, but Daisy was used to doing what she was told, unquestioningly. She counted odds, and Spencer held up a finger for each number she said. When Daisy reached eleven, Spencer was showing six fingers.

"So," Spencer said, walking around the side of the building. He counted six windows from the end on the second story. The drapes were open wide and the flashing, bluish light of a television could be seen in the oncoming darkness.

"I need a broom."

Daisy dug in the bush, accidentally handed him a mop, then traded it for the broom.

"Spencer?" his mother said. But this was beyond her now.

Spencer jogged to the wall, estimated the distance to the window, and tapped his broom on the ground. He floated up slowly, using one hand to guide himself along the wall. Staying clear of the window, he peeked sideways into the hotel room.

An old man was lying on his back under the covers, his fat stomach rising and falling with the rhythm of his snores. The TV blared a rerun of *Wheel of Fortune*.

Spencer descended to the ground next to Daisy, shaking his head. "Not it. Must be on the other side," he said.

Suddenly, Alice snatched the broom from Spencer's hand. "What is . . ." She shook it, like she was strangling the broom handle. "Spencer! This is . . . dangerous, crazy—I don't know! Where did you get this?"

"This," Spencer took the broom from his mother, "is just the beginning. We're up against worse things than this, Mom. I told you it was real."

"You shouldn't be . . . you can't . . ."

Just then the officers emerged from the hotel. Spencer, Daisy, and Alice ducked into the concealment of the bushes.

" . . . the lady's son was probably confused," said the woman officer.

"Yeah," chuckled the other. "Who's going to abduct a school janitor?"

"Probably a high ransom. Didn't you know that janitors make millions?"

They both burst into laughter, climbing into the police car. The automobile pulled out of the parking lot and disappeared down the highway.

"Did you hear that?" Daisy whispered. "I had no idea Walter was a millionaire!"

"Yep," said Spencer. "And Marv's a brain surgeon." He tightened the straps on his pink backpack and dug into the bush for the other supplies.

"So, what does *that* do?" Alice pointed to the mop. "Does it fly, too?"

Spencer grinned. It was weird to know so much about something that his mom had never even imagined possible. "There's no time to explain it all, Mom. The BEM knows we're coming. I'm sure the police gave us away. The longer we wait, the better chance for them to get away."

"Hold on, son," Alice said. "You are *not* going in there to take them by force. Do you remember that you're only twelve years old?"

Spencer didn't want to argue with his mother. This was the risk of bringing her along. She had been supportive so far, but no mother would knowingly let her son go into a fight.

"What should we do, then?" Spencer asked. "If the police won't get involved, who will?"

"Oh, the police are getting involved, so help me." Alice slapped her pockets. "Shoot, I left my phone in the car." She turned to Spencer. "You two—*stay*."

Spencer fidgeted as his mom jogged across the parking lot. "Daisy," Spencer said without breaking his gaze toward his mom, "I need you to follow me."

"But we can't. Your mom said *stay*."

Stay was a dog command, meant for animals. But dogs didn't plot or plan. Dogs didn't have the weight of the world on their shoulders, the future of education hanging over their heads. *Stay* was fine for a dog . . . but not for Spencer.

Alice had just looked up from the station wagon, cell phone in hand, when Spencer and Daisy bolted into the hotel. The kids sprinted through the lobby, mops and brooms in hand, backpacks jangling. They saw the stairs, but that wasn't the plan.

Spencer and Daisy exited the hotel as quickly as they'd entered. But now they were on the other side of the building, the side that Spencer was sure had a window to room 211.

"This has got to be it," Spencer said, counting six windows again. "You still got the nail?" Daisy patted her pocket, face grim and nervous.

"I need you to stay down here," Spencer explained. "In about a minute, my mom is going to show up. Try to calm her down, convince her that I know what I'm doing." As he talked, Spencer slipped the latex glove onto his right hand and hastily stocked both pockets with quick-access vac dust. "Okay. I'm going up."

It was almost fully dark outside and a narrow strip of light leaked out where the curtains didn't seal together. That gap was all Spencer needed.

He floated up to the window and pulled himself close until he was almost standing on the narrow brick ledge. All Spencer could see was a dim corner of the hotel room. But tied in that corner was big Marv Bills.

Spencer strained around, trying to locate Walter and see how many BEM workers were in the room. He didn't have

235

much time to decide how to attack. His broom was already trying to descend. The window was wide open, so only the screen and the curtain kept him out.

"Is that someone at the door? *Again?*" Garth Hadley's voice drifted out the window.

Someone at the door? But who? For a moment, Spencer wondered if the police had returned.

"I'll get it," answered a woman. It was Leslie Sharmelle, or Sarah Bently, or whoever she was. "Put the Rebels in the bathroom again."

Spencer pressed his ear to the screen. He heard the door open. "My son!" shouted a frantic voice. "Where is he?"

Spencer nearly toppled from the windowsill. It was his mother at the door! Alice must have thought he and Daisy had gone upstairs . . .

There was no time to lose! His mother was in danger and the opportunity for a surprise attack was dwindling. He acted—impulsively, instinctively, but not without surprise. A twelve-year-old boy flying through a second-story window was always going to be a surprise.

CHAPTER 36

"THANKS, KID."

Spencer used the mop, flicking it at the screen as hard as he could. The Glopified strings ripped off the screen and entangled the curtains, stripping them from the curtain rod.

Spencer didn't have time to wait for the mop to retract, so he threw it down. At the same moment, he lunged through the open window, striking his broom against the sill to give him an extra boost.

Spencer's mother was standing in the doorway, fear and surprise flashing across her face. Only a few feet before her stood Leslie Sharmelle wearing a baggy sweatshirt and stretch pants. The pink streaks were gone from her spunky hair and now she was platinum blonde. Leslie barely had time to turn away from the doorway before Spencer hit her with a palm blast of vac dust, suctioning her to the floor.

Garth Hadley was in a much more strategic position. As Spencer shot across the room, the strong BEM worker seized the boy's foot . . . only to find that it slipped through his hands like Jell-O.

Spencer noticed an adjoining door that linked rooms 211 and 209. In the corner, Marv was struggling to his feet, hands still bound. Walter was nowhere to be seen. Perhaps the warlock was in the next room.

"Gloves!" Garth shouted as he scrambled toward Marv. But Spencer was already there. The broom clattered against the wall as Spencer ducked behind the big janitor, checking the knots at his wrists. He tugged at them for a moment, but the ropes were too tight.

Garth leapt forward and grabbed Marv by the front of his shirt, Spencer cowering behind. Garth would have punched the big janitor square in the nose, but Marv suddenly slipped through his grasp.

"Ha ha!" Marv exclaimed, feeling Spencer shove the sweaty latex glove onto his bound hand. Marv flexed, but the ropes still held.

"What the . . . ?" Hadley said. Marv threw his full weight forward and checked Garth Hadley to the floor.

Out of the corner of his eye, Spencer saw his mom lunge forward, tackling Leslie as she recovered from the vac dust. "Mom!" he shouted.

Alice had Leslie's arms pinned. She blew at an errant strand of hair in her face. "Don't worry about me, Spence." She drove an elbow into the middle of Leslie's back. "Get out of here and find Daisy!"

Spencer gave a half grin. If Alice was anything, she was independent. Spencer ducked behind Marv. "Go!" he shouted, using the big janitor as a shield to cross the room.

With his hands tied behind his back, Marv lowered his head like a charging ram and burst into the adjoining room, Spencer close behind.

Walter was strapped to a chair, a lamp illuminating his face as in a professional interrogation. Five angry BEM workers were scrambling around the room, gathering supplies to fight the intruders. Among them, Spencer recognized the skinny man with the pointy nose, the pimply recess aide, and the fat guy from the gym's emergency exit. The other two were strangers.

Marv and Spencer paused in the doorway, surveying the area. The room was set up like Walter's Rebel Closet, minus the vat of gurgling gray Glop. Vacuums, mops, brooms, and a myriad of other Glopified tools were ready for use. But Spencer was only searching for something sharp to cut the janitors free.

"Chaaaarge!" Spencer shouted when he spotted an open pocketknife on top of the little refrigerator. Like a faithful warhorse, Marv galloped forward. He head-butted the skinny dude and sent him sprawling on the floor. The pimply guy bounced from the bed and grasped a handful of Marv's shaggy black hair, but it was impossible to hang on while Marv wore the glove.

One of the strangers tossed a well-aimed fistful of vac dust, and Spencer's shield finally went down. At the same time, the fat BEM worker donned his own latex glove and grabbed Marv by the throat.

Spencer dove aside, springing from one queen bed to the next. On his way, he grabbed a pushbroom from the wall. If he remembered correctly from Walter's training, the pushbroom should send his enemies flying. Spencer struck the nearest man once . . . twice.

Yes! The pushbroom flung the BEM worker helplessly toward the ceiling. Another man was charging, but Spencer hurled the pushbroom like a javelin and the man floated backward over the bed.

Marv was thrashing on the floor, his face turning beet red as the fat BEM worker continued to choke. Spencer reached the fridge, grabbed the pocketknife, and ran to Walter. With two cuts from the sharp blade, the warlock was free.

Walter Jamison leapt to his feet, snatched a mop from the rack, and dealt a painful blow to the back of the fat man's head. Marv gasped for breath, veins still bulging across his forehead.

Walter grabbed a second mop, stepped over Marv's body, and began casting an impenetrable network of elongated mop strings. Spencer rolled Marv onto his side and cut the ropes around his wrists.

"Thanks, kid," Marv huffed. "That was brave of you to come alone."

"I didn't come alone," Spencer said. Suddenly he remembered his mom, wrestling with Leslie in the other room, and Daisy waiting nervously outside.

"My mom's over there," he said. "She was supposed to stay with Daisy outside. We've got to help her! She doesn't know what she's up against." Spencer stepped forward, but Walter cut him off.

"Marv," Walter said, still spinning a defensive net with the mops, "take Spencer to help Daisy. I'll hold off these three and get Mrs. Zumbro."

"Come on." Marv grabbed Spencer's shoulder and steered him toward the window. In the lighted parking lot below, Spencer saw Daisy sprinting away from the hotel. Close behind, and gaining fast, Garth Hadley and Leslie Sharmelle descended on brooms.

"Oh, no!" Spencer cried. "Daisy has the nail. If they catch her . . ."

"Get a broom." Marv jerked open the window and pulled off the screen. With a broom in hand, the big man clambered onto the sill just as two BEM workers launched from the next window.

"Hey!" Marv shouted, striking his bristles on the ground and jumping into a collision course. Spencer followed, leaving his mother tied in the next room and Walter to rescue her.

Once in the air, the broom's course was unalterable. Marv sped forward and smashed into the skinny guy. Marv's bulk won out and the BEM worker's broom was knocked askew.

Spencer's launch had set him higher than all the others. From his bird's-eye view, he saw Garth Hadley and Leslie Sharmelle close the gap on Daisy.

Spencer heard the faint suction of vac dust and saw Daisy topple to the blacktop. Her broom dropped and shot off on its own. The mop tumbled from her grasp.

"No!" Spencer shouted, anger flooding through him. Garth picked up the mop and stood guard while Leslie pried open Daisy's clenched hand. Spencer floated, trying uselessly to make his broom descend.

"Got it!" he heard Leslie shout. Spencer felt his stomach sink. The Barbie woman stood up and tossed the tiny object to Garth Hadley. They had found the bronze nail!

Too far away to do anything, Marv was fistfighting the two BEM workers in the parking lot. Spencer finally touched ground as Leslie and Garth reached a silver Lexus sports car.

Spencer had a chance to reach them if he stayed low and kicked off with enough force. The boy sprinted a few steps, angled his body forward, and whacked the broom bristles on the blacktop. The broom streaked forward, Spencer swinging a leg over the handle and riding it like a stick horse.

Leslie was in the driver's seat and the motor revved as she turned on the car. Given his current angle and speed, Spencer guessed he would hit the car's windshield in about a second and a half. Whether he had enough thrust to break through, Spencer never got to find out.

In the split second before impact, Garth Hadley leaned out the passenger window and cast the mop he'd stolen from Daisy. The strings wrangled Spencer from the broom and the mop retracted as Leslie peeled out. Spencer was caught like a bug in a butterfly net as the car sped for the exit.

Suddenly, big hands snatched him out of the mop strings, and Spencer felt totally disoriented. Marv held Spencer like he'd caught a touchdown pass. Momentum and gravity pulled the two of them over. They collapsed in the parking lot as the silver sports car took the corner too sharply and scraped the exhaust pipe on the curb.

"Daisy?" Spencer whispered, sitting up painfully. The girl was walking toward them. Her face was tear-streaked and her hands and knees were scraped from her fall.

"You all right?" Spencer asked, stumbling to his feet.

"They got the nail," she sobbed. "I tried to get away, but they came too fast."

"It's okay," Spencer tried to comfort. He clenched his fists in frustration. He never should have left her alone. She really could have been hurt.

Marv stood up, dusting his big belly. The burly janitor was equally scraped and bleeding, and he already had a black eye and loose tooth from his fistfight with the BEM workers. Spencer glanced across the parking lot. The skinny guy and the pimply guy were collapsed on the grass nearby. Apparently, Marv had won.

Suddenly, the side door of the Best Western burst open. The last three BEM workers charged forward, arms laden with Glopified weapons. Spencer felt a surge of fear. What had they done to Walter and his mom?

Weaponless, Marv stepped forward, clenching his beefy fists. Marv was never truly weaponless as long as he had hands. But the BEM workers were coming fast, the first one almost within mop range.

The screech of tires caused Spencer, Daisy, and Marv to whirl around. The Zumbro station wagon rounded the corner of the Best Western, single headlight shining on them. The BEM worker struck at Marv with his mop, but the car intercepted, brakes squealing to a halt in front of Spencer.

Walter rolled down the passenger's window.

"Get in!"

CHAPTER 37

"THE SCHOOL BOARD."

L ooks like we got to you just in time," Walter Jamison said as the station wagon pulled onto the highway. "Those three BEM workers weren't going to show you any mercy. Mrs. Zumbro and I barely got away."

Alice hadn't said a word. She gripped the steering wheel, unblinking. Spencer noticed the ash-white color of her face. *Welcome to my world, Mom.*

Spencer and Daisy were squeezed in by Max's crumb-filled car seat while Marv sprawled out in the back. There weren't many cars on the two-lane highway, and Spencer could see the Lexus's taillights far ahead.

"We'll never catch them," Spencer whispered. "They're driving a sports car."

This seemed to snap Alice out of her trance. "Hey!" she said. "This baby's never let us down." She patted the dashboard. "And she's been with us as long as you have, Spencer. Is your seat belt buckled, young man?"

Peering over his mom's shoulder, Spencer saw the speedometer's needle rising past 70. The whole car was shaking like a jackhammer. He quickly sat back and snapped the seat belt securely across him.

"Your mom gave an impressive show back there," Walter said. "Knocked two of those guys over with a mop. And she didn't even use the Glopified end."

Spencer tried to imagine his mom swinging a mop like a club. It was a stretch of his imagination.

"Turn here," Walter pointed. "We'll take the back roads through Welcher. Cut them off at the intersection by Maple Park."

"You know where they're going?" Spencer asked anxiously.

"Welcher Elementary School," Marv said. "It's a sure bet."

"But why? If they got the hammer and nail, why would they go back to the school?"

"The School Board," Walter explained. "Hadley needs it to replace me as the next warlock."

"What's the School Board?" Daisy asked.

"When the Founding Witches placed their power into the bronze hammers, they recognized the need for a transfer of power for someone to become a witch or warlock—a rite of passage that would complicate the procedure and discourage thieves from stealing the hammers.

"The Witches formed the School Board—a plank of

magical wood that would transfer the power from one warlock to his successor. After the Witches died, the Board was cut into thirteen square pieces. The idea was that each American colony would safeguard one piece. In order for Garth Hadley to take my power, he must pound the nail into the School Board. That resets the nail—kind of like wiping a computer hard drive.

"If Garth manages to do that, he'll be cloaked in a magical Aura and no one will be able to touch him until he sets his domain. The Aura will provide him a safe walk. All he'll have to do is choose a building for his domain, pound the nail, and he'll be the new warlock."

"But why would he risk going for the Board in Welcher?" Spencer asked. "Why not drive it into one of the other twelve pieces?"

"Welcher is the most accessible," said Walter. "With time, eight of the pieces were destroyed. Four of the five remaining have been appraised as antique hardwood and fashioned into items that are now safeguarded in museums: picture frames, a historic plaque, an antique clock. Nearly impossible to reach. That leaves one."

"At our school," Spencer mused. "But how'd it get there?"

"I brought it with me." Walter grinned at an old memory. "A year ago, when the BEM withdrew support from the schools, I stole Ninfa from a factory in Florida. With a little help from some Rebel spies, I managed to drive the nail into the remaining School Board. From there, I was protected by the Aura, so I took the Board and established my first domain in Arkansas. The BEM tracked me down, so I moved to Welcher. You know the rest."

Walter pointed. "Turn left." Alice spun the wheel and the station wagon squealed around a corner.

"What'll we do once we reach the school?" asked Spencer.

"Mrs. Zumbro will drop me and Marv in the parking lot and take you two out of harm's way."

"But we can help!"

"NO!" Alice and Walter shouted in unison.

"I need to make sure you kids are safe," the warlock said. "You've become too involved already. Marv and I can handle this. If we beat Garth to the School Board, we should be able to defend it."

"That should be no problem, right?" Spencer said. "Garth will have to search every room to find the School Board, but you guys already know where it is."

Walter grimaced. "I'm afraid the BEM already did the searching. Why do you think Miss Leslie Sharmelle came to your classroom as a substitute?"

Daisy and Spencer shared an astonished glance.

"The School Board is in Mrs. Natcher's room?" Spencer couldn't believe what he was hearing.

"And if you haven't guessed it yet," Walter said. "It's actually *your* desk."

CHAPTER 38

"INTO THE SCHOOL!"

W ait a minute," Spencer muttered. It took a second to process what Walter just said. His desk? It seemed so ordinary. "My desk is the School Board?"

"Part of it, anyway," said Walter. "About a square foot. In an attempt to disguise the magic wood, we inlaid the School Board into your desktop."

Spencer tried to imagine his battered desk, wondering which part was the crucial magical wood. Was it the part with that funny message about Mrs. Natcher smelling like cabbage?

The station wagon rounded the last corner and Alice gunned it down the straight road into Welcher Elementary School. As he craned his neck to see out the windshield, Spencer's heart sank.

The blue Toyota Garth had once driven was parked askew, the doors wide open.

"Couldn't be," Spencer whispered. "Garth was in that silver car with Leslie."

"More BEM workers," Marv guessed. "Preparing the way so Garth will have an easy entry once he arrives."

They didn't see the worst part until Alice swung the station wagon into the parking lot and its single headlight flashed across the school. The double doors that led into the middle hallway were smashed open. Glass lay in glinting shards, leaving a jagged, dark opening into the school.

"Drop us here." Walter's voice was an urgent whisper. Alice screeched to a stop.

"We're unarmed," Marv said from the backseat.

"Thanks for mentioning that." Walter gripped the car door, ready to spring out.

"Take this." Daisy swung Spencer's backpack over to Marv. "It's got vac dust."

"We'll need it."

"Let's go!" Marv flung open the door and shouldered the backpack. Spencer watched the two janitors cautiously approach the broken school door.

Headlights suddenly flooded the parking lot. Spencer and Daisy whirled around to see a big vehicle speeding toward the station wagon. Squinting against the lights, Spencer saw what it was.

The white BEM van.

Alice threw the car in gear and slammed on the gas. But the acceleration on the old station wagon made a tortoise look fast. Before the tires had made a complete revolution, the BEM van slammed into the side of the Zumbro station wagon.

Metal folded and glass crunched. Airbags deployed in the front, slamming Alice against the seat. Daisy flew into Spencer and he knocked his head against the window.

"Mom!" Spencer cried. "You okay?" He didn't have to ask about Daisy. She was clinging to his sleeve, whimpering but unharmed.

"I don't know who these people think they are!" his mother shouted from the front seat. "But somebody's going to pay for that!" She was twisting the key in the ignition, but the attempt was futile. The station wagon was parked forever.

"We gotta get out," Daisy said. Marv and Walter were racing back toward the station wagon.

Spencer tested the door. It was stiff, but with some pressure from his shoulder, it popped open. Daisy followed him out as Alice climbed across the passenger seat. Marv ripped open the door and helped her to her feet.

"Into the school!" Walter cried as the BEM van doors opened and several angry workers leapt out. Daisy led the group through the shattered opening in the door, Marv bringing up the rear.

The first BEM worker tried to follow them in, but Marv was ready for him. A fistful of vac dust struck the enemy, suctioning him onto the shards of broken glass.

"They're trying to get in!" Daisy pointed down the hallway where two BEM workers knelt at the lock to Mrs.

Natcher's door. One held a flashlight while the other fiddled with slender lock-picking tools.

Walter knocked them both back with a palm blast of vacuum dust. Marv stepped over the pinned bodies and inserted his key into Mrs. Natcher's doorknob.

"Inside! Quickly!" Walter ushered the others into the classroom. Just as the BEM workers poured into the hallway, the warlock slammed the door and twisted the lock.

Marv started shoving desks against the door for a barricade. Walter retreated to the center of the room. He exhaled a sigh of relief and briefly touched Spencer's desk. Then he crossed to the window, pulling things along to block it.

Spencer glanced at his mom. She didn't look so good. It looked as if the evening was turning out to be more than she could digest. As soon as she saw Spencer staring, Alice grabbed a desk and shoved it toward the door.

That was Mom. Strong and independent, if not a little frazzled. She clearly couldn't let her son see a weakness. Especially not now, when courage was being stretched like taffy.

"What now?" Daisy pushed her own desk and Marv picked it up to make a stack.

"We hold out," Walter said. "The BEM will have to retreat before school starts in the morning. That should buy us at least eight hours to smuggle the School Board safely away. All we need to do is survive tonight."

Mrs. Natcher's room seemed foreign in the darkness of night. Alice reached for the lights, but Walter stopped her.

It was better if the enemy couldn't see them. Spencer strode over to his desk, the object of so much attention. It was funny. He'd been so close to the School Board for weeks.

"Hadley already has Ninfa and the nail. If he gets into this room, all could be lost." Walter dumped over a table and propped it against the window. "The most important thing is to keep Garth Hadley away from Spencer's desk."

"I think we have a problem." Spencer looked up. "This isn't my desk."

CHAPTER 39

"ACTUALLY . . . THAT WAS ME."

Everyone stopped. Marv dropped the desk he'd been holding. All eyes were on Spencer, begging for him to be mistaken so they could ignore his last statement.

"This desk isn't mine," Spencer repeated.

"What do you mean? It's got your name on it." Marv stomped forward.

"This is my name tag, but it isn't my desk."

The others gathered closer, abandoning their efforts to fortify the room. Spencer felt his stomach sinking.

"Are you sure?" Walter asked.

"Positive," said Spencer. "I know, because some dummy wrote *Mrs. N smells like cabbige* on mine. Some dummy who couldn't even spell *cabbage*."

"Um," Marv grunted. "Actually . . . that was me. *I* scratched that into the School Board."

"You?" Daisy said. "Why?"

"Well, she *does* smell." Marv shrugged.

"But why'd you write it?"

"Walter told me to add some subtle marks to make it look more like a normal desk instead of a magic board."

"Very subtle," Spencer said.

"Enough!" The warlock waved his hands. "If this desktop doesn't have the School Board, then we've got major trouble."

"They switched it," Spencer said. "They switched my desk for a fake."

Walter nodded. "They knew we would stop at nothing to get in this classroom. All our attention was focused here."

"But what about the guys picking the lock?" Alice asked.

"A decoy."

Marv grabbed the stack of desks and threw them away from the door, breaking down the barrier that he'd so desperately built.

"And now," Walter muttered. "Now they have us right where they want us—trapped in a classroom."

Marv uncovered the door and threw himself against it. He shouted with rage as Walter's prediction became reality. The door to Mrs. Natcher's classroom was blocked. Alice ran to the window, but shadowed faces of BEM workers already clogged the escape.

"We're surrounded," she said. Marv slammed against the door again. The big janitor was determined, and Spencer was surprised to see the blockade hold against such a force as Marv.

"We need to find out where they've taken the real School Board," Walter said.

Daisy suddenly dropped to her knees and started emptying Spencer's fake desk. "If they really switched them, then all we need to do is find out whose desk this really is." She pulled out a notebook. On the cover was a label: *Haley Rasmussen's writing notebook.*

"Haley Rasmussen," Daisy muttered. "She's in Mrs. Cleveland's class. That's only two rooms down!"

Marv threw his bulk against the door, but it still didn't budge. Alice ducked out of sight by the window.

"We need another way out," said Walter, as though no one else were thinking it. "Every moment we wait brings Garth Hadley closer to the school. Once he's here, nothing will stop him from becoming a warlock."

"Let me just open this door and we'll stroll on down to Mrs. Cleveland's room," Marv said sarcastically. He threw his shoulder against it once more, but it was still solid.

Spencer glanced at Daisy, who was staring at the ceiling. "The vent!" she said. "We could climb into the air vent and escape."

Spencer sized up the vent. It was small, but they would be able to fit. "Nice one, Daisy!"

In no time, Walter was standing atop two stacked desks, straining on the vent cover. "Marv!" he said, jumping down. "I need you."

Marv lumbered over and climbed up. He was a frightening sight, gingerly balancing on two desks, like a circus elephant standing on a tiny ball. With one meaty hand, Marv seized the vent cover and ripped it from the ceiling. White dust snowed down on the shaggy man as he looked up.

"No way I'm fitting," Marv quickly determined. He and Walter traded places on the desks.

The warlock grasped both sides of the open vent and tried to pull himself in. His bald head disappeared into the ceiling. But, to everyone below, it was obvious that Walter's shoulders were too broad to fit.

"Useless," he said when his head reappeared.

"Wait." Spencer stepped forward. "What about us?"

Before Walter could answer, Alice was climbing up next to him. "Fine," she muttered. "I guess *I'll* go."

Spencer knew that his offer had prodded his mother into action. Her motherly instinct would be too strong to let her son enter into potential danger.

"This isn't going to be good," Spencer whispered to Daisy. He had to avert his eyes from the scene. His mother was atop the desks now, clinging to Walter Jamison. "My mom's terrified of heights."

"I got you, I got you," Walter assured. He helped her grasp the vent. With his hands, Walter made a cradle for her foot. Her head disappeared into the vent.

Spencer covered his ears. Any moment now, his mother would start screaming.

And she did. "Get me down! Down right now! NOW!"

It was something Spencer had learned on a family vacation three years ago. They'd gone to Mesa Verde to tour the Native American ruins. Mom had gotten halfway through one of the cliff dwellings when she just froze. It had taken two park rangers to get her back on level ground.

It wasn't just the twelve-foot height of Mrs. Natcher's classroom ceiling that got Alice Zumbro screaming. It was a deadly combination of . . .

"Heights *and* tight spaces," Spencer whispered.

Normally, Spencer would have been embarrassed by his mother's outburst. But there was no time for that now. As Walter and Marv got Alice back on flat ground, Spencer volunteered again.

"You've got to let us try. Garth Hadley could be here by now."

Walter glanced at Alice for parental approval.

"Please, Mom. I can do this. I'll be careful."

Still flushed and out of breath, Alice nodded wordlessly. Spencer scampered up the desks and stepped into Walter's cupped hands.

"I don't know what you have planned," the warlock said, "but you better be careful. Your mother will never forgive me if something happens to you." Without waiting for a response, Walter boosted Spencer into the metal air vent.

It was a tight fit with the princess backpack. Movement was limited to something between a crawl and a slither. Daisy's face suddenly appeared behind him. Spencer reached back and took her hand.

She was still pulling her legs into the vent when a loud crash filled the classroom below. Shouts drifted up, filling the vent.

"What's happening?" Spencer hissed.

Daisy twisted around, peering over her shoulder. "They've come into the classroom!" she whispered back.

"Must have seen us escaping and tried to stop it," said Spencer.

"Walter's down," narrated Daisy. "He looks hurt. Your mom's all tangled up in a mop. They got Marv, too. No, wait. He's breaking free. He's heading to the door!"

Suddenly, Glopified mop strings shot up from below and filled the vent opening.

"Spencer!" Daisy cried as the strings twisted around her leg. He reached back desperately, grabbing for anything. His hands found something and he pulled . . . on her braid!

Daisy yelped from the pain as she became the victim of a human tug-of-war. At last, the mop strings retracted and Spencer let go.

"Ow," Daisy whimpered, grabbing the top of her head. "Who do you think I am, Rapunzel?" She stroked her thick braid. "This isn't a rope, you know."

"Sorry," Spencer said. "Let's get out of here before they attack again."

CHAPTER 40

"STOP SINGING!"

Spencer and Daisy snaked their way forward through the vent system of Welcher Elementary School.

"If we go two rooms over," Spencer whispered, "we'll come out right in Mrs. Cleveland's room. They won't expect us to pop out of the ceiling."

Spencer sounded much more confident than he felt. A million things could go wrong between here and there. He had no idea what they would do once they dropped into Mrs. Cleveland's room. How could they get the desk safely away when all they had was a pink backpack full of vacuum dust? Besides, Garth might already be in there, pounding the nail into the School Board.

I've still got the Vortex, Spencer reminded himself.

"I think this is it," Spencer whispered. The vent shaft branched, leading to a downward drop into a classroom.

"Have you ever noticed how shiny this vent is?" Daisy asked. Spencer glanced over his shoulder to see that she'd fallen behind. "And it's kind of cool how they hook all the different pieces of metal together. I really like this vent."

What was Daisy *talking* about? How could she pay attention to the vent when they were so close to Mrs. Cleveland's room?

Then he saw it, and everything made sense.

A pale Grime was only inches behind her. Bulbous fingertips clung to the metallic vent shaft. The Toxite was enjoying Daisy's brain waves while sending out strong waves of distraction to confuse the girl.

"Behind you, Daisy!" Spencer hissed. "There's a Grime right above you."

"Come back here, Spencer," she said calmly. "You've got to see this."

"No!" Spencer said. "You have to listen to me." But it was too late. The Grime breath was doing its trick. Daisy wasn't hearing anything else.

"I *love* this vent! I think this is the coolest place I've ever been."

Spencer was torn. He needed Daisy's help, but if he went back to vac dust the Grime, he'd waste precious time in reaching the School Board.

Daisy was beyond reason. Now she was singing a lullaby to the vent, her voice getting a little too loud. If the BEM workers below heard the noise, Spencer's surprise attack would be ruined.

"Quiet!" Spencer urged. "Stop singing! You've got to be quiet!"

Suddenly, the Grime scuttled away, aware of its detection. Before Spencer could breathe a sigh of relief, before Daisy could come to her senses, a hand clamped over the girl's mouth from behind.

Daisy tried to scream, but the sound was muffled. Someone had followed them into the vent! But who? It had to be someone small enough . . .

A blast of flowery perfume hit Spencer as a face appeared behind Daisy. It was Leslie Sharmelle. And if Leslie was here, that meant Garth would be . . .

"I found them!" the thin woman shouted. Her voice echoed down the resonant vent, sounding in every nearby classroom. "They're up in the—"

Spencer hit Leslie with a fistful of vac dust from the backpack. Her voice cut short as the suction dragged. Daisy was trapped helplessly beneath the BEM woman, but Spencer had no choice.

Spencer reached the branch in the vent shaft and entered feet first. He wriggled backward until he arrived at the drop into the classroom. Reaching down with a palm blast of vac dust, Spencer hit the vent cover. Suction ripped the bolts out of the ceiling and sent the slotted cover crashing into Mrs. Cleveland's room. He pushed his legs through the blown-out opening and peered into the classroom.

There were at least half a dozen BEM workers prowling the room with a myriad of Glopified weapons in hand. The door was barricaded by a few stacked desks, just as Marv had done in Mrs. Natcher's room. The window, too, was blocked and under watchful eye.

Garth Hadley was at the center of the room. The bronze hammer flashed in his hand. His other hand was in a fist, undoubtedly clenching the nail. Garth was bent over one of the desks, scrutinizing the wooden surface. But the clattering vent cover caused him to look up.

A pair of sneakers emerged from the ceiling. Garth set the point of the nail against the desk, but before he could swing the hammer, Spencer jumped.

In midair, Spencer hurled a dose of vacuum dust. The controlled funnel throw struck Garth in the chest and suctioned him to the floor. A split second later, Spencer landed painfully on the teacher's desk. He bounced and crumpled to the floor.

The pain was intense and throbbing. Spencer felt blackness clouding his vision. If he passed out, all would be lost. Garth would recover from the vac dust and drive the nail while Daisy was trapped with Leslie in the vent above.

Spencer blinked hard. The BEM workers were converging on him. A mop lashed out. Spencer was immediately wrapped and turned upside down. The mop dragged him across the classroom floor. He tried to scream Daisy's name, but couldn't muster the strength.

The barricaded door suddenly shuddered. Spencer craned his neck to see. Something struck the door again. This time the stacked desks tumbled and the door slammed on its hinges. A shaggy form filled the doorway, a sawed-off pushbroom in his hands.

"Marv!" Seeing the burly janitor infused Spencer with an unknown strength. His painful fall was numbed by adrenaline.

The BEM workers swarmed at Marv, desperate to repel the intruder and give their boss time to drive the nail. A handful of vac dust struck his side, but Marv groaned like a Titan and resisted the suction. He was immobile, but still on his feet.

Spencer wormed his way out of the tight mop strings. Marv was going to need his help. The boy was reaching for the mop when something jerked him off his feet and threw him onto the nearest desk. Garth Hadley had him pinned, holding tight to the pink straps of Daisy's backpack.

"Fighting us is the wrong choice, Spencer," he said. "You showed promise. You could have been one of us."

"Help rot kids' brains?" Spencer shouted. "Never!"

"It's for the good of all. If only you'd believe me."

"You lied about the janitors!"

"Not *everything* was a lie, Spencer. Some of it was true. And I can explain the rest if you'll give me a chance."

"I'm not letting you change colors again!"

"Change colors?" Garth asked.

"You're a chameleon! And them's the worst kind of folks!" Spencer kicked savagely, landing his foot in Garth Hadley's stomach. Then, fumbling in the side compartment of the desk beneath him, Spencer grabbed a textbook. With all his strength, he swung the book like a baseball bat, clobbering Garth on the side of the head.

Garth Hadley staggered, momentarily stunned. Spencer

glanced at the weapon in his hands. A math book. That had to hurt—433 pages of mathematical pain.

Let's times that by two! he thought.

Spencer swung again, dealing a blow to the other side of Garth's head. Then he threw the textbook and lunged past the dazed man.

Spencer reached his desk, the School Board. Atop the wooden surface, the bronze nail had toppled. It spun lazily next to Marv's misspelled inscription about Mrs. N. Spencer snatched the nail and found the hammer on the carpet nearby.

There was a great deal of thumping and banging resonating from the open vent. No doubt Daisy was putting up a fight.

Marv was still battling the other BEM workers. Some had collapsed on the floor; others were sent spiraling upward as Marv wielded his short-handled pushbroom like a knight's sword.

Spencer turned as Garth Hadley charged. The boy started to brandish the bronze hammer like a weapon. Then a better idea came.

At his feet was a broom. Kicking it up, Spencer struck the bristles and launched to the ceiling. Garth cursed as Spencer rose out of reach with Ninfa and the nail.

He hit the ceiling only a foot from the open vent. Spencer carefully reached out and shoved the bronze hammer into the air vent. Leslie might reach it before Daisy, but at least it was momentarily out of Garth's grasp.

Daisy's face suddenly appeared in the hole. "Spencer!"

she shouted. His broom was starting to descend. Desperately, he reached out with the bronze nail. Daisy's hand closed around the item as Spencer slipped out of reach.

"Yes!" Daisy cried. But her celebration was followed by a scream. Daisy's face disappeared into the vent again, Leslie Sharmelle dragging her backward.

Garth was waiting for him when Spencer touched down. The boy felt the air whoosh out of his lungs as Hadley tackled him to the floor.

Marv bellowed as mop strings tangled around his arm. He shook free and somersaulted across the classroom, his weight and momentum making him unstoppable.

Marv struck the School Board desk and bowled it over. All of Spencer's school supplies tumbled across the carpet.

"This is the right one?" Marv asked.

"Yes!" Spencer shouted.

With a roar, the big janitor hefted the desk above his head and threw it. The desk tumbled across the room with a tremendous clamor. The metal legs bent and the wooden desktop cracked. Which was exactly what Marv wanted.

Marv leapt into the air and body-slammed the desk. The desktop splintered violently and came totally free. Marv picked up the wood and stripped away loose slivers. At last, he was holding a fragment of wood about a square foot in size—the School Board.

Marv quickly tucked the magic wood under one arm for a quick escape. Garth Hadley saw the plan and abandoned Spencer.

"Look out, Marv!" Spencer screamed. The janitor turned to face the oncoming BEM rep.

Garth swung a fist. Marv caught it and threw him back as more workers came at him. Others had turned to the classroom door, blocking it again to complicate Marv's escape.

Spencer grimaced at the noise coming from the overhead vent. The shaft was probably too narrow for Leslie to get past. Daisy seemed to be holding her own, but it was only a matter of time before Leslie overpowered her. If that happened, Daisy would need a fast way out of the air vent.

Searching quickly, Spencer found the broom he'd used before. He aimed the broom, struck the bristles, and let it go. The broom shot out of his hands and entered the vent's dark opening in the ceiling.

Marv was surrounded, Daisy was trapped. Spencer felt hope slipping away. Where were his mother and Walter? Daisy had last seen them mop-tied in Mrs. Natcher's room. Spencer could only assume they were still there, powerless to escape. Wherever they were, Spencer couldn't count on them for help.

Marv was still fighting like a giant, holding the School Board securely under his arm. He had taken several blows to the head, and dark blood streamed down his face into his shaggy black beard. The bearlike man was grunting and groaning. Struck from the side by a puff of vacuum dust, Marv dropped to his knees.

"The vent, Marv!" Spencer shouted. It was their only chance. The janitor met his stare across the room.

Straining against the vac dust, Marv grabbed his sawed-off pushbroom. Pulling the School Board from under his arm, Marv took careful aim and hit the wooden board with the Glopified pushbroom.

The School Board rocketed upward and clattered noisily into the metal vent shaft. Everyone watched it sail out of reach.

All hope was on Daisy now. She had everything that Garth needed to become a warlock. But Leslie was still up there too.

"No!" shouted Garth Hadley, thrusting his mop at Marv. The strings elongated, wrapping multiple times around the big janitor's pained face and pulling him to his stomach. The pushbroom fell from Marv's hands and another worker grabbed it. He swung, hitting Marv across the back and sending him into the air.

Garth Hadley laughed cruelly, dragging Marv through the air with his mop like a clumsy, injured bird on a leash. At last, Garth threw Marv against the chalkboard, where the big man collapsed in a motionless heap, suffocating from the strings around his face.

Spencer watched the torture in stunned silence from across the classroom. He remembered the first time Garth Hadley had put a hand on his shoulder, enlisting his help to catch the "criminal" head janitor.

Lies! Garth Hadley was a liar. A cruel, mean liar.

"Give me a broom," Garth demanded. "I'm going up." One of the BEM workers stepped forward with a charged broom. Daisy would never survive an attack from both sides.

Garth would claim Ninfa and the School Board. He'd become a warlock.

But Spencer couldn't let that happen—no matter what!

Spencer pulled the pink princess backpack from his shoulders and ripped open the zipper. Vacuum dust was useless now. Spencer stared at the other object in the backpack, a wild thought forming in his head. It was too risky. He couldn't possibly . . . but his hands were already moving.

The spilled contents of his desk were all around him. He snatched a sharp pencil from the floor and lifted out the overcharged Vortex vacuum bag. Spencer was breathing hard, wishing there were some other way. Walter had warned about the Vortex; it was unstable, unpredictable.

Overhead, Spencer heard Daisy scream. It reverberated in the metal vent, amplifying the sound of her terror. Garth Hadley took aim and struck the bristles of his broom against the floor.

Without another thought, Spencer stabbed the sharp pencil into the vacuum bag.

CHAPTER 41

"*SOMEONE* HAS TO END THIS!"

As soon as the tip of the pencil pierced the papery fabric of the vacuum bag, a deafening suction sound filled the classroom—three hundred times louder than any puff of vac dust.

Spencer held onto the pencil, clenching the bag with all his might. Everything around him went black and he struggled to maintain consciousness.

On his knees, Spencer saw a funnel of dark dust issuing out of the bag. It grew, twisting and pitching like a giant tornado with Spencer at its root.

At the opposite end of the shifting tornado, Spencer saw dim visions of the classroom: Marv's limp body, a mangled desk, Garth Hadley rising on his broom. But these scenes seemed miles away, frozen in time.

Then something crashed down the dust funnel, spiraling

toward him. Spencer flinched, seeing a math book and a chair come hurtling at his face. At the last moment, both objects were sucked into the vacuum bag in Spencer's hand, passing the boy without so much as a scrape.

But that was just the beginning.

The Vortex was soon tearing everything inward. There were so many objects twisting toward him that Spencer could see only glimpses. The teacher's computer, an overhead projector, desks, cabinets, fragments of chalkboard . . . everything!

But the worst part was the bodies. Spencer saw human figures, indistinguishable among the rubble. He tried to count them, but it was impossible to see anything clearly at the base of the tornado.

Spencer cried out, screaming against the deafening squall. His own voice seemed to get caught in the dust funnel and sucked into the Vortex. Spencer felt tears flinging off his face. The sharp pencil slipped from his hand and disappeared into the vacuum bag. He felt the pink straps of the princess backpack snap. It swirled above his head and then vanished.

It took everything Spencer had not to let go of the dangerous bag. Still, his grip was slipping. Spencer had no doubt that he would end up inside the bag just like everything else unless he could hang on . . . just hang on!

Whoosh!

The tornado suddenly folded in on itself, crackling and hissing as it was sucked into the Vortex bag. Spencer felt the vacuum bag shudder in his hand. It felt no different from how it had been before—no heavier, no bigger. But as moonlight angled through the classroom's blown-out window, Spencer saw that *everything* was gone.

The classroom was utterly destroyed. He was kneeling on bare concrete. The force of the suction had imploded the walls, tearing the sheetrock like paper. The sink in the back of the classroom had been pulled into the bag. A surge of water shot from the broken pipe, running across the floor like a river.

He was alone in the desolation.

Glancing up, Spencer saw that the ceiling tiles were gone. The insulation, too, had been sucked away. Sparking wires hung where the lights had been. Cracks angled across the bare ceiling, almost wide enough to expose the night sky.

But among the crooked roof trusses, a twisted, metal vent shaft remained, bent askew and dangling precariously.

"Daisy!" Spencer whispered hopefully. Through some stroke of fate, the vent had survived, held in place by the metal roof supports. And if the vent had survived, then Daisy might have, too!

Then, as if the vent had sensed his optimism and wanted to dispel it, the damaged shaft slid from the metal roof truss with a groan. The vent fell in slow motion, Spencer wishing he could intervene. But what more could he do than watch helplessly and hope for the best?

The vent made a mighty crash as it hit the concrete floor of the skeleton classroom. Overhead, the weakened roof creaked.

Spencer raced forward. Water from the busted pipe was already forming a puddle, so he carefully set the Vortex on top of the twisted vent.

Please, he silently hoped. *Let her be in there!* Falling to his knees, Spencer peered into the narrow chute.

An arm stretched out of the dark vent, barely visible. In desperation, Spencer grasped the hand. To his relief, the hand grasped back.

The roof rasped as something fell from above and crashed onto the floor behind him. Spencer risked a glance upward. A patch of starlit sky winked through a new hole in the roof.

It's coming down, he thought, his throat tightening. *This whole room is going to collapse!*

Spencer glanced at the door, mentally preparing his escape. But the doorway had been sucked into the Vortex, and rubble blocked the exit. Gasping, Spencer turned to the window. The glass was gone, but he might be able to climb out with Daisy before the roof caved.

"Come on," Spencer whispered. He pulled on the hand and felt Daisy trying to work free. The flooding water, the groaning roof . . . it was enough to make his head spin.

Another portion of the roof caved in. Plumes of dust rose from the rubble like swirling, pale ghosts. A foreshadowing of death and a tomb of rubble if they didn't get out soon.

"Come on, Daisy!" Spencer called into the vent. He could see her head and shoulders now.

"Spencer," the girl moaned, an eerie sound that

resonated in the metal shaft. Sliding her other arm forward, Daisy opened her hand. The bronze nail was clutched so tightly that it left a red mark on her white palm.

Her dedication was admirable. Through all the danger and commotion, even as the vent plummeted twelve feet to the hard floor, Daisy had kept an iron grip on the nail. She knew what was at stake if Garth took Ninfa and the nail.

"It's okay," Spencer called into the vent. "It's over now."

Right then, something slammed into him from behind. Spencer's head clanged against the metal vent shaft. In a dazed stupor, he saw Leslie Sharmelle reach down and pluck the bronze nail from Daisy's open palm.

"How . . . ?" Spencer tried. Leslie must have also survived inside the vent. Then, as he was distracted with rescuing Daisy, Leslie had slipped out the other end of the metal shaft. The thin woman, covered with cuts and bruises, glanced around the gutted classroom. In one hand, Ninfa glistened, wet from the rising water. Under her arm was the splintery School Board. And now she had the nail . . .

"Devil knows what happened to Garth Hadley," she screamed, her face contorted with madness. "But *someone* has to end this!"

Leslie placed the School Board on the vent and set the sharp tip of the nail against the wood. With a wicked shriek, Leslie raised Ninfa to drive the nail home.

Rubble crashed down from above. The roof gave the most terrifying groan yet, causing Leslie to glance up. In that crucial moment of distraction, Spencer leapt forward.

Slipping the wet hammer from her hand, he lunged at the School Board.

Leslie was still holding the bronze nail to the wood when Spencer struck with the hammer. Once—twice. She cursed as the hammer smashed her fingers. But, with a third strike from Ninfa, the head of the bronze nail was smooth against the School Board.

The room was dreadfully silent. Even the roof stopped its creaking—the calm before the storm.

Leslie backed away from the Board in shock. Spencer gripped the hammer, his eyes wide in disbelief at his own actions. *He* had driven the nail! But Leslie had been right; *someone* had to end this.

Then the roof cracked violently, as if to make up for its moment of silence.

"Daisy," Spencer cried. "You've got to get up!"

Leslie had fallen to her knees, hands outstretched, as if the world had just slipped through her fingers. With such a dazed, blank stare, Spencer would have thought her a mannequin if it hadn't been for the slight tremble of her chin.

Dropping Ninfa, Spencer grabbed both of Daisy's hands and jerked the girl out of the bent air shaft. Beside her tumbled the broom that Spencer had launched into the vent.

"Hang on!" Spencer shouted. Her arms feebly clung to his neck and Spencer helped her straddle the broom handle. He picked up Ninfa and shoved the hammer into Daisy's hand. Turning back for the School Board, Spencer saw that Leslie Sharmelle was holding it tightly.

As the roof sloughed inward, Spencer leapt sideways,

slamming the broom bristles against the floor as hard as he could. Spencer's left hand reached out, grasping the papery Vortex bag from the broken air vent. The two kids shot sideways, sailing toward the blown-out classroom window and into the dark sky.

Behind them, the room crumpled like a cardboard box. The sound was sickening—the kind of crunching and crashing that the kids would never forget.

Spencer and Daisy drifted into the parking lot as the weak broom struggled to keep them both aloft. The landing was awkward and they both tumbled to the blacktop.

"What happened?" Daisy said. She had found the strength to rise on her own feet.

Spencer looked at the crumbled, moonlit wreckage of Mrs. Cleveland's classroom. "I think we won."

"No," Daisy whispered. "What happened to *you*?"

Spencer stepped away from her, wondering what she meant. He looked down and gasped.

"You're glowing."

CHAPTER 42

"WHAT HAPPENED TO ME?"

The classroom accident made the news. A janitor by the name of John Campbell was the first responder. He'd been at the school late, shampooing carpets, when a violent crash led him to discover the ruined classroom and call 911.

Not only was the accident newsworthy, but several mysterious events surrounding the collapse of the classroom also gained the media's attention. Police were still investigating.

Only one person was found in the rubble of the broken room. She was quickly taken by Life Flight to the hospital. The young woman was in critical condition, having suffered broken bones and a concussion to the head. Police scoured the area, but no other individuals were found.

News reporters commented that, as the debris was cleared, the classroom was found to be completely stripped.

Desks, computer, carpet, even the classroom sink was gone. Authorities believe the operation was some kind of massive classroom theft.

To make things worse, the woman had stolen a vehicle from Hillside Estates. Fortunately, John Campbell was able to cripple her escape by driving a BEM van into the stolen station wagon.

Police were waiting until the unnamed blonde recovered before interrogating her about the alleged station wagon theft and total destruction of school property.

There was much hearsay and speculation as to the cause of the classroom cave-in. Answers to these questions would be resolved only when the victim regained stability.

But there were many things, of course, that the news would never know. The true story went more like this:

Spencer and Daisy raced into Mrs. Natcher's classroom. Walter and Alice were on the floor, tightly mop-tied. The kids untangled them, and Alice fell on her son with hugs and worried exclamations. But it was Walter's reaction that really frightened him.

"Spencer," the warlock hissed. He put a hand to his bald head. "The Aura."

"What do you mean?" Alice asked, pushing Spencer back for inspection. "What happened?"

"You drove the nail, didn't you," stated Walter.

Spencer stared down at his body, cloaked in a warm, gold glow. "What happened to me?"

"Since you drove the nail," Walter explained, "you're protected by the magical Aura until you set up a domain."

"Set up a domain . . . ?" Spencer mumbled in disbelief. The consequences of his actions were uncomfortably starting to set in.

"Aura? What Aura?" Alice started combing over Spencer like something was hidden in his hair.

"You can't see it because it exists on the same plane as the Toxites and you haven't been exposed yet," the warlock explained.

Daisy handed Ninfa to Walter.

"Where's the School Board?" he asked.

"It's under the rubble in Mrs. Cleveland's room," Spencer said. "There wasn't time to get it away from Leslie."

Then Walter noticed the vacuum bag cradled in Spencer's arm. The boy clung to it, the only tangible evidence of what he'd done. A memorial to utter destruction.

"You did what you had to, Spencer," Walter said.

"Marv," Spencer whispered. "I killed him." He remembered the burly janitor rolling across the classroom, fighting like a dragon. The Vortex had claimed Marv just as it had the other BEM workers and Garth Hadley. Spencer felt his eyes welling with tears.

"I didn't mean to," he mumbled. "He saved my life . . ." His mom put an arm across his shoulders. Daisy stared unblinking at the bag.

"Marv knew the dangers involved in this kind of janitorial work," Walter said. "There was nothing else you could have done. Marv would be proud of you—and your decision to use the Vortex."

Spencer swallowed hard. He held out the Vortex, begging

Walter to take it. The janitor held up his hands. "He may not be dead," Walter said. "The Vortex is a mystery to us all. Keep the bag. If there's a way to recover him, we'll find it."

Walter strode purposefully out of Mrs. Natcher's room and disappeared down the hallway. The others stood in reverent silence for a moment. When Spencer finally moved, his feet seemed heavy and sluggish.

By the time they caught up to Walter, he'd been to the Rebel closet and stood before the wreckage of Mrs. Cleveland's room with a pushbroom.

"Stand back," he cautioned. The janitor struck the rubble of the collapsed doorway and sent it floating.

"Be careful," Daisy said as he tunneled out of sight, bits of brick and twisted shards of metal flying out of his way.

A moment later, Walter returned with the School Board, the nail set firmly in the magical desktop. He handed the board to Alice and glanced back at the crumpled classroom.

"I've got to get back in there. Leslie's still alive, but she's going to need first aid." He dug in his pocket and pulled out a car key. "Mrs. Zumbro, I need you to get the children out of here before the police arrive. Please go. Take my car." Walter handed her the key. "Red Pontiac Grand Am."

"What about you?" Daisy asked.

"I'm calling 911. I need to get Leslie out of there." The warlock looked once more at Spencer and gave him a stoic nod. Then he sent the rubble flying again as he burrowed into the wreckage to rescue the enemy.

The two kids followed Alice through the school's

broken doors and into the parking lot. Spencer couldn't help but notice how Daisy stared at him while they walked. The Aura illuminated the whole hallway, powerful and frightening. Spencer bit back the urge to cry.

What had he done?

CHAPTER 43

"IT'S A BIG DECISION."

Thanks for coming," Spencer said, clearing a spot on the leather couch for Walter to sit down. "Sorry about the mess," he added. "My family's not the cleanest."

"Don't worry about it," Walter answered with a smile, sliding one of Max's toy dump trucks aside with his foot. "I'm a janitor. I'm used to messes."

It was Saturday afternoon, cool and rainy. A quick phone call had brought Walter Jamison to the house.

"I saw you on the news this morning," Spencer said.

"Oh, no. Did my hair look all right?" Walter asked sarcastically, running a hand over his bald head.

"How's Leslie Sharmelle, or Sarah Bently . . . or whoever she is?"

"She'll survive," Walter said. "But when she wakes up, she'll wish she hadn't. Everyone thinks she stole your station wagon and emptied Mrs. Cleveland's classroom. By the time I was finished talking to the police, I even had her blamed for the mysterious cave-in. I don't suspect we'll be seeing much more of Leslie Sharmelle."

Alice Zumbro entered from the kitchen, a few store-bought cookies on a plate. "It was all I could find," she said. "Wish they were homemade."

The janitor took a cookie and sat back. "I'm really proud of you," he said. "Both of you." His eyes looked exceptionally tired and weary. "Insurance will cover the station wagon," Walter said. "Once they prove Leslie guilty, you should get a new car."

"The old station wagon suited us fine." Alice shook her head. "Twelve years of safe driving, and then—*wham!*" Alice clapped her hands. "Some jerk totals it in a parking lot."

"How is Daisy holding up?" Walter asked. "She showed such courage."

"She was pretty shaken up last night," Alice said. "Luckily, I was able to calm her parents when we dropped her off."

"Everyone that discovers the truth will be in danger of the BEM," Walter said. "Poor Daisy's involved, whether she likes it or not. But I'm counting on you to keep her safe, Mrs. Zumbro. We really mustn't bring Mr. and Mrs. Gates into this."

"I'll watch Daisy," Alice promised. "And it shouldn't be a problem to keep her folks innocent. They're quite clueless about a lot. Surprisingly gullible."

They chewed the dry cookies in awkward silence.

"Oh." Spencer reached over to the coffee table. "Here's the School Board and Ninfa." He picked up the hammer and the heavy piece of antique wood. "I'm ready to get rid of this Aura." Spencer glanced down at his shimmering arms. "You don't know how hard it was to fall asleep last night. I was like a walking nightlight."

"You seem the same to me," Alice said. It was a simple statement, but she had no idea how much that meant to Spencer. He felt so foreign, so alien. It was comforting to know that his mom couldn't see anything different about him.

Walter chuckled. "Regretfully, Mrs. Zumbro, we don't keep a stock of revealing soap at the school. Too risky. Spencer will have to create a new batch if he chooses to expose you. It might take some time, but he'll get it." Walter nodded at Spencer. "There's a lot you have to learn about being a warlock. I don't claim to be an expert, but I'll help you as much as I can."

He took another cookie from the plate. "Where will you drive the nail? Give it some thought. It's a big decision."

"Not for me." Spencer held out the objects to Walter. "I don't think the Rebel Underground should have to rely on a twelve-year-old warlock," Spencer explained. "You can keep supplying the Rebels, and maybe the Toxites won't take over *every* school."

Walter reverently took the bronze hammer and School Board from Spencer's outstretched hands. "I'm honored."

"Now will I stop glowing?" Spencer glanced at his arms.

Walter placed the tip of Ninfa against the head of the bronze nail. A magic bond formed instantly and started lifting the nail free of the wood. The small bronze nail fell tinkling onto the coffee table.

Instantly, the protective Aura around Spencer began to fade. He closed his eyes and sighed. When he opened them again, the glow was completely extinguished.

Spencer retrieved the fallen nail and handed it to Walter. "Just promise me that you'll Glopify some really cool stuff."

Walter grinned. "I told you once that I feared a war might be brewing. The BEM's new experiments will redefine the world of Glopified equipment. They're not out to fight Toxites anymore. They're fighting *us*."

"Well, I hope they know what they're up against," Alice said. "Because *nobody* messes with my kids."

Spencer had taken that for granted until he had seen his mom tackle Leslie Sharmelle at the hotel. It was nice to have a mom who cared.

"There's one more thing," Spencer said. He stepped into the other room and returned with the Vortex. He had debated giving it up. The vacuum bag represented painful memories, true. But to Spencer it was also an icon of sacrifice and friendship. "I want you to have this." He handed it to Walter.

The janitor accepted the bag with a sad smile. "Spencer," he said, "Marv would want—"

"I don't . . ." Spencer held up his hands. "I don't want to talk about it."

Walter sighed and pulled on a baseball cap. "Thank you for the cookies, Mrs. Zumbro." He pocketed Ninfa and the nail and tucked the School Board under one arm.

At the door, Walter Jamison turned. He stared hard at the boy. "Thank you, Spencer. For everything." Then he disappeared into the rain, sidestepping a puddle on the sidewalk.

"Until Monday," the boy whispered. So why did Spencer feel like that was good-bye?

CHAPTER 44

"A VAN?"

Daisy Gates reached her goal of being the first student to enter the school on Monday morning. Close behind was Spencer.

Bright and early, the two kids had met on the playground and entered Welcher Elementary, anxious to see how Walter had reestablished his domain. The kids walked briskly to the janitor stairwell only to stop short, their hearts beating fast.

Boxes.

Cardboard boxes were taped shut and piled on the stairs. Spencer and Daisy waded past a stack and were starting down the stairwell when they came face-to-face with a somber Walter Jamison.

"What is this?" Spencer asked, pointing at the stuff piling up.

Walter set down the box he was carrying and rubbed a hand along his bald head. "Ah, glad you're here. I need some extra helpers to carry things out to the van."

"Van? What are you talking about?" Daisy cried.

Walter nodded. "I'm done here," he said quietly.

"What?" Spencer and Daisy shouted in unison.

"I've been fired," Walter explained. "We knew it would happen. The BEM is still in charge."

"I don't care!" Spencer said angrily. "We beat the BEM!"

Walter shook his head. "We beat Garth Hadley and stumped the BEM's plans to make him the next warlock. But one doesn't *beat* the Bureau of Educational Maintenance."

"But," said Spencer, looking for an excuse. "But the nail and the hammer . . ."

"They are safe," Walter said. "I re-drove the bronze nail into the School Board yesterday. Then I chose my new domain. I'm a full-fledged warlock again, ready to experiment—thanks to you two."

"But where will you go?" Daisy asked.

Walter lowered his voice. "The BEM will track me down wherever I set up. But if I can remain in motion . . ." He grinned to himself. "I have established my new domain in a van."

"A van?" Daisy asked.

"A fifteen-passenger vehicle," he replied. "It should be large enough to experiment with Glop. And since the van will already have wheels, I'll be able to make deliveries to the Rebel schools without ever leaving my domain."

"No," Spencer interrupted. "I won't let you leave. Who's going to replace you?"

"The Bureau has hired two new janitors," said the warlock. "They'll arrive at Welcher in a few days."

"BEM workers? Here?" Spencer stomped his foot. "But they'll let the Toxites take over. Without you, I'll be sleeping through every lesson!"

"Haven't we taught you anything?" Walter asked. "The Toxites will multiply, true. But as long as you can see them, *you* can fight them." He picked up the box. "I'll be around to give you new supplies as often as I can manage. As long as you two are here, I'll consider Welcher Elementary part of the Underground."

Spencer clenched his fists. It couldn't be true. Soon he would wake up and know that this whole scene was nothing but a nightmare. Walter couldn't leave now! Not after Marv had died. Not after all they'd been through together.

"Look," Walter said, "I know it's hard to accept. It isn't like I *want* to go. There's nothing I'd rather do than stay here and watch out for you kids. But I won't leave you totally friendless."

"What do you mean?" Daisy asked.

"Principal Poach just hired a new lunch lady." Walter lowered his voice. "Her name is Meredith List. She's an old friend of mine. She knows about Toxites and she's loyal to the Rebel Underground. If you ever need to contact me, just tell Meredith."

Spencer slumped down onto a nearby box. A lunch lady

wasn't the best trade for a warlock, but at least there would be an adult in Welcher who knew about Toxites.

"Ten minutes till the bell rings," Walter said. "Do you kids mind giving me a hand with some of this stuff?"

Spencer, Daisy, and Walter waddled out to the parking lot, their arms laden with boxes, janitorial equipment, and half-completed warlock experiments. A brown fifteen-passenger van was parked in the nearest stall, the back open. It was stripped of its rear seats, much like Garth Hadley's BEM van. But Walter's brown van seemed a hundred times friendlier.

The three of them piled their armloads into the back of the van. Walter dusted off his hands and smiled. "I'll go back for the last load," he said. "You two run along to class before the bell rings."

"Where are you going after this?" Spencer asked, stalling—anything to avoid saying good-bye.

"Oh, I don't know," Walter said, looking up into the bright blue sky like he could see forever into space. "First thing I need is an assistant. My niece has volunteered to go with me. She's young, but she's worked as a janitor since she was seventeen, so she knows a few tricks. She should make a good replacement for . . . um . . ."

"For Marv," Spencer said. But he knew that wasn't true. Nobody could really replace Marv Bills.

"We'll head over to some Rebel schools in Wyoming and Colorado, keep moving south." Walter shrugged. "There's endless work to be done, and when we're finished with that, there'll still be gum to scrape. You kids can't seem to keep it in your mouths." Walter smiled, a transparent attempt to lighten the mood. Spencer stared back gloomily and Daisy gazed down at her shoelaces.

The three of them stood awkwardly in the September morning, Spencer having a stare-off with Walter Jamison.

"Listen, Spencer," the warlock said, rubbing his forehead. "There's something I should probably tell you. I was going to tell you sooner, but then I thought maybe I should wait. Now, since I don't know when I'll see you again, well . . ." Walter sighed.

"What?"

"I just wanted to let you know . . . I think your father would be proud of you."

Spencer heard his heartbeat in his ears, growing steadily faster. Was that supposed to be a compliment? Didn't Walter know that Spencer's dad had disappeared years ago?

He's got to come back, Daisy had said when they were scraping gum. *Nobody loves their work more than their family.*

As if reading Spencer's mind, Walter said, "He meant to come home, Spencer. Alan Zumbro was a good man."

"You knew him?" Spencer asked in utter disbelief.

"Your father was an excellent Toxite biologist. He was part of the BEM before the Bureau went haywire. Smart man. Once I sat in on a lecture he gave at a Bureau conference. The topic was Filth anatomy—way over my head. The BEM really valued the experiments that Alan did to understand the anatomy and physiology behind Toxites."

Spencer almost had to gasp for breath. His father! A Toxite scientist? It was almost impossible to believe. Yet it made perfect sense. Spencer's mother was always annoyed by Alan's secretive behavior—his mediocre explanations of where he'd been and why he'd been out so late.

"You're just like your father sometimes!" Spencer's mother had told him. Suddenly, he realized how right she'd been.

"I'm sorry, Spencer," Walter said with a curt nod.

Sorry? Sorry for what? Spencer had never felt better in his whole life! But the solemn expression on the janitor's face quickly killed his joy. At last, Spencer asked the unanswerable question.

"Why hasn't he come home yet?"

Walter exhaled slowly. He made eye contact, then broke it before answering. "Your father went to Texas for an experiment with the Toxites . . ."

"Yes, I know," Spencer interrupted. "He went with Rod Grush two years ago—"

Walter silenced the boy by raising his hand. "The experiment was very dangerous; lots of unstable variables—"

"What was he doing?" Spencer cut him off again. "What *was* the project?"

"Alan was attempting to trace Glop back to its very source. He was on the cusp of discovery when it happened."

"What happened?" shouted Spencer. "What?"

"Your father disappeared."

Silence.

Spencer felt it starting in his stomach. A sick rejection of the truth, pulling at his insides. This was unacceptable.

"Poof? Gone?" Spencer cried. "That's not good enough! What happened to him?"

"I'm telling you," Walter said, "no one knows what happened down there."

Spencer felt like all his bones had turned to jelly. So close to learning the truth about his dad . . . nobody just *disappeared*. His dad had to be *somewhere*.

"Tell you what," Walter said, changing his tone of voice. "Since I'm headed south, I'll do my best to pick up some new clues. In my opinion, the case was never investigated as much as it should have been." The warlock smiled. "I promise, Spencer. I'll do as much as I can."

The bell rang, shrill and obnoxious. Daisy tugged at Spencer's sleeve. "We'd better go," she said.

"Yeah," said Spencer, taking a deep breath. Walter extended a hand and Spencer shook it.

"Get going," Walter urged them.

Daisy and Spencer turned to face Welcher Elementary School. With Dez back from suspension and a school full of toxin-breathing Toxites, who could tell what new adventures the day might hold?

The adventure continues in
Book Two of *Janitors*

TYLER WHITESIDES

JANITORS

SECRETS OF NEW FOREST ACADEMY

COMING IN
2012

Visit www.tylerwhitesides.com

SHADOW
MOUNTAIN

ACKNOWLEDGMENTS

It seems like every time I turn around, I meet someone new to thank. So many awesome people have helped me transform *Janitors* into what it needed to be.

Thanks to everyone at Shadow Mountain for doing so much to help launch this series—especially Chris Schoebinger for believing in the story and having the vision of where this could go. I'm also grateful to Heidi Taylor for patiently working through the rough spots with me, and to Emily Watts for her excellent editorial work.

Another big thanks goes to my wise agent, Rubin Pfeffer, for starting me off on the right foot. Thanks to Brandon Dorman for bringing the story to life with his amazing artwork and illustrations.

I want to acknowledge and thank my good parents for always fostering my creativity and supporting my hobbies.

Now, for the team of family and friends who read the early manuscript and gave me feedback: Mom, Dad, Jess and Dave, Laura (for countless drafts) and Martin, Molly and Mike, C and Hil, the Dykstras, Lance, and two of my youngest readers, Anna and Maren. Thank you all so much.

A shout-out also goes to the dark hallways of Mount Logan Middle School for inspiring me, and to the mysterious custodians who wandered those halls: Ray, Glenn, Mike, and Paige.

Of course, I owe a special thanks to my wonderful, patient wife, Connie, for supporting me along the road to publication.

And thanks to you, reader, for picking up this book! Now, grab your mop and get back to work. There are lots of Toxites out there, and someone's got to stop them!

1. Spencer knows he saw some creatures in the school, but he denies it when Dez threatens him after lunch. Have you ever had trouble standing up for something you know is right? What made it hard?

2. Mr. Gates says that a chameleon is someone whose story changes depending on who he's talking to. Is it important to always tell the whole story? Why, or why not?

3. Daisy tells Spencer that he needs to believe that his dad will come back. Why is it important to have hope? What kinds of things should we hope for?

4. Garth Hadley tricks Spencer and Daisy into doing things for him. How can you know when someone is asking you to do the wrong thing? What should you say if that happens?

5. Spencer waits till after the ice cream social to tell his mom what is going on. By then, he has already caused a lot of problems. How could Spencer have handled that situation differently? What kind of things should we talk to our parents about?

6. Garth Hadley communicates with Spencer via e-mail. Spencer continues to e-mail even after he's been told not to. Why was that a dangerous choice? How can you be safe on the Internet?

7. If you could have one Glopified cleaning supply, which would it be? Why?

8. For unknown reasons, the BEM has stopped fighting Toxites. The Rebel janitors continue to fight the creatures so that kids can keep learning. Would you join the BEM or the Rebel janitors? Why is it important to get a good education?

9. Spencer and Daisy discover that the Toxites stop kids from learning by creating sleepiness, apathy, and distraction. What are some things in school that make it hard for you to learn? How can you overcome them?

10. Walter tells Spencer that Toxites work harder on kids who really try to learn. Why don't Toxites "waste their breath" on kids like Dez? How hard would the Toxites have to work to get you?

11. If you could Glopify a new cleaning supply, what would it be? What magical power would it have?

12. At the end of the book, Spencer temporarily becomes a warlock. If you had that power, would you give it back to Walter Jamison? Why, or why not?